BY

THE

TIME

YOU

READ

THIS

YANNICK MURPHY

BY

THE

TIME

STORIES

YOU

READ

THIS

FC2

TUSCALOOSA

FC2 is an imprint of the University of Alabama Press.

Inquiries about reproducing material from this work should be addressed
to the University of Alabama Press

Book Design: Publications Unit, Department of English, Illinois State
    University; Director: Steve Halle, Production Assistant: Steven
    Lazarov
Cover Design: Lou Robinson
Typeface: Adobe Caslon Pro

Library of Congress Cataloging-in-Publication Data is available from
the Library of Congress.

ISBN: 978-1-57366-189-8

E-ISBN: 978-1-57366-891-0

TABLE OF CONTENTS

FOREWORD

BY RENEE GLADMAN

EVERYTHING IS OFF in Yannick Murphy's *By the Time You Read This*. The field is too wide, the view too long. The characters are too sad, the tone of their narration too casual. The women are not protected well enough; the girls are left too alone. The men are depressed and lost, or they are absent. The further into the collection I go, the more desolate I feel. But I can't stop reading, and when I do manage to stop, my mind continues to worry over the details of what I've read, and it tries to anticipate what's to come. Something nails me to the walls of these stories. They are languid, absurd, desperate, long, and quiet. Something nails them inside me.

I chose this collection of stories as the winner of the 2020 Catherine Doctorow Innovative Fiction Prize because it haunted me. It disturbed my sense of time and it made my heart ache. I also was drawn to it because there was something phenomenal happening in the writing. I keep returning to the sensation that standing at the opening of each story is like holding a glass enclosure containing some kind of matter: grain, beans, tiny rocks; the specificity of what's inside is less important than the feeling of holding something that's contained and finite. That's where you stand at the beginning of each of the stories in the collection *By the Time You Read This*, but then within the first page or so, it's as if the jar has fallen from your hands and crashed disastrously upon the floor. It's the same measure of content but now scattered everywhere, even crossing the threshold into the next room, soon to be inadvertently kicked into the rooms beyond.

What I'm trying to say is that many of these stories have novel views. They elongate the space around them, elasticize our seeing and reading. They are the same, but we are changed. These are stories that have no intention of ending. They emerge in waves; lifetimes seem to pass. I don't mean that they are the same; it's more that they have a sense of time that appears foreign to the form through which they emerge. Like, they know they are novels and don't understand why we're looking at them like they're stories. They think they are hundreds of pages when they are in fact thirty or forty. Some of the stories also seem to not know which century they are in, which decade, or rather, not to know that whatever time to which they are referring may not be the same time in which they are being read. The view renders time irrelevant as it simultaneously uses time to create its own expanse. We are always only ever seeing because of time, and it is time we're only ever seeing. Now, pull that fact through the perpetuation of the oldest and deepest human crisis—that of *living*—then pepper it with a tongue that's been *in-cheek* for so long it no longer remembers any other way of being, and meet these fourteen stunning, strangely plain, exquisitely crafted, sometimes funny, often lonely-inducing bouts of trying.

BY

THE

TIME

YOU

READ

THIS

THE GOOD WORD

ON VACATION WE MET A GERMAN. He wanted to go south to the ocean for two nights. He invited us along. There were many buses to take, he said, but in the end, we would stay in a place he knew on the beach. He had stayed there once before. His name was Jurgen. We said okay while eating dinner in the dining room of the boardinghouse that we shared. We were tired of the food they served us. We were tired of the same old tablecloth that was never washed. We ate with our plate rims shadowing stains from our breakfasts of black beans spilled days before. We could use a few days' vacation from our vacation.

He explained a German word for which there was no translation in English. It means a good feeling people have when they are together, he said, and then he said the word. We could not pronounce the word. Iris said how trying to say the word hurt her throat. She took a drink of her water; he touched her pale skin at her small Adam's apple.

We left the next morning. There were many buses. Each time we boarded a new bus we noticed how the people all looked like they had been on the last bus, and the chickens on their laps looked the same as the chickens who had been on the last bus. After the buses, there was a small boat. We had to wait for it to come. We waited at a bar that was outside. The roof was made of dry grass, and we ordered ceviche along with our beers, and Jurgen said we had best squeeze as much lime juice as we could on the ceviche so that we wouldn't become sick.

Jurgen's cheeks were always red and we told him we imagined him as a boy wearing lederhosen and standing on a mountain top covered with snow. He told us we imagined right.

When we boarded the boat, the people who had been on the buses, and their chickens, boarded too, and so all the while sailing on the river, we heard the chickens cluck, and it was louder than the chug of the outboard motor.

When we reached the shore where the place was, Jurgen led us down a road. We walked for a while, and then we cut in to the beach. We were on the ocean side, and the waves were big. The house we stopped at had a porch, and there was an old man sitting on the porch and smoking a pipe. Jurgen waved to him.

Here we are, Jurgen said. We set our backpacks down on the porch. The old man said hello and sucked in on his pipe.

You've got a nice view, Iris said, and the old man nodded and looked Iris up and down.

I'm dying to swim, Iris said.

Iris and I changed in our room. There were only two cots in the room. There was no other furniture. The window had no glass. It was just an opening cut into the wall. A large branch from a tree growing outside reached into the room. A few of its leaves had fallen to the floor.

We went into the hall wearing our bathing suits with our towels wrapped around our waists when we saw Jurgen come out of his room wearing his bathing trunks. I caught sight of Jurgen's room as he came out of it. There was just a cot in his room too, only there was no window at all.

The old man went into the water with us. He stood in the shallows still smoking his pipe. The water came up to his knees, but then when a wave came the water rose higher, above his waist.

Iris went deep. She yelled for me to come join her. She liked riding waves. Jurgen swam to her, and I watched them a while. Iris always rode farther in on her waves than Jurgen. The old man laughed.

Didn't you learn to swim in Germany? he called out to Jurgen.

I was standing in a bad place. The breeze was onshore. The old man's pipe smoke traveled to me. The waves broke right where I was standing, hitting me down low. I kept losing balance. I swam out to Iris in the deep. It took me awhile. I kept having to duck my head and swim into the tall oncoming waves. Something brushed against my leg. I thought it was Jurgen, horsing around, pretending to be a monster from the sea. But when I turned to look for him swimming around me in the water, he wasn't there. He had ridden a wave all the way in. He was on the beach now, shaking his head back and forth, drying his hair the way a dog would dry his coat.

I rode the next wave in. It was small, without much push. When I stood up, I was near the old man. So far as I can tell, he said, only one of you knows how to swim.

Iris was catching another wave, disappearing for a long time before she finally came up.

Later we lay on our towels on the beach, and Jurgen, since he did not have a towel, lay on the sand. The old man did not have a towel, and so Iris sat up and patted one side of her towel. Share with me, she said, and he sat down next to her.

The old man was not so old. He was sixty or so; he said he could not quite remember since he had been living here so long and he had not celebrated birthdays. He did not know the date. His pipe was no longer lit, but still he sucked on it. Iris asked about a wife, about children. Jurgen slept, his chest turning red where his ribs poked out, the closest thing on him right then to the sun.

The old man once had a wife. He had left her in an apartment in a city with a river that turned to ice in the winter and that she would walk on with her toy dogs, schnauzers or Shih Tzus, he could not remember which. She threw them balls, and it was something to watch the dogs skitter and skate across the ice in pursuit of the balls. The old man shook his head, remembering. There was a son who came to visit once. It was he who had helped build the porch and the back rooms where we slept, our room with the window without glass. Now the son built bridges. I call him The Connector, the old man said.

What does he call you? Iris wanted to know.

Old man, the old man said.

We were all hungry, but it wasn't quite dinner yet. The old man said he had beers, but we would have to pay for them. Of course, we said. We drank them on the porch. All of Jurgen had turned red now in the sun and with the beer. Even his eyes were red, and he said it was from the salt. He said he always kept his eyes open when swimming underwater, just in case there was something to see.

Then the old man said it again. He said, As far as I can tell there is only one of you here who knows how to swim.

I can swim, Jurgen said. Germany has pools. Everyone is expected to know how to swim.

You all sink though, what with all that bread and beer, the old man said.

What is it you've got against Germany? Jurgen said. The old man shook his head.

Not much, he said, maybe I just have something against Germans.

Iris laughed. Where is there to eat around here? she said.

There is only one place, the old man said. I always have whatever fish they have caught that day. You'll like it, he said to Iris.

We went to change out of our bathing suits and when I walked past the old man's bedroom, I saw that he had left the door open and in there he too had a cot and a window, but his window had glass and the glass needed cleaning. It was yellow with what must have been pipe smoke. It was hard to imagine how much light it let in.

We walked with our beers on the beach to the one place that served food. Ordering was fast, the same all around of what the only meal was, blind river dolphin. We touched the necks of our beers together in a toast. To our vacation from our vacation, Jurgen said.

You won't like the blind river dolphin, the old man said to Jurgen. It doesn't come with heavy bread and a slab of butter.

Maybe I won't like it because it's blind, Jurgen answered. We laughed. The old man nodded.

How did someone like you get to know these two lovely women? The old man asked, looking at Iris while he spoke.

It's German, Jurgen said, to be friendly to everyone while on vacation. It's sort of an unwritten rule that when a German goes on vacation, he goes to meet people and not just to take in the sights.

Tell me, the old man said, you weren't taking in the sights when you spotted these two girls.

The food came. Iris and I ate small bits of the blind river dolphin, but mostly we drank beer. The old man ate very little too, and he kept ordering more beer for Iris and me, but he told Jurgen he could pay for himself.

All right, Jurgen said, and Jurgen took big mouthfuls of his blind river dolphin.

Then, when Jurgen had finished a few beers, he patted the old man on the back and said the word in German again, the word he called the good word that meant the good feeling between people in a group, the word that hurt Iris's throat to say it.

Can you say the good word? Jurgen said to the old man. The old man shook his head. I can't, he said.

Try, Jurgen said. The old man then stood. In one hand he held his beer, and with the other hand he pushed on Jurgen's shoulder, sending him backward onto the floor of the place where there lay scattered sand that had blown from the beach in the breeze through the open doorway or had come in on the bottoms of our shoes. One of the legs on Jurgen's wooden chair was now split. He got up and righted the chair. He sat back down on it and while he did, I could hear the sound of the wood splintering, splitting some more. He would fall again soon. Jurgen reached up and smoothed down his hair.

I'll pretend that didn't happen, he said.

The old man did not sit back down. He stood by the table as if waiting for the check or someone to come.

We must all be tired from the sun, Iris said. Jurgen, you're burnt, she said.

Vinegar can help, I said. Iris nodded.

Yes, vinegar, she said.

It's a good word to know. Everyone should know it, Jurgen said. Germans, Americans, everyone because it's about everyone getting along.

The old man hooked his foot around Jurgen's chair leg, and he pulled. Jurgen fell off. He stayed on the floor this time and did not bother to try and sit back down again in the chair whose leg was now completely broken. He crossed his legs there on the floor. He reached up and found his fork and took another bite of his blind river dolphin without being able to see what portion the tines of his fork had pierced.

I can eat like this. Who needs a chair? he said.

We should leave, Iris said.

No, the old man said. More beer, he said. He called to the waiter. Just for the girls, he said.

Iris stood up and went to an empty table and found another chair. She brought it behind Jurgen.

Take a seat, she said, and he did.

Tell us more about your son, Iris said to the old man. When will he come next? she said.

The Connector? the old man said, and he shrugged. Hell if I know, he said.

Do you miss the city? I asked the old man.

Iris was drunk now. She stood up to use the restroom and she teetered as if the floor beneath us had shifted. The

7

old man went to her and took her by the arm and helped her find her way.

Let's go, Jurgen said to me.

Go? I said.

They won't miss us, he said. That old man's on his rocker. Let's swim, he said.

I looked out at the ocean. The sky was so dark, I could barely see the water. I just had the sense that it was there.

You go on, I said. I'll wait for her. Sometimes her shoulder gets loose, and she needs me, I said.

Loose? Jurgen said.

Mmm, I said. When she drinks like this sometimes it goes and then I have to push it back in. I have to stand her up against a wall and push with all my might, until she tells me it's back in.

In Germany there's a simple operation for that, Jurgen said.

Yeah, well, we have it in the states too, only difficult part is paying for it. Costs money, I said.

You're American. You're rich. You can pay for it, Jurgen said.

Oh, sure, I said. Go on and swim, I said. I moved my head in the direction of the ocean I could barely see.

All right, but then come join me later, won't you? Jurgen said.

Sure, I said. He left and he was drunk too; again the floor beneath us seemed to shift as he walked across it, like a man aboard a ship rolling in the waves.

They did not come back. I waited a while. I could see the blind river dolphin that was cooked in a white sauce, starting to turn brown. I went in search of Iris. I opened the bathroom door, and both Iris and the old man were in there. He had Iris up against the wall and was pushing on her hard. Her eyes were closed because of the pain. When he got her shoulder back in, she smiled and opened her eyes. All better, she said and reached for her bottle of beer that had been set on the porcelain sink and she took a long drink.

Back at the table she said, Where'd our German go?

He said for a swim, I said.

A swim, doesn't that sound like fun? Iris said to the old man.

The old man said he would enjoy that, watching her swim.

No, all of us. Let's swim, Iris said. She started walking out the door, hitting the doorjamb accidentally and then laughing and saying, Oh, excuse me, to the doorjamb.

The old man paid while I followed Iris out onto the sand. The top layer of the sand at first was still warm from the sun, but then after a second it felt cold as my feet sunk down beneath the top layer.

Jurgen! Iris yelled. There was no answer from the black ocean water.

Iris bent over and pushed her bottle of beer upright in the sand so it would not tip over, and then she took off her clothes.

The old man helped her with her shirt. Watch that shoulder, he said.

Naked, Iris's thin body glowed, and then she ran and dove in and disappeared.

I wish I were young, the old man said to me, watching nothing or the place where Iris disappeared.

All along the beach the sand shone with bits of phosphorous.

Looks like snow, I said. I kicked it up.

It was Jurgen who came out, as if Iris had turned into him beneath the water, and it was he who walked toward us now, naked and shaking the water from his hair.

Come on in, Jurgen said to me.

I shook my head.

I'll help you, Jurgen said. He went to lift up my shirt, but I held my shirt down.

Where's Iris? I said.

I don't know. Where is she? Jurgen said. Then he looked down and saw Iris's beer planted in the sand and he picked it up and drank the rest of it down.

The old man yelled for her. He ran into the ocean. He dove down and then came up and then dove down again.

The current had carried her. She came out of the water farther down the beach than where she had gone in. She walked back toward us while the old man was still looking for her in the water, yelling out her name.

He'll give himself a heart attack, Jurgen said.

I ran in after him. She's here, I yelled, but he was yelling so loud and diving back down so often, he could not hear me.

I stepped on him. I think it was his back I stepped on. He must have been down low, on the bottom's surface, reaching and digging for where she might be. I went under and pulled him up. We found her, I told him. He gasped. Thank God, he said.

We went back to the old man's place. He wouldn't let Jurgen in until he was dry. He told him to stay on the porch and let the wind dry him. Meanwhile the old man himself was very wet. The shirt and shorts he wore dripped on the floor in his hallway as he made his way to the closet and brought towels for Iris.

One's enough, she said, thanks. He had brought her four.

Well, thanks for the dinner, Iris said to the old man, and then Iris and I went into our room and shut the door.

Before I fell asleep, I could hear the old man lock the front door and then I heard him go into his bedroom and shut the door.

I'm wide awake, Iris said while she lay on her cot, but then a second later I could hear her softly snoring.

I woke up later to Jurgen. He was climbing down the large branch that came in through the open window of our room.

More leaves fell down because of him climbing on it, and it reminded me of rain.

Bastard locked me out, Jurgen said, jumping down onto the end of my cot. My body bounced up on the cot's mattress when he did it.

Jurgen didn't leave. He stayed sitting on the end of my cot that was now covered with leaves, leaning his back against the wall.

He asked about America. He wanted to know where I lived. I described for him the building and the heating duct in the building that ran through all the floors and how it was easy to hear what the neighbors upstairs or downstairs were talking about because the sound carried up and down the duct. I told him it wasn't that good German feeling thing, either. I didn't like hearing other people talk. I didn't like knowing they were so close by. He wanted to know if I had a boyfriend. I told him I didn't think I did when I left, but I might when I get back.

Americans don't talk straight, he said. Germans do. Ask me a question, he said. Any question and I'll answer it.

I didn't want Jurgen any longer at the foot of my cot. I couldn't stretch out my legs and lay down. I wanted to lie down and sleep.

All right, one question, I said. I tried to think of what to ask him. I didn't know. I pictured him again at the restaurant, how he got back on the chair with the broken leg after the first time he fell.

All right, I said. If Hitler were around again today, would you join him? I asked.

Jurgen shook his head. Hitler, Nazi Germany, that's all foreigners seem to remember about Germany.

Not true, I said. I remembered how they ate heavy bread and drank beer.

Do you think when Hitler and all of them decided to go after the Jews together that they had that feeling, the German word you know I can't say? I said.

Jurgen said the word.

Yes, that. Did they have it? I asked.

Yes, no, maybe, Jurgen said.

That's not a straight answer; you're answering like an American now, I said.

Yes, they had it, Jurgen said.

I shook my head. That's funny, I said, to think they had the best feeling of all to do the worst thing.

Then Iris said it. She said the word. She must have been listening. When she said it, it sounded like she was German, like she was Jurgen saying it.

Jurgen jumped off my cot, trailing some of the leaves with him, sending them to the floor. Perfect, Iris. You said it perfectly, he said, going over to her.

It didn't hurt my throat this time, Iris said. I'm getting the hang of it, she said, and then she closed her eyes and started softly snoring again.

The next day, the old man knocked on our door. He had breakfast on a tray. He said he had walked to the restaurant early in the morning and had asked them to fix it for her. But Iris was sick from drinking too much. Ugh, she said when the old man brought the tray close to her, lifting a napkin, showing her fried eggs and fried silver sardines, still with their heads and their eyes, their mouths partly open, showing small sharp teeth.

The old man started to walk away with the tray and back himself out the door, but then Iris said, Not the coffee, leave the coffee, and the old man lifted the coffee for her and held it to her mouth so she could drink.

Iris did not leave the room. The sun outside was too strong for her eyes. The old man, every so often, would open up the door and look in on Iris, and then he would close the door and tiptoe through his house. I think he even stopped smoking his pipe, so as not to let the smell bother her. Jurgen and I sat on the porch and Jurgen talked. The old man came out and told us to keep it down, to let Iris sleep. Jurgen would keep his voice down for a while. Then, forgetting, he would raise it again. The old man was telling Jurgen to keep it down again when the Connector walked up the beach. At first, of course, we did not know it was the Connector, but later we learned.

Old Man, he said to the old man, I wrote to you. I told you I was coming.

I never received the letter, the old man said to his son. The Connector shook his head. He went into the old man's room. When he came out, he was holding up a piece of paper.

It was on your desk, he said to the old man. The old man took the paper and he read it.

This is the first I've seen of this letter, the old man said.

The Connector laughed. Oh, Old Man, he said, and then he put an arm across his father and brought him close, a kind of half-hug.

Later, when the old man went to check on Iris, the Connector and Jurgen and I sat outside on the porch, and the Connector said he had been worried about his father here all alone. Did we notice anything peculiar about his behavior? he asked.

Yes, Jurgen said.

No, I said. We don't know him. How could we guess what was peculiar and what wasn't? I said.

He's a nut work, Jurgen said.

Nutjob, you mean? the Connector said.

Exactly, Jurgen said. He tried to fight with me.

I'm thinking, the Connector said, that I can't leave him here alone much longer. He'll have to come back with me. I can get care for him at home, he said.

When Iris finally came out of her room, the Connector smiled.

How do you do? The Connector said and he stood tall and straight and shook Iris's hand for a long time, as if Iris were famous and he was so glad to meet her finally.

The old man hurried onto the porch behind Iris. Don't listen to a damn thing he says, the old man said, looking at Iris. He's all his mother, the old man said.

I'm you too. What about our thumbs? the Connector said. He held up his thumb and made his father hold up his too. See, look, the Connector showed Iris. We have the same thumbs.

And they did. Except for the Connector's thumb being paler, not darkly weathered by this country's sun, their thumbs could be the same.

We all laughed. Drinks, we need drinks, Jurgen said, and for once the old man agreed with Jurgen and sent Jurgen into the house to get beer from the cooler.

Iris wanted to know where he was from. Did the Connector live in that city? The one with the river that froze in winter?

The Connector said he did. He told Iris how she would have to come and visit. He would show her the river; it was beautiful and the water turned pale green when it froze. The Connector said he would take her to restaurants in buildings reaching high above the city's skyline.

Iris smiled. How nice, she said. She looked out at the ocean, and then she said, anybody up for a swim? I think it'll clear my head, she said.

The Connector was the first to say yes; then the old man said yes. Jurgen said he was going to stay and take a nap. He was tired from drinking beer in the afternoon and in Germany, that's how they did it: they sometimes drank in the afternoon and then took a nap and later they could embrace the night.

The Connector could swim. He and Iris went far out. The old man stood in the shallows watching. They did not ride the waves in. They stayed in the deep, floating, treading water, talking, I could tell. I went up to my waist. I rode the small waves that lacked push. Once in a while I could catch a bit of what they were saying. The Connector talked about bridges and his projects and how he sometimes stood on the supports and girders and felt the wind off the river trying to knock him down.

At the restaurant that night, the Connector had us play a game. Guess what I'm thinking of, he said. We guessed and guessed, using questions requiring yes or no answers. Oh, come on, the Connector said, ask better questions.

We don't want to play this game, the old man said. We're not in school, he said.

It's all right. I can guess this, Iris said, and she did. She guessed anchor. She was right. The Connector said, Bravo! And because she won, she had to drink a shot of tequila.

She guessed correctly often. She drank a lot of shots. Then again, after our meal, she wanted to go swimming.

Come this time, Jurgen said to me. So I did. We were all in the water. The old man came out with us. He had left his pipe behind. Race me, the old man said to his son. The Connector looked out across the water, to the deep where his father was facing. To where? he said.

Afraid? the old man said. I'll beat you, he said. Come on, he said. On the count of three, he said. One, two, three. Then he swam hard. He swam and soon the sound of his kicking in the water and his arms splashing became distant. The Connector did not race.

Come on back, Old Man, the Connector said. Old Man? he said. The Connector went out after his father. Iris and Jurgen and I went back on shore. We put on our clothes.

He builds bridges, Iris said. Quite remarkable, she said.

It's not like he builds them with his hands; he just draws them on paper, Jurgen said.

The Connector and the old man came back, but the old man would not walk back with us to the house. The old man walked ahead, almost running. Come on, can't you keep up? he said over his shoulder to his son.

On the walk back to the house Jurgen said we should get to bed early, as we planned to leave the next day to catch the boat and the many buses back to the boardinghouse where we had started our vacation. I agreed with him and we left Iris and the Connector and the old man on the porch, still drinking what was left of the beers. Jurgen went to his bedroom and I went to mine.

When I woke up Iris was loose, her shoulder was out of its socket, and she was standing by my bed, waking me up, moaning with pain.

Please, put it back in, she said. I got out of bed and stood her up against the wall. I began to push on her shoulder hard. When I did it, I heard something coming from the hallway. It was the sound of a fistfight. I heard grunts and I heard the old man saying, Stop, stop. Still, I hadn't put Iris's shoulder back in yet, so I did not go and see what was the matter. I tried to push as hard as the sound of the fists hitting. It was more like slamming is what I was doing. I did it in time with the hits. I think it helped. I slammed into Iris hard. I threw my weight into her. There, it's in, she said. But I still kept slamming. It wasn't until she cried stop that I stopped.

I helped Iris to her cot and then I looked into the hallway. The old man was down, and the Connector was standing over him, holding a wet cloth and wiping his father's brow.

When the Connector saw me, he said, more to himself than to me, I really think it's time I took him home.

When we left in the morning neither the old man nor the Connector was awake. We went walking with our backpacks down the beach, heading for the boat on the river side that would take us to the buses.

On the first bus back home to the boardinghouse, we sat again with more people and chickens. It was hot and Iris said what she would not give for a drink. An old woman beside her understood, and she pulled out a bottle that looked old, that looked like it had spent years lost at sea. The liquid in the bottle looked old too: it was pale yellow and reminded me of the color of the window glass in the old man's room. She passed Iris the bottle, and Iris drank and drank. The old woman smiled and nodded her head and lifted her hand in a gesture, letting Iris know she could drink more. When Iris was finished, she said the word, the German word, to Jurgen and me and then she taught the old woman how to say the word, and the old woman learned how to say it too. Then the entire bus wanted to learn the word. They all said it. All the men and women with chickens on their laps practiced saying the good word. Jurgen stood up in the aisle saying the word so they could repeat it after him. He lifted his arms, palms up, getting everyone to say it louder, and they did. Everyone was saying it; even the chickens seemed to be saying it, their clucks really the good word and not clucks at all.

I WOULD GET A LOT OF PHONE CALLS for my boss from men who said they were Deep Throat. Usually I assumed they were really the boyfriend I was seeing at the time so I would say, "Lou, is this you? Lou, I have work to do," and hang up.

My boss was having work done on his apartment, and the two construction workers wanted to know what I knew about him, him being famous, and since I worked out of his apartment, I showed them a pair of alligator boots he kept under his bed. The workmen, covered in sawdust, put down their hammers and saws and handled the alligator boots, whistling while they did, letting me know they knew the cost of things like boots made of exotic animal hide. When I put the boots back under the bed, I turned them over first to shake out any wood chips or sawdust that may have fallen inside them.

Sometimes when the phone rang and the caller said he was Deep Throat, I would crack the workmen up by screaming into the phone, "Is this Deep Throat really? Well this is Mary Fucking Poppins!" They would get a kick out of that. Other days I was Little Bo Fucking Peep or Little Red Fucking Riding Hood, but I think the day they laughed the loudest was when I yelled into the phone, "Well this is Aretha Fucking Franklin!" All that afternoon we sang all the

Aretha we knew while I paid my boss's utility bills, balanced his checkbook, booked him a flight, and made sure the dry cleaner was going to deliver his clothes on time.

My boss wasn't often at home, and when he was, he was in his office working on a book at the opposite end of the house where the sun shone in brightly on his desk and made all the wood surfaces glow. He was not fond of metal, and once I had to call about thirty shops just to find one that sold the kind of filing cabinets he wanted which were not made of metal but brown wicker. He was on a diet where he only ate brown rice for every meal, and my job was to make him the brown rice. I don't think I ever made it the same way twice only because I didn't know how to cook it, but he never complained and when I brought it in to him, he seemed happy. He was seeing a woman at the time. He liked to buy her things and often he would call from a shop and describe objects to me that he held in each hand, asking me which one I thought she would like better. "Take the one on the right," I would tell him, cutting him off sometimes, the descriptions pointless since I didn't know her and I couldn't possibly see what he was holding. He would laugh when I said things like that. "I know, I know, I'm being ridiculous. But I love her so much. I just want to make the right decision," he would say.

Once the other man my boss had become famous with called, and when he told me who he was I did not believe him. I had, that morning, received numerous Deep Throat calls, and so when this man told me his name and said he wanted to talk to my boss, I said, "Right, and I'm Linda Fucking Lovelace." The workers liked that one too, and in the background, where they were building a new room and framing the walls, I heard them catcall and then start panting like the person had just called some porno set and we were in the middle of hard-core filming. When I hung up and the man called back, angry now, so that I could hear spit hitting the mouthpiece of the phone, I decided to put the man on hold and use the intercom to call my boss in his office in his woody, wicker-filled room (which I had started referring to as Bali since it was so far at the end of the house that it seemed like another part of the world) and ask him if, indeed, he would like to talk to the man. "Of course, put him through," said my boss.

Right then I started to worry that maybe Deep Throat really had been calling all along. Maybe there was another lead or tip or who knows what information that my boss needed to hear. I was quiet while I sat at my desk in front of all of my boss's bills from stores where he had been buying his girlfriend gifts. One of the workmen, Eddie, came over to me, still holding his hammer. He was tall and had hair the color of the pine sawdust that he was always creating with his band saw. When I first met him he was painting a wall in the house with a first coat, and he said he was a painter and I said, "Yeah, right," and what he meant to say was that he really was a painter and had studied at school all the famous artists I'd ever heard of. Eddie put the hammer on top of the table, on top of all the bills from the store from where the girlfriend had received her gifts, and I looked at the pocked metal of the hammerhead, thinking how my boss probably hated hammers and tools because of all the metal, and Eddie took his raspy fingers and put them under my chin and lifted my face up to his. I thought he might kiss me. "What's the matter, kiddo?" he said. I was a little younger than he was, but not by much. Lou, my boyfriend, was my age.

Lou wanted to know a lot more than I did about my boss. He wanted to know, for instance, what kind of shampoo my boss used. I have no idea, I told him. "Don't you look in the shower?" Lou said. "No, I don't," I said. "What does it matter what kind of shampoo he uses?" I said. "It says a lot about him. Is it salon shampoo or drugstore?" I shook my head. Lou had started to smell. Before he had never smelled, but now he was on a new kick where he didn't wash his clothes very often because he didn't want them to wear out quickly or fade. He said it's what the Spanish did. He had lived in Spain for a while. He would now only wash his clothes if they were stained.

Lou was baby faced and I'd never seen him shave once, but Eddie, with his face up close to mine, I could tell was one of those guys who could have shaved twice a day. Because his hair was blonde, his five-o'clock shadow came in kind of shimmery and sparkly, reminding me of flecks of fool's gold you can find in the bed of a stream. "I'm all right," I said. I looked at the clock. It was time to cook lunch for my boss. "Hey, anyone want some brown rice?" I said overcheerfully and loudly, trying to be funny.

Sam, the other workman, groaned. "I hate that shit. My wife's always trying to get me to eat it. I don't eat anything that I can't tell the difference if I'm eating larvae or not."

Eddie peered over my shoulder, watching me cook. "Hey, can I have some of that rice when you're done?" he said.

"Sure," I said and when it was done, I placed it in three bowls, one for my boss and one for Eddie and one for myself. I wasn't making enough money at the time to be able to afford to buy my lunch. I had asked my boss for a raise, but he said it was all he could afford. I put my boss's bowl on a tray with a napkin and a fork and a bottle of soy sauce, just in case he had taste fatigue and wanted to liven up his meal a bit and then I walked to Bali with the tray.

When I opened the door, my boss had his back to me and his bare feet on the windowsill. It was warm in the room because the sun was shining in through the long windows. My boss was looking down the avenue at all the old buildings that, when I was a kid, were once places like slaughterhouses or places where pickles were set in barrels to soak in brine but were now restaurants and apartments with doormen. When I was a kid the sidewalks of those streets were slick, either with the blood from cows or the brine of pickles, and you often slid walking down them, and once I even slid off the sidewalk and onto the street, where the worn cobblestones glistened and looked like humps popping out of the ground, as if they could no longer be contained by the dirt beneath them and were breaking free of their hold. My boss didn't turn around to look at me. He was just staring out of the window. I placed the tray on his desk and took letters from the tigereye-maple wooden box on his desk where he kept mail that he wanted me to put stamps on and take to the post office. Just as I was about to leave the room he spoke. "What would be the perfect gift?" he said. I almost kept walking out the door. It didn't seem like a question he wanted me to answer, but I wasn't sure, so I stopped and turned toward him. He turned and looked at me now. He ran his hand through his hair, and it made him look like he had just woken up. He wore a shirt with the cuffs loosely rolled up and the collar wide open, the buttons unbuttoned far down on his chest so that I could see his graying chest hairs. I knew he was talking about the perfect gift for his girlfriend. I didn't have an answer for him. "How's the book going?" I asked him instead. He smiled and then laughed quietly, and maybe the only reason I knew that he was laughing was because I could see his chest moving up and down a little bit. I didn't have an answer for him. I left Bali, shutting the door behind me. I walked down the long expanse of the house back to the area where I had my desk and the phone and the computer. "Come look at this," Eddie said before I sat down in my chair, and he showed me his paintings.

They weren't really his paintings, just photographs of them he kept in a binder. They were of flowers. Every single one of them. The flowers weren't growing up from the ground. They weren't set in vases on tables. They were just all over the canvas set against dark backgrounds of what looked like thick globs of paint that with time would peel off because the canvass wouldn't be able to hold their weight. Eddie put his face close to mine and looked at me looking at his paintings. I raised my eyebrows. I nodded my head. I pursed my lips. "I like your petals," I said. The petals he painted all had pointy tips at their ends. Not one of them looked like a pansy flower or a mum petal. Eddie nodded. I went back to the beginning. I began to look through them again. I was lucky when the phone rang. It was a long phone call. I had to convince the telephone company not to cut the phone service off. "My employer will be paying the bill right away," I said. The late bill was my fault. I had forgotten to put the envelope in the mailbox. I still had the payment envelope in my bag with the stamp on it that I had put there myself. I took the envelope out while I was talking to the phone company and held it up in my hand, as if the phone company, being the phone company, had a way to see it through the phone. When another call came through while I was talking to the phone company, I asked the phone company if they could hold. The phone company said they couldn't hold. I would have to call them back. "What do you mean you can't hold? You're the phone company," I said. The phone company hung up. I nodded. "Yes," I thought to myself, "they can hang up too."

The other line was Deep Throat. It was a good deep throat. It sounded like this guy had put some thought into it. Maybe he was speaking into a salad bowl, because it seemed like it had an echo to it. I wondered how he fit his face into the bowl along with the phone receiver. "You must be crowded in there," I said out loud. "You have no idea," Deep Throat answered.

"Well, what can I do for you, Deep Throat?" I said, and as I said it, I swung around to see if Eddie was there, listening to what I was saying, but he wasn't there. I could hear him in the back room. He began to pound a hammer into a partition they were building. I didn't have any witty thing to say to Deep Throat. "Let me talk to your boss," Deep Throat said.

"Oh, sure," I said. I held my hand over the mouthpiece of the phone.

"Eddie, Eddie, it's for you. Telephone!" I yelled toward the room where Eddie was hammering. Eddie came to the phone and held his hammer in one hand and the phone in the other hand. I set the pot with the brown rice in it to soak. I wasted rice when I cooked it because I never learned how to cook it properly. I always had a hard layer of rice left at the bottom of the pot that was impossible to scrape out, so that after it soaked, the remaining grains became loose and bloated and it always looked like there was enough rice there to serve a person an entire bowl.

"I see," Eddie said. I didn't catch all of his conversation with Deep Throat. I put the soy sauce away in the cupboard and squirted liquid soap into the rice pot I had set to soak. When Eddie got off the phone, he came up behind me and put his face against my cheek and then turned me so that he could kiss me. I thought he tasted like beer, and I wondered if inside his tool bag he kept some beer bottles alongside his ball-peen hammers and his screwdrivers.

"Guess what?" he said, after he drew back from kissing me. His five-o'clock shadow was very shimmery now, and I looked at it because the overhead light in the kitchen was casting reflections on it, and it seemed like it was moving, as if it really was fool's gold being turned over and skittered in a gentle stream's current.

"I sold a painting!" Eddie said.

"Just now?" I asked.

"Yes, of course just now. He wants to pick it up at my house tonight. He's coming with cash!" Eddie said. Eddie said the word "cash" so loud that I put my fingers to my lips.

"Shh," I said. I did not want my boss, all the way down the house in Bali, disturbed.

"Deep Throat bought your painting?" I said. Eddie lifted back his head and laughed so loud that I caught sight of one of his back teeth. It was gold, and in its surface, I could see how it was made to look like his other teeth, complete with bite marks.

"No, an art dealer bought it. That was an art dealer on the phone. I've got to pack up. I've got to go!" he said.

He left, running down the stairs, leaving the door partway open.

Later, when I was in my place, Lou stopped by. We sat on my futon bed. Before I moved into the place, the landlord had told me that the former resident had been found dead in his bed. I told Lou that where we sat was exactly where the man had died. Lou wanted to know how I knew. "Look around," I said. "Where else could you put your bed?" The other three walls had windows, or a fireplace, or the wall was too short, because there was a doorway next to it to the kitchen. I lived in such a small place because I couldn't afford a bigger place. I barely could afford to pay the next month's rent on the place that I had. I lay back on the bed and looked up at the ceiling. I saw a spot there that I bet the man who died saw every night and every morning. It looked like a grease stain, and I wondered how it got there. Did the man, one day, tackle the fine art of pancake flipping and flip too high? Lou turned me over and rubbed my shoulders. He did not rub hard enough. His hands were not much bigger than mine. Down around his thumbs he had needle-thin strips of skin missing from where he bit and chewed off hangnails. "Did you call me at work?" I asked, sitting up, going to the kitchen for a glass of water.

"Uh, was I supposed to?" Lou said. I shook my head and said "no" into my glass. I sounded like I was deep inside the glass when I said it, as if I was backed up far into some cave. The water even tasted like minerals, heavy and metallic, the drippings from the pointed ends of some stalagmite that had formed centuries ago.

Lou's radio went off. He worked as a grip and often came to see me on his breaks since most of the films he worked on were filmed in my neighborhood. The radio crackled and hissed, and a kid with a voice that sounded like a twelve-year-old's said,

"We need more water in the trailer. Who's out there that can get some more H_2O?"

"Do you have to answer that?" I asked Lou. He shook his head. "Who needs the water?" I asked. I pictured a famous actress in the trailer demanding more bottles of Perrier.

"The grips need more water," Lou said. I nodded. Then another crackle came through. It was a girl's voice.

"Lou, are you there? Are you coming over tonight? I miss you," the girl said. She had some kind of an accent. It might have been Spanish. It was news to me that Lou was seeing someone else. It made me sad how naïve I was. He had obviously been seeing her a while.

"I bet you have to answer that," I said.

"This isn't working out," Lou said.

"There's the door," I said and pointed to my door with its peephole and its dead bolt locks and its layers of countless paint jobs. Lou looked at the door. We both did.

After he left, I could still smell him. I opened the window wide that faced a small backyard. There were overgrown trees in the yard and some grass that once was maybe a mowed lawn, but now it was weeds and vines with petals as large as grape leaves. There was rustling down there too, probably from a cat or a rat. That night, even after I had turned the light off, I could see the stain on my ceiling. I put my hands behind my head and stared at it, still wondering how the old man had done it.

In the morning, Eddie didn't show up, and neither did the other workman. I guessed they had taken the day off. I fumed a little about Lou. I called myself stupid for ever having gone out with him in the first place. I should have known. I pictured his girl as some Spanish girl who wore the same beautiful clothes every day. I filed some bills for my boss. I didn't know if he was awake or not. The door to Bali was closed, but it was usually closed, and so was his bedroom door. I figured he'd want his brown rice soon, so I started to cook it. When the phone rang, the rice was on the stove. It wasn't Deep Throat. It was Eddie. He said, "This is Deep Throat," but I knew right away it was Eddie. "Let's go out to breakfast," he said.

"Now?" I said.

"It's morning, isn't it?" he said. I heard him rub his chin. I thought I could hear the roughness of his hand rubbing against his gold-flecked stubble. "Meet me at the restaurant on the corner," he said.

I left with the rice still cooking. I didn't think about it while I was with Eddie. What I thought about with Eddie was how his fingernails were purple and black from paint and did not look like colors of flowers at all. I ordered blood sausage and cooked apples on the side. Lou had once told me blood sausage was a specialty in Spain, and I had never seen it on a menu before. Eddie said it was his treat. He was going to be rich soon. He walked back up to my boss's apartment with me after the meal. He was finished as a carpenter, but he wanted to pick up his bag of tools, just in case some day he had to return to his trade. On the first flight of stairs he stopped me and kissed me. I could feel Eddie pressing into me and the banister digging into my back. It wasn't going to be a quick kiss. He slid his hand up my skirt. I could feel his fingertips reaching up to the elastic of my panty leg. I smelled the burning rice then. It was a faint smell. Eddie probably couldn't smell it, but I knew right away what it was. I pushed Eddie back and ran up the stairs. By the time I got the door open, Eddie was cursing at me from the staircase.

"You cunt. You don't walk away from me. I could have anybody I want," he said. Because they had been working on the apartment's electrical system, they had temporarily disconnected the smoke alarms, so there was no loud beeping; there was just the rice pot burning and then the water sizzling while I filled up the pot. I turned on the fan above the stove and I opened up some windows. I saw Eddie down the street.

"What about your tools?" I called to him. He heard me and stopped and turned around. He grabbed himself between the legs.

"I don't go anywhere without 'em," he said. He threw his head back and laughed. The day's sunlight was growing stronger, and it hit the gold tooth in his mouth and made it look like a flame, like he was a man eating fire.

My boss wasn't in Bali. He wasn't in his bedroom either. I knocked first and opened up the door after I didn't hear a response. His alligator boots were by his bed. They were not too big on me. When I put them on and walked into the bathroom, they did not slip in the heel. I pulled back the shower curtain and looked. The shampoo bottle was one I recognized. I had used the same brand once before. I thought I should call Lou to tell him. But I knew that if I called him, he would have egged me on. He would have asked me to find other belongings. He would have made me put him on speakerphone while I walked around the house, opening drawers for him and reading labels on shirts. I was tired now. I went to Bali and opened up the door. I sat in my boss's chair and put my feet with the alligator boots still on them across some papers that had a seal from the Vatican on them. They were written on paper that was as thin as tissue, and I'm sure the hard heel of the boot was about to rip a hole on one page. My boss's chair could swivel, and when I sat in it, it creaked like a hammock that was swinging, roped between two trees. The window was open, and a breeze came through that carried with it the smell of the Puerto Rican vendor on the corner selling chipped ice in a paper cone that could be drizzled with any color of food coloring and smelled of a mixture of lemon and lime and coconut syrup. I closed my eyes. I remembered being a girl and how my mother always cautioned me not to buy those treats from the vendors. The ice, sitting out all day, my mother said, was peppered with city soot. "You might as well lick the pavement," my mother had said one hot day when I did not want to walk any longer and the sun hit me with a force that felt like a grand piano falling down on my head.

I dreamt of her then, while I slept in my boss's chair. In my dream she had died and I cried in my sleep. It was my boss who put his hand on my shoulder and shook me from the dream. When I looked at him, I didn't know who he was. For a moment I thought he was the Puerto Rican street vendor and that he had come upstairs to give me a cone. He wanted me to try one after all these years. "I burnt the rice," I said, taking my feet off the desk, and a little bit of the Vatican's letterhead with it.

"I can't eat it anymore," my boss said. "Shall we go for lunch instead?" he said. "I would like a burger and fries and a Coke," he said.

I was standing now. I could see afternoon clouds rolling in. It became darker in Bali.

"This isn't working out," I said. "I don't make enough money here." My boss scratched his chest. Beneath the gray and white hairs there, his skin was sweating.

"I have to quit," I said.

"Let's go to lunch now," my boss said. "I could eat Chinese too," he said. "I could go for some moo shu pork."

I took off the boots and changed back into my shoes, while my boss stood in the doorway waiting for me to join him. My boss never seemed to notice I was even wearing them. I left the boots by the chair at my desk, as if someone invisible were sitting in the chair, still wearing the boots, still answering the phone calls and talking to Deep Throat.

I walked down the stairs with my boss. I looked at the steps, and they seemed like they had flecks of gold in them, and I wondered if while Eddie was kissing me so hard some of his beard hairs had come loose and floated down the stairs.

I left my boss at the corner. "I have to go home now," I said. My boss said he would call me later. He said I needed time to think. "Think about this," he said. "I may not be able to pay you more money, but I could make things happen for you," he said.

At home that night the phone did ring. I heard it while I was lying in my bed. The moon was full. Its silver light was everywhere, reflecting off mirrors and the glass in picture frames on my walls as if I were in the dark watching an old black-and-white movie flickering on the television. I didn't answer the phone. I let it ring and it stopped after a while. I stared up at the ceiling, at the stain. Maybe there was something up there that had been bugging the old man who had died in the place before me. Maybe he had gone into the kitchen and grabbed a mop and stood on the bed and tried pounding on the ceiling, trying to get the thing to stop. There was a mop in the kitchen when I first moved into the place. I got out of bed and grabbed the mop and stood on the bed. Sure enough, the stain on the ceiling was the size of the head of the mop. When the phone rang again, I picked it up. I didn't say hello. I just said, "What kinds of things can you make happen for me?"

"A lot," he said. "The world is your oyster," he said. Then it started happening. The ceiling started shaking and I heard music without words coming from a stereo. My upstairs neighbor was dancing, or doing calisthenics. I couldn't be sure. He was loud though, and I thought I could hear him breathing too, right through the plaster ceiling. He could have been lying beside me in bed right next to my ear, his breathing was so loud. "Can I ask you something?" I said to my boss.

"Shoot," he said.

"Do you ever talk to Deep Throat when he calls? Do you ever just talk to him because you have no one else to talk to?" I said.

My boss laughed. "I have a lot of people to talk to," he said. I nodded. The neighbor's dancing was getting frenetic. I could feel the frame of my bed slightly bouncing. The music was so loud that my boss must have thought it was my music playing and not my neighbor's.

"What do you say? Will you come back?" he said.

I told him no, while still holding onto the mop, while I was lying in bed. The handle of the mop was on the floor, and the head of the mop pointed at the ceiling, and I held it like it was a scepter and lightly banged it up and down, as if I were making a point or wanted everyone in the room to be quiet, but the music kept playing.

I took another job, which paid me more money, working for a company that made hair transplants for men. The head of the company wanted me to videotape how everyone did their job in the building. Before the job I called Lou and told him I didn't know the first thing about taking video; could he help? "Is that why you're calling?" he said. "Yes, that's the only reason," I said.

"Move slower than you think you have to," he said. I slowly videotaped a warehouse where hairpieces made from the hair of Asians, because it was said to be the strongest, sat on the heads of mannequins that filled the room. I slowly videotaped a worker opening up complaint letters from men whose hair transplants had come off: one while he was breakdancing, spinning on his head at a wedding, another who had walked behind the running engine of a jet airplane, and his hair was blown off. I slowly videotaped a worker opening the photographs men sent of allergic reactions they had to the hair transplants and how their heads looked like they had been burned in different places with the butt of a lit cigar. I videotaped so slowly, I ran out of tape, and when I asked my boss for more, he said it wasn't in the budget. He said he was sorry, but he wasn't interested any longer in the project where everyone's job in the building was videotaped. He was going to retire now, and someone else was going to take his job who did not care about the videotapes. The day I was let go, Lou came over to visit. He still had a key to my place, and when I got home, he was sitting on my bed. "I think the old man who died in your place could have died by the window too. He could have set up his bed so that his head was by the window," he said.

"Show me," I said, and Lou showed me how the head of the bed could have been at the window and the foot of the bed could have reached out into the middle of the room. Lou then said he was hungry.

"What have you got? Can you make some brown rice? Sometimes all I feel like eating is a big bowl of brown rice," he said.

"I thought we weren't doing this anymore. I thought it was over," I said. Lou nodded. His brown hair fell in front and covered one of his eyes entirely, and for a moment he looked like a girl. "How can you do this? How can you just walk into my place and tell me where the old man died and that you want brown rice for dinner after you're the one who started seeing someone else?" I said.

Lou shrugged, "It's not so hard to do. You still like me," he said, and he moved closer to me, holding out his arms to take me in them.

"What about the Spanish girl?" I said. "Isn't it time you go to her place? She misses you. Oh, I understand now," and I really was beginning to understand it all. "She dumped you. You need to leave," I said. Lou smiled. He sat on my bed. I was the one who left.

I still had the key to my old boss's place. I walked up the stairs of his place and unlocked the door. I knew he was away that week. I was the one who had booked the plane reservations for him to fly to Rome on business. I looked around the place. The other workman had finished building the extra room. There were no signs of tools or sawdust anywhere. I slept in my boss's bed that night. I turned down the covers and checked the label on the sheets. The sheets were cotton, a high thread count. They were so high in thread count that they felt thin to the touch, and I worried that just by sleeping on them my elbows and knees would wear them and cause them to rip. When the phone rang and woke me up, I jumped to answer it. I talked to

35

Deep Throat for a long time. He was close to the ocean, and his true voice seemed masked by heavy rollers pushing in to shore. He told me what the weather was like where he was, and it was not so different than the weather in Bali. He told me birds took flight from saltwater rivers and moved their great long wings. He said I would like the huge leaves on the trees that shaded him on shore when he sat beneath them watching the sunlight hit the water. Over the sound of the waves, I heard a creak on the other end of the line. I figured it was the wicker chair he was sitting in. I heard the lazy whir of a ceiling fan on low. I could almost smell coconut and pineapple, or was that just the smell of my shampoo that I had used to wash my hair with before I went to bed? "What about the food?" I asked.

"Do you like seafood?" he asked.

"I love it," I said.

"The oysters are huge here, and for nothing you can have as many as you'd like. Think oyster city, think oyster to the hilt, think oyster ad infinitum," Deep Throat said.

It was early morning by the time we got off the phone. I slept late, and I felt hot in the bed with the late morning light streaming in. Even after showering, I was still hot, so when I left the place, I stopped at the Puerto Rican street vendor. He had just arrived. His block of ice was still covered in cloth that looked like it had been ripped, with threads dangling here and there, from a pair of faded denim jeans. I ordered a blue frozen ice. When he poured on the blue syrup, I watched it flow through the ice, spreading quickly, turning into some kind of snowball found only on Mars. I looked around me. I expected to see my mother. I expected to feel her grabbing the snow cone away from me and throwing it to the pavement.

She wasn't there. I walked away from the Puerto Rican vendor to the sound of him chipping ice to make more snow cones. When I got home, Lou was there. Either he had let himself in again or he had never left. In my hand, all that was left of my treat was a soggy paper cone colored bright blue, and the tips of my fingers were blue and my palm was blue. I held up my blue hand to Lou, showing him. "I'm from another planet," I said. "And I'm not here to help you." Lou laughed.

"God, that's awful," he said. "What color is that?" he said. "It's all over your mouth and your teeth," he said.

"You have something we need. It's crucial to our civilization," I said.

"Yeah?" Lou said.

"Yes, give me the key, and I will spare your human race," I said. I went up to Lou, ready to dig my hand into his pocket, but I didn't need to. He took the key out, his face changing, his smile disappearing. He threw the key where it landed on the bed. "You're acting like a jerk," he said.

"We take pity on your kind," I said.

"Fine, I'm out of here then," he said. I followed him out the door. I stood at the top of the stairs, watching him go down.

"We will come back light-years from now to check on your progress as a species," I said. The door slammed open, letting in a whiff of hot smelly chemical air from the vent located on the ground floor by the dry cleaners. I breathed in deeply; on my planet, I imagined, it was the only air we could breathe.

Later that night, when the neighbor upstairs started his loud music and his wild dancing, and the light fixture swung, and my bed shook, I went for the mop quickly. I pounded it against the ceiling. I added to the stain that was already up there. I thought if only I could smash the mop through the ceiling, then my neighbor would stop, and all the noise would cease. I was breathing hard. I was sweating. My arm hurt. I stopped and sank down to sit on my bed. "Is this how you died?" I said out loud, wanting an answer.

BY THE TIME YOU READ THIS

"DEAR PAUL, BY THE TIME YOU READ THIS, I will be dead. If you don't stop seeing that other woman, I will come back to haunt you. I will be the face in the mirror when you shave. I will be the wind you hear at night. I will be the creak in the stairs and the loud shudder of the settling roof beams that wakes us up from our sleep."

"Dear Cleo, I hope you never understand why your mother did this. If you ever find yourself close to understanding, I want you to call and get help right away. Please promise me that. There are plenty of numbers to call on the fridge in case of an emergency. (You might even consider calling Irving Propane. Their staff has always been helpful and ready to come out to the house at a moment's notice if we think we hear even the slightest hissing sound of gas leaking from our pipes.)"

"Dear Paul, have you ever noticed the birthmark on my labia? If not, you should look now. I'd hate to go to my grave thinking that I was married to a man all these years who didn't even notice such an intimate detail about me."

"Dear Paul, I'm doing this because I want you to respect my last wish, and that last wish is that you stop seeing that woman because I don't want Cleo to know the woman you left me for, even if she might be some amazing person you think

Cleo should get to know — a choreographer or symphony musician or nuclear physicist. All that she'll ever be to me is a slut."

"Dear second grade teacher Miss Debbie, thank you for always letting me come to class early so I could help you set up the classroom. Even though you were hugely overweight, I liked the way you looked and smiled at me. I liked the candy you would give us when we behaved well, and I am sorry that I told you that I thought you were bribing us. That was just something my father said, and I was repeating it. At times he takes things very seriously, and once, while watching election results, he threw our television out the window when a certain president was elected that he didn't like."

"Dear Cleo, I want you to throw away what you don't want and keep what you want of all that I owned. I think my pearl ring would look good on you, so don't throw that away, and don't throw away my mother's sorority pin, as there are little diamonds embedded into it, and it might be worth something someday. Also, even though the brown Le Creuset baking dish in the pantry looks old, it's French and very good for roasting new potatoes, so I would say don't throw that away either. Don't throw away the handheld eggbeater. Those are quite rare, ever since whisks became the rage, and you can't even buy one on eBay these days. Remember not to put the colored Pyrex bowls with the white interiors into the dishwasher, as their colors on the outside will fade. Definitely throw away all the boxes and boxes of colored slides your father's parents took on their trip to Alaska. They are just pictures of icebergs and flowers."

"Dear Mom, I hope I did this right. My biggest fear is that I wake up in a hospital room and you are staring at me with fear in your eyes, the same fear you had when we were in that car accident and I hit my head on the windshield, and there was so much blood that you had to take off your shirt to stop the blood from flowing, and I was so embarrassed when the police came because you were wearing a white bra that looked dirty, like you had just come out from under the wheels of our car."

"Dear Dad, I hope I do this right, and really cleanly, because I want you to shake your head and say what you always used to say, which was, "That girl can do anything once she puts her mind to it." I want you to tell Mom that crying won't make me come back. I'm never coming back. (Well, if I do come back, it will just be to haunt Paul if he's still with that slut, so don't worry because I won't be coming back to where you and Mom are.) Tell Mom something like the load of life was too hard for me to take, and now it's her job to hold it for me, just like when I was a girl and we would walk along the road back from school, and my backpack was too heavy and I would ask her to carry it. Make it sound like she still has a purpose in life."

"Dear Paul, tell me that you'll be so bent out of shape after my death that you'll fall into my grave after I'm lowered into it. Tell me you'll take out all of my pictures and put them on display on the dresser. Tell me you'll sleep with a pile of my clothes you pushed together to make look like a body and that's the only way you can fall asleep at night. Tell me you'll take Cleo to every place we've ever been together so you can say, 'and this is where we held hands, and this is where we kissed, and this is where I told her I loved her.' Tell me you will remember that love more strongly than when I was alive so that it almost hurts, but not too much of course. I still want you strong enough to take care of Cleo. Tell me you'll remember she has an appointment with the orthodontist in two weeks. It should take over an hour, so tell her to bring a good book to the office, and not one of those trashy YA books with the airbrushed cover. Tell me you'll bring her something good to read. She's almost ready for *The Lord of the Rings*. Maybe they have redone the cover, and there's a trashy-looking YA cover with a swarthy shirtless Frodo on it that you will have better luck getting her to read than that old edition we have with its spine breaking off and thread hanging from where it was bound."

"Dear UPS man, thank you for all the years when you saw my car parked in town and decided to open the hatch of my unlocked car and put my package into it so that you could save time and gas by not having to drive all the way up the hill to my house. Thank you for always waving at me on any country road I ever saw you on, which was sometimes towns away from our town. (You certainly put in a lot of miles.) Thank you for always handing my dog a biscuit when she climbed into your truck, and thank you for not yelling at our chickens that also climbed into your truck and pecked the corrugated metal steps, and instead you just said, "shoo, shoo," in almost a whisper. I think we will see each other again someday. I really do. Don't forget to wave like usual. Maybe then I will find out your name."

"Dear Cleo, when you get your period, start off with tampons right away. Those pads can be uncomfortable, and with all of your swimming you'll want the tampons anyway. But of course, you probably know this, and you are probably saying, 'Geez, Mom,' right now. Don't let your father get his panties in a wad about you dating boys. You've got good sense, and tell him you'll use it. He might bring out a baseball bat and sit out on the front porch the first time a boy comes calling on you, but kiss him on the cheek before you leave on the date and tell him you studied a self-defense book at the library and you know how to rip the guy a new asshole if he tries anything on you."

"Dear sixth grade English teacher Mr. Sun, despite all of your grand teachings (I will never forget the meaning of "hyperbole," one of your vocabulary words, for example), I have not retained the knowledge of when to use "lay" or "lie." They say "lay" takes an object, but I still don't understand that. And the title of that book *As I Lay Dying* has screwed me up for years. Then there was that billboard when I was a kid: "Winston tastes good like a cigarette should." What was the matter with that grammar? I'd like to know. Anyway, I do thank you for a great sixth grade class. I loved that short story called 'The Ledge' about the man and his son and his nephew who lose their skiff on a hunting trip to a small island and when the tide comes in the father has to hold the boys aloft for as long as he can before they all drown from the freezing water that encroaches upon them from all sides. You might have known then that I would grow up to be the type of woman who would do this act now, which is what I have done by the time you read this, since I loved those morose stories so much. (Was that just a run-on? I apologize if so.) You might have said then that I was a dead ringer for this kind of act I'm about to commit now."

"Dear Paul, I'm sorry I did this, in a way. I mean, maybe all men are going to cheat on their wives eventually. You're certainly not the first. Maybe I'm just sorry I'm the type of woman who got upset enough about it to take her own life. I'm sorry you didn't marry the type of woman who just said, 'Fine, you want to fuck someone else, then I'll fuck someone else too.' I guess I should have gone out and found myself some other man and then let it subside and let us be together again. I couldn't do that, though. I couldn't stand to think about you with someone else. I think I did what was best. Don't you? Stupid how, after all these years, I still want your approval. I should have been the type of woman who could just leave you and wish you well and feel sorry for you and maybe, from time to time, even stomach you and meet you for lunch and notice you were wearing your hair still in a ponytail after all these years and recognize the sweater you were wearing as one I once gave you but that you've now forgotten where it came from. Listen, I'm going to throw that sweater out right now before I finish this note because, damn it, I don't want you wearing it in the presence of that slut. I've been thinking about that other lover I should have taken, instead of taking my own life. I mean, I don't know who I would have taken anyhow. There are all those fathers of the girls on Cleo's swim team. They're all smart and in shape or at least they care about being in shape. I think I like one of the head lifeguards at the pool. He is younger than the rest of the fathers of the swim team girls, but I have noticed him noticing me. I think you know him. He's the one with the big sparkling blue eyes. He's tall. He's got a chest broader than yours, and he's got more muscle than you do. (Oh, did I just write 'got'? Yikes, I mean to say, 'he has more muscle than you do.')"

"Dear whatever your name is, of course, in my eyes, you are Dear Slut, but I should really take the 'dear' out anyway because 'dear' and 'slut' are probably too incongruous to appear one right after the other, and there is probably some rule my sixth grade English teacher, Mr. Sun, could tell me about placing two incongruous words right next to each other. So, Slut, I am writing this to let you know that even though I have never met you, I feel I should let you know that it's probably your fault I have taken all these pills because I know Paul, and really, I don't think he would have let himself go this far with you if you hadn't probably pushed yourself on him in some way. I wondered for a while what you looked like, but now I really don't want to know. I'm sure you're beautiful and thin and have something unusual about you that Paul found irresistible. Maybe you have a lisp. Maybe you even have a limp or one hand that is missing a finger. Has Paul taken you to the restaurant that's a house with the famous shepherd's pie and the jazz band whose drummer in the warmer months has to fit himself inside the massive fireplace because there is no other room for him, what with all the tables they try and fit in to accommodate the crowd?

Has he held you the way he held me from behind at night where he is able to whisper in your ear? Has he told you about that dog he had when he was younger that followed him everywhere and then got killed by a tree his father felled and how his father chainsawed the tree in pieces to move the log off the dog, but it was too late—the dog was not going to make it, and a gun had to be used? Does he hold your hand when you walk to hurry you along the way he does me? Has he told you his favorite time of year is winter? Has he made you take long walks in the snow and pointed out the tracks of snowshoe rabbits and families of deer? Has he told you about Cleo? How beautiful she is and how when she was first born, he suddenly became more frightened than he ever had in his life because he realized he now had something he could lose and afterward he would never be the same? Has he told you how she inhales books and is really witty in a dry way you would not expect a girl her age to be? Has he told you she looks like me? She does. Our baby pictures are almost identical. Do you know Paul eats his chicken with two forks? I could never understand that, but the next time you see him eat chicken, notice how he will ask for an extra fork and not a knife. That is, if you really decide you are going to keep seeing him after I have killed myself and after he has grieved and realized I was his only true love. Are you really still going to want to be with him after all of that? I would think not. He might be somewhat of a basket case for a while. We've travelled all over the world together, and I know things about him that he hasn't told anyone else. He knows almost everything about me, except there are things, private things I am not going to discuss with you, that I think he has overlooked, but in the scheme of things, they are not so important after all. They are just minor blemishes, in a manner of speaking.

Once we traveled to Spain, and I fell off a moped that I was trying to start and I gave it too much gas, and the moped reared, and I fell on the ground, which was littered with big rocks, and I cut my knee terribly. He said he thought I was trying to show off when I did it. We didn't have disinfectant, but we did have Grappa di Julia, a liquor that bubbled when it came into contact with my deep cut. He might tell you, after he finds me, how I was unstable anyway and that it was not finding out that the two of you were seeing each other that made me kill myself. He might tell you how I hitchhiked while I was six months pregnant on the French island of Réunion and that I could have been kidnapped, but he would not be telling you the whole story because he did not know the whole story. The whole story is that I did not hitchhike anywhere. I just told him I did to make him feel bad that he had left me for the day to go to the caldera of a volcano. (I wasn't supposed to travel to high altitudes while pregnant so he went without me. I was jealous that he got to go see the active volcano and I didn't.) I came back to the house we were staying in with two very long baguettes I bought on my long journey home that did not involve my thumbs for hitching a ride but only involved my legs with the swollen ankles from carrying a child curled like a pill bug inside of myself. So, you see we cannot believe everything people tell us because sometimes they do not know for sure themselves."

"Dear Mom, you will probably react in the worst way to my death, and you are the one person I least feel like writing to. I bet you might have some advice for me now if you saw how I was thinking about killing myself. In this circumstance, you might have quoted some religious line you heard in *The Sound of Music*. If you were here with me you would say, "Whenever god shuts a door, he opens a window." And I would look around the room and say the windows are already open. They've been open a while, and there are no more to open."

"Dear UPS man, Cleo is ordering a goose egg that she bought. She has an incubator for it. Please put the package inside the door. I would hate for the egg to become overheated and for the poor little chick to die before it has even had a chance to break free. I hope she has enough time to let the goose, when it hatches, imprint on her. She has little time these days since she is on the swim team such a far drive away, and they practice so often and they go to so many meets. She is getting quite good and just bought one of those Fastskin suits that are so tight that I almost need a crowbar to get it on her. I wonder who will help her into the suit when I'm gone?"

"Slut, if you are still with Paul after I've hung myself, do me this one favor, and make sure he compliments Cleo a lot. I believe there is nothing more valuable to a girl than a father who is able to tell his daughter how smart and beautiful she is. I think sometimes he doesn't want to tell her how beautiful she is because he doesn't want her to become full of herself and conceited. But I don't think there is a chance of that. If you haven't met her already somehow, you will realize when you do meet her (and of course I'm hoping you don't meet her and that Paul, in his grief over losing me, breaks up with you) that she is unassuming and forthright and also very beautiful. She is one of those girls whose eyebrows you wish you had because they taper so nicely. She is tall and slender and can make you laugh easily. I guess I would be wrong to say I will miss her since I will no longer "be," but I miss her right now, and she is just in the next room reading, only a plasterboard's thickness away. It is inconceivable to think that I won't miss her when I am dead; that's how much I love her. Do you have children? Probably not, since I have decided you are most likely young. I was kind of hoping that you did have children, or at least one child, and when trying to convince Paul to stay with you after I killed myself, you would have the monumental task of trying to sell not only yourself to Paul but your child. Maybe he is a son and has been having a hard time of it in school. Maybe he is a "different kind of learner" and needs aides to go with him from class to class and take notes for him and give him the first lines of essays to get him started. Maybe someone holds the pencil for him and does the computation for math homework while he watches, wondering about what will be on the lunch menu that day. Maybe you don't tell Paul any of this, and what you tell Paul is that your son has the uncanny ability to tell who it is when you hear the phone ring. You make it seem like your son has some kind of powers the average child does not have. He can tell the minute he sees the color of a license plate what state it's from. I suppose you are questioning why, if I love Cleo so much, am I willing to leave her? I think maybe I have raised her too well. Let me explain. She can bake. Cream puffs and biscotti are in her repertoire at the tender age of twelve. She can sew, not just mend. A quilt she made lays/lies on her bed that she tells me is the flying geese pattern. She quotes Shakespeare verbatim after just reading lines of him in one sitting. She can scoop up her pet goose in her arms and walk with it in the field and stroke its head and imitate the goose when it hisses. She is armed for the world, you see, and hardly needs me anymore, except of course for getting that Fastskin racing suit on."

"Dear Paul, by the time you read this note, I will have asphyxiated myself in the garage, but I did want you to know that I was thinking beforehand of the time we traveled to Madrid and you tried your hand at the Spanish tongue and kept asking the bank teller, "Do I have a pen?" instead of correctly asking, "Do you have a pen?" and I remember how I could not stop laughing, and when you realized your mistake, how you started laughing also, and the people on the line behind us were getting angry and started saying things we could not understand and throwing their hands up in the air, which we thought was very Spanish and made us laugh harder. I remember the time in Scotland, when we were worried about waking up in time to catch our train back to London and the proprietor of the bed and breakfast said not to worry, that he would come knock us up in the morning. Do you remember how hard we wanted to laugh then? We had to run up to our room while we covered our mouths to make sure we didn't laugh in front of him, and then after we made it to the room and slammed the door behind ourselves we fell onto the bed laughing, with tears streaming down our faces, and behind us a window with a breathtaking view of the Edinburgh castle and black clouds sailing in the Scottish sky. Paul, I killed myself because I couldn't imagine those memories living alongside the more recent memories of you cheating on me."

"Dear coach of the swim team, I shot myself because my husband and I were having some marital infidelity problems, nothing more than that. I don't believe I'm insane or that some kind of insanity or psychological neurosis runs in the family. I'm telling you this because I want you to treat Cleo as fairly as possible. Understand that she's no different than all of those other kids. She's not suddenly going to get so upset at not winning an event that she's been training for months for that you feel you have to put her on a suicide watch. (By the way, she has been telling me lately that she would like to improve her butterfly. I think she thinks she comes out of the water too high when she takes her breath, so maybe if you have time some time you could work with her on her body profile.)"

"Slut, I slit my wrists because, well, you know why. I don't want you to be a mother to Cleo, but maybe, once in a while, you could tell Cleo things a mother might tell her daughter.

Things like, after changing into your swimsuit, don't forget to reach inside and to, one at a time, lift each breast up higher so it looks fuller and doesn't look like your breasts are silver dollar pancakes."

"Dear UPS man, I ran in front of your truck because I got tired of waiting for a package that was never delivered. What I mean to say is that I was hoping my husband would fall back in love with me after having a torrid romance with a younger woman, and he never did. Did you ever have that package in the back of the truck and maybe it was undelivered? Maybe it is sitting in some holding facility in Maine where outside blueberries grow this time of year and seagulls alight on the rooftops. (Maybe you have seen Paul with his slut on your rounds, and you are shaking your head reading this, saying you could have told me all along that he would never leave the little hottie and that I was history long before the Christmas rush began last year.)"

"Dear Paul, I walked off into the woods alone one winter's night because you were the one who always told me that dying from the cold was probably the nicest way to go, that even right before I died I would not feel cold at all any longer and I would see everything around me more clearly than I ever had before. It was very Native American of me to do it this way. By the time you read this letter, you will have to imagine me leaning up against some maple tree having died feeling very alive, every leaf blowing past me sounding like a roar."

"Dear Mom, by the time you read this I will have jumped off the bridge over the falls. Please keep an eye on Paul in the future. After all, the women he dates will leave an impression on Cleo. Feel free to let Cleo know your opinion of these women. I won't be there to teach her the meaning of 'slut,' 'whore,' 'wanton,' 'cradle robber,' etc."

"Dear Mr. Sun, do you happen to know of any other expressions or words for women who would try to land a man at any cost? I would look those words up in a thesaurus or dictionary myself, the way you taught us to in sixth grade, but I am a little caught up right now, and it is more time-consuming than I thought. When you get them would you please write them on a list and send them to my daughter, Cleo, at the following address:

'Dear Cleo, I did this because I love you.'

'Dear Paul, I did this because I hate you.'

'Dear Mom and Dad, I wish there was a way you would never have to learn I did this.'

'Slut, it's none of your business why I did this.'

'Dear Mr. Sun, I did this to myself. I have done this to myself. I will have done this to myself. I shan't have done this to myself. I had to do this to myself. I have had to do this to myself. I will have had to have done this to myself. I, myself, have done this. I done did this.'

'Dear Paul, just one last thing: I'm putting a roast in the oven, so by the time you read this letter, it will probably be done. I wanted to leave Cleo one last good meal. Don't make her that cube steak again, even if it is on sale. It was way too tough, and bits of it got caught in her braces, and every time she flosses, she pops a spring and has to make a new appointment.'

'Dear Death, here I come. Be forgiving, be swift, be the answer.'

'Dear Death, you will have to take a rain check. I don't really want an answer. I can't really remember the big question anyway. All of my questions are small. Where is the hydrogen peroxide? I need to use some on Cleo because she has come down with swimmer's ear. Who has fiddled with the water heater, and why am I stuck in a lukewarm shower? If lightning, when it hits the air, is hotter than the sun, then why doesn't everything around the lightning bolt melt? Why aren't the nearby trees reduced to just puddles of sap? Can I pass a school bus on the road if it's stopped to drop off kids but the stop sign hasn't been extended by the driver? Besides, there are too many things going on here for me to want to kill myself right now. There is a goose egg coming that we will have to turn around in the incubator every morning and night. There is a storm coming, and I love how the lightning lights up the sky and the gray barn looks almost white. Also, there is a new barred owl in the tree by our window, and I'd like to hear his call again tonight, as it is peaceful right to the bone. Also, the dog needs her second dosage of heartworm medication, and I better be around to give that to her. And one more thing, I am too tired right now to tie a noose/slit my wrists/pop pills/run the engine in the closed garage/jump off a bridge/pull a trigger/freeze to death/get run over. I think I just might lie/lay down for a while and close my eyes and when I wake up I can decide what's the best thing to do, but right now, I am so tired, and the bed looks so comforting, and the sheets, just off the line, smell like flowers and sunshine.'

CAESAR'S SHOW

"THESE?" THE BOY SAYS, rolling two race cars across the wooden hallway floor when his mother, Sarah, asks him where he got them. "My teacher gave them to me," he says. Outside the dog barks and whines. The dog is in the yard, his nose against a chain-link fence, wanting to get closer to a litter of stray kittens whose eyes are still closed. Rats are scurrying across the phone line that runs to the house, their shapes black in the dying light. "Really? Your Kindergarten teacher gave you those two cars? Why?" Sarah says while standing at one end of the hall.

"I don't know," the boy says. Sarah wishes that her husband, Benjamin, were home so she could tell him that she thinks their son has stolen the cars. She would like to discuss what to do about the stealing and about the lie. Sarah never feels confident reprimanding her son. She always thinks she is being too easy on him. But Benjamin will not be home for a while. He is at the airport, waiting for a foreign client he's supposed to pick up and escort to a meeting with the senior partner. Sarah hears the rats jump from the phone wire to the top of a palm tree. The palm tree leaves rattle and shake. Everything in the yard sounds like it's moving because of the Santa Anas. They blow and the hot air moves across her yard, shaking the grapefruit tree. Its fallen leaves skitter across the paved walkway.

Sarah picks up the phone and calls Benjamin. "How much longer?" she asks.

"An hour at least. The plane's delayed," he says.

She picks up the broom. The house is so dirty. There are bits of food on the floor and balls of hair, but just as she lifts the broom, she hears the dog barking again. He won't stop barking at the kittens that were born on the other side of the chain-link fence where rough grass grows in clumps and bare old tires lay. With her broom she goes out to where the dog is, his nose in between the diamond-shaped spaces of the fence, and she tells him to hush, just hush. "I'll hit you with this broom if you don't," she says, but she knows she would not and instead she sits down beside Bob. She pets his fine broad head and runs her hand down his thick black fur. She looks at the kittens too. "Oh, they are cute. No wonder you like them. Yes, you would be a good father to them if they were on our side of the fence," she says. Her son comes out with the cars and sits down next to her. They all look at the kittens, and her son shows the kittens his two cars and then he rolls the cars up and down the dog's back, which spreads the fur apart so that the dog's pale skin shows brightly against the black fur. Sarah still holds the broom and looks down at the bristles, noticing how they are bent backward, as if every time she ever swept, she swept too hard, as if everything she tries to sweep up is ground in or stuck on the floor and will not come loose.

The phone rings and it is Benjamin saying, "The good news is the plane is landing now. The bad news is, Rogers, who is supposed to meet him for drinks, just got a flat tire on the expressway, and it looks like I'll have to be the one taking him for drinks." Sarah can hear the rumble of the planes flying low. "Call you later," Benjamin says.

The two cars are on the table at dinner. Her son slides them between the salt and pepper shakers, and Sarah asks again, "Did your teacher really give you those cars?" The boy doesn't answer. He decides to put his fork into his mouth instead. "She did not give you those cars, my love," she says. The boy continues eating. He takes his fork and pierces as many pieces of chicken as he can on the tines. Then he stuffs the forkful in his mouth. Sarah can see the white pieces between his lips because with all of the food inside, he can't keep his mouth closed.

"When your father gets home, I'll tell him that you stole the cars. I bet he'll say that tomorrow, at school, you will have to give the cars back," Sarah says. The boy continues to chew. Later, when she clears the table, and her son has gone into his room, she notices the cars are gone. When she is finished with the dishes, she goes to his room to check on him. He is reading on his beanbag chair, but she does not see the cars, and the cars don't seem to be in his pockets either. She feeds the dog after dinner, because someone told her once that dogs should always be fed after the family is fed because that puts them in their place, and they know they are not the alpha dog and that you are the alpha dog. Really, though, she has no interest in being the alpha dog and likes to feed the dog after the family eats because after dinner there are always scraps from their plates she likes to give the dog, and the dog's food that they buy is like rolled-up balls of chewed cardboard and who can live on that? Not my dog, she thinks, not a dog who is still so protective over the newborn kittens that he has not even come into the house for dinner but is still out there in the darkness, still barking, but barking with a sore-sounding throat that sounds very sad to Sarah. It seems to strike a chord inside of her, and for once she knows exactly how that expression came to be, because she feels as if somewhere inside of her that sore-sounding bark is resonating against a piece of her, such as her breastbone, so that she feels the bark as much as she hears it.

"Let's jump," the boy says, and he takes Sarah by her hand and leads her to her bedroom and tries to get her up onto her bed with him. It is close to the boy's bedtime. She should not be letting him jump because he will become too excited and sleep will take too long to come to him, but she is feeling sorry that she accused the boy of lying and so she takes off her shoes and starts to jump with him. Holding hands, they are jumping high. The bedcovers beneath them become jumbled under their feet. "In circles, Mommy," the boy says, and so they jump going in circles now, and she's laughing with her son, because she is out of breath and her son is saying, "Higher, Mommy, higher," and so she is trying to jump higher now and when she does she sees that she can see into the neighbor's bedroom across the way. It is easy to see because it is such a short distance from their house that if she were to open the window and lean out, she could probably touch the window of the neighbor's bedroom. The neighbor is Caesar. He does not have children or a wife. His wife died a year ago. At first it looks like Caesar is watching a television show, but then she realizes it is Caesar on the screen having sex with a woman in his bedroom. Sarah knows the woman. She realizes that Caesar filmed himself and his wife having sex years ago, that he must have set up a tripod and a camera and let it roll. Sarah, when she realizes what she is seeing, falls down to the bed, bringing her son down with her.

"What? Let's keep jumping!" her son says.

"No, we're done jumping. It's your bedtime. Tomorrow is a school day," she says.

When she tucks him in, she says, "Close those brown eyes, and we will see each other in the morning." She puts her mouth against the top of his head to kiss him, feeling with her lips the softness of his hair. Outside again they can hear the dog barking and whining.

"He loves those kittens," her son says. "Can't we go to the other yard and pick those kittens up and give them to Bob?" her son says.

"No, they are not his kittens. It's best if we leave them over there. The mother of those kittens would not want us touching them. If we do, she might not take care of them anymore."

"Why?" the son asks.

Sarah shakes her head. "It's just what mother animals sometimes do," she says.

After she kisses her son good night, she leaves the door open for him because sometimes he gets scared. Then she goes to her bedroom and she turns off the light. She stands on her bed and peers out through the window. The Caesar in the show, the Caesar who was once married, is getting head from his wife on the screen, and the Caesar who is now is touching himself while lying on his bed watching his dead wife giving him head. When the phone rings and Sarah answers it she whispers, "Hello," and Benjamin says, "What are you whispering for?" and so she tells him what she is seeing right now outside their bedroom window, and Benjamin says that is so sad, and Sarah says how it is also disgusting. The man should buy some curtains, and she wonders if that makes it more sad that it is also disgusting or if it is less sad.

"Well, my client's plane landed and I'm waiting for him to go through a long line at customs," he says. "Tell me, what else is new there?"

"Your son is a thief," she says. Benjamin laughs. "Really?"

"He stole two cars from school. He said the teacher gave them to him."

"Well, maybe she did," Benjamin says.

"No, she did not. He practically admitted to stealing them in his own way. What should we do about it?" she asks.

"'Do' about it? Nothing. He knows you know he did something wrong. He won't do it again."

"Nothing? Shouldn't we punish him in some way?"

"I suppose we should make him return the cars," Benjamin says. Sarah hears the dog now. He is no longer barking. Now he is wailing.

"Maybe he should do something more. Maybe he should write about it. He should write fifty times that he will never steal cars again," Sarah says.

Benjamin laughs, "Does he even know how to write that?"

"I'll show him," Sarah says. "I'll write the first sentence down and then he'll write the rest."

"What else is going on?" Benjamin says.

"Our dog thinks he's a cat," Sarah says.

"A cat? Oh, here's my client. That was fast," Benjamin says. "I've got to go."

Sarah hangs up the phone. She thinks having her son write fifty times that he will never steal cars again is a good punishment. She wishes Benjamin had agreed with her or told her he thought it was a good punishment too. She decides that she will definitely make her son do it. I'm his mother. I can decide my own son's punishment, she thinks, and then she wonders, if her son wakes up early, will he have enough time to write fifty times on a sheet of lined paper that he will never steal cars again before she has to take him to school.

When the dog wails again, she goes outside. She doesn't need a flashlight to see when she sits down next to the dog because there is light enough to see by from Caesar's sex show and light enough from a nearby street lamp. The dog is panting heavily, and the kittens are awake and mewling. The mother cat is not there. "Come inside now," she says to the dog, worried that the mother cat will never come back now to feed her kittens, but she cannot budge the dog. She pulls up on the scruff of his neck, but the dog is a large breed dog, and he weighs more than Sarah. The dog cannot just be lifted and made to stand and come away. The dog turns his head toward her, and Sarah wonders for a moment if her dog will bite her if she keeps pulling on him, even though the dog has never attempted to bite anyone in his life. Sarah goes inside. In her bedroom, when she is ready for sleep, the light from Caesar's show is too bright. She wishes she could just get up and go over to Caesar's house and ring the doorbell and tell him to turn it off and tell him to buy some curtains. If Benjamin were here, he would probably do it, she thinks. He would know exactly how to talk to Caesar and ask him kindly and smile, but she cannot do it. She would never talk to him about his sex show. The only way she has ever talked to Caesar was when Benjamin was standing right there beside her, and even then, she did not talk to him directly. It was Benjamin who did all the talking and she just nodded. She thinks how that is usually the case with everyone they know. Benjamin does the talking, and she just listens. If she does say anything, it is a short answer or she will ask a question, anything to prevent herself from having to speak for too long, because it is so much easier to let other people do the talking.

The light comes in through her curtains, and to make matters worse, the moon has now risen, and it's coming up from the opposite direction of Caesar's screen so that Sarah feels like she's now living on a two-moon planet with so much light bathing her room and her body. Just when she thinks it can't get any brighter in her house, that even daylight would be less glaring, there comes a chopper. It is flying low and loud, its searchlight landing on her yard and on all the yards around their house. She can hear it heading for the nearby stretch of freeway, and she can hear it circling back again, over her roof and down her street. Its beam of light comes right through her window and onto her body where she's on top of the covers wearing just a short nightgown because the night is such a hot one. She gets under the covers, pulling them over her head.

When she hears a creak and then footsteps on the linoleum floor, just inside the back door, she takes her head out from under the covers. She thinks of running out of bed and grabbing the phone, but it's too late. There is already a man standing in her room. She thinks she can smell him first. He smells of sweat and of the city itself when the endless car tires rolling over the pavement on the hot days smell like burning rubber, and he smells of the stale dust that blows down from the palm trees in a Santa Ana and swirls at your feet on the burning hot sidewalks.

But there is no man there. It's just her imagination. It's just a hot Santa Ana wind that has come through the window and is trapped against the wall of her room so that it feels almost like a man is standing there. Outside the dog howls and barks, and every once in a while, she can hear the chain-link fence ring after being struck by the dog's paw as he hits it in his frustration to be closer to the kittens.

Out her window, she hears what sounds like the wind rustling the fallen leaves from the grapefruit tree, and then she hears a voice. "Sarah?" she hears. She sits up in bed, clutching her covers to her front. She peers out the window. "Yes?" she says, her voice sounding like she is answering a telephone instead of leaning out her window late at night talking to a dark unknown figure.

"It's Caesar. Your neighbor. Sarah, your dog keeps howling and barking. I can't sleep," Caesar says. She does not recognize Caesar at first because he isn't wearing his glasses that she always sees him wearing, that and the fact that he is just wearing his boxer underwear.

"I'm sorry. I'll bring him in right away," Sarah says.

"Thank you, Sarah," he says. After he walks back to his house, she goes outside to the dog.

"Come on now. It's time for bed. It's time to go inside, you big pain," she says. She lifts up on the scruff of his neck, but he hunkers down, whining. He is so big that she cannot lift him or even push him or pull him. Every time she tries to pull on his neck, she gets a handful of fur instead. She goes back inside the house, not needing a flashlight of course to see the way because Caesar's show is still on, and she can see the cracks in the paved walkway as easily as if it were daylight. What does he mean he can't sleep? Does he fall asleep every night to that show? Is that the only way he can fall asleep? She thinks to herself. In the house she takes some leftover chicken out of the refrigerator and brings it back out with her to the dog. He is usually quick to grab the food from her hand. He is usually so hungry all of the time, but now he does not have any interest in the food, and when she lets him smell it from her hand and takes a few steps backward toward the house, he doesn't even look at it. All he wants are those kittens.

Her hand is small but not small enough to fit through the chain-link fence. If only her hand were smaller. There is only one person she knows whose hand is small enough to fit.

Her boy is sleeping peacefully on his back. She gently shakes his shoulder, saying his name, but he is deep in sleep. In each hand he is holding a race car. "Wake up," she says, and when he does not, she picks him up and carries him out with her to where the kittens are behind the fence. In his sleep, he still holds onto the race cars. As she's carrying him, he starts to stir. "Hmm," he says, and then his body becomes more rigid as he wakes up completely. "My cars!" he says, and then he looks down at his hands and realizes they are still there and relaxes. "Mommy, why are we outside?" he says.

"I need for you to do something. Bob needs one of those kittens. The mother cat was out here earlier, and I talked with her. She said Bob could have one."

"Really?" her son says.

"Yes, it's okay," Sarah says. "Go ahead, you reach through and take one. My hand is too big," she says. The boy does not want to put his cars down. "I'll hold them for you," Sarah says, she holds out her hand so he will give them to her.

"Mommy, you have to give them back. Give them back, okay?" her son says.

"I promise," she says.

"Then I get to keep them for tonight. Right? I don't have to give them back until tomorrow at school. Right?" her son says.

"Yes, okay. They're all yours tonight," she says, anything, she thinks, to keep Caesar from coming back over without his glasses, wearing his boxers. He lets her take the race cars and then he reaches in. "Which one?" he says.

"Any one, the mother cat said I could take any one."

Her son grabs an orange kitten, smaller even than his own hand, who mews when he lifts it and pulls it through the metal of the fence. Bob jumps up immediately when he sees that her son has the kitten. "He's so soft," her son says. She takes the kitten from him and gives him back the race cars. She holds the kitten up high because Bob is now jumping up and down, trying to get the kitten. "Run back into the house," she says to her son, and they both run into the house, Bob running behind them and then in front of them, his paws stepping on her, his claws digging into her bare feet and scraping her instep, drawing blood.

Once everyone's inside, she slams the door behind her, so the dog cannot get out again. "Give him the kitten. He wants it, Mommy," her son says. But Sarah is afraid to give Bob the kitten. If she gives it to him, she's not sure what he'll do. The length of Bob's tongue is even longer than the entire kitten. Just by licking it he may hurt it.

"Get me a towel," she says to her son.

"What?" he says. He cannot hear her because Bob now is barking louder than ever. He's frantic, jumping up onto her, placing both paws on her chest so that she has to lean against the wall so he doesn't knock her down. Standing at full height, the dog is even taller than she is. "A towel!" she yells. She knees her dog hard and she kicks him, but he doesn't care. "No! Knock it off, Bob!" she says to the dog, but he doesn't listen.

After her son comes with the towel, she wraps up the kitten while still holding it high in the air. "You can't hold him up forever, Mommy," her boy says.

She knows he is right. Eventually she will have to give Bob the kitten. The kitten is so small. It feels as if she could be holding just an empty towel in the air. "You go back to bed," she says to her son.

"But what about the kitten . . ."

"No buts. If you want to keep those race cars for the night, you march back to bed right now."

"But you already said I could keep the race cars tonight, Mommy."

"Yes, I meant it, too. Just go to bed, please," Sarah says. "I will take care of this kitten. The kitten will be fine." Her son walks back to his room, looking over his shoulder as he walks down the hallway.

She takes the kitten to her room and sits up in her bed with him. Bob of course comes bounding onto the bed too. In her arms she holds the kitten wrapped in the towel, and Bob sticks his huge head into the towel and starts licking the kitten. She lets him lick it a few times, and then she pushes his head away. "That's enough. Let it breathe, Bob," she says. When he doesn't get to lick it, though, he starts to bark.

"What's he barking for, Mommy?" she hears her son call from his bed.

"Go to sleep!" she says back to her son.

Bob paws at the kitten now, his heavy paw pressing into its body, making it cry. She gets up from the bed. "This isn't working, Bob," she says, and she puts the kitten in the towel in a shoebox. Then she goes in the hallway and puts it in the linen closet on the top shelf and closes the door. Bob scratches the door and barks. She goes back to her bedroom and lies down in bed, holding her hands to her ears, but she can still hear everything.

"You didn't really talk to the mother cat, did you?" her son says loudly from down the hall so that he can be heard over the barking. She doesn't answer him.

"You lied about the mother cat!" her son yells.

"You lied about the race cars!" she yells back before she can stop herself from saying it, before she realizes how immature it sounds and how she doesn't want her son to know how adults can be so stupid sometimes that they sound like children.

Her son doesn't say anything. She is hoping that maybe he did not hear her.

"I can't sleep. Bob is barking too loud," her son says.

"Just let him bark. He'll stop soon," she says. Bob barks for a long time, though, and she's awake listening to him. Even if he were not barking, she thinks, she would not be able to sleep because the light from Caesar's show is still on. She thinks about going over there and telling him to turn it off, to get some damn curtains, that his show is keeping her awake, but she doesn't dare. She doesn't want him to know she knows he is watching a show of himself having sex with his wife who's now dead. She doesn't want to know herself, even, that such sadness exists. Eventually, in the middle of the night, Bob stops barking, and she falls asleep. Sarah doesn't even wake up when Benjamin drives home and gets into bed next to her. She only wakes up when he leaves the house at daybreak to go back to work, and she hears the front door close and his car engine start.

She gets up from bed and sees the hall closet door is open. In front of it is a stool. The kitten and the towel are no longer there. For a moment she has a ridiculous thought. She thinks the dog was able to drag the stool to the closet to reach up and get the kitten. Then she opens the door to her son's room, and there is the dog curled in a ball beside her son's bed. Between the dog's front legs is the towel the kitten was wrapped in. When she goes to unwrap the towel, the dog is too tired to wake up and doesn't stir. The kitten is in the towel, and she puts her hand on it.

"The kitten's dead," her son says, still holding his race cars. "Bob licked it to death. I couldn't stop him, Mommy. He held it between his paws so he could lick harder, and he pushed so hard on it. I'm sorry. I gave it to him so he would stop barking. He was so happy to have it, Mommy," her son says, crying. She hugs her son. "It's okay," she says. "The kitten was so little. It couldn't survive without its mother. I shouldn't have taken it away from her in the first place," Sarah says.

She takes the towel and wraps it so that it covers the entire orange kitten. They take it outside, and the dog, who is still sleeping, doesn't follow after them. They use a large spoon to dig up the ground and bury the kitten under the grapefruit tree, which her son says is the best place because it is cool under there in the shade and the kitten will not have to be hot during the day. They check on the other kittens. They are all gone. "The mother cat must have moved them. That's good," Sarah says.

After that they eat breakfast, and then her son gets out two lined sheets of paper and two of his pencils from his pencil box. He gives her one sheet and one pencil. "Let's start writing," he says.

She sees he is writing, "I will never steal race cars again" over and over again. She rubs her eyes. She is so tired from the night before. She feels so bad for the kitten that had to die by Bob's incessant licking and pawing. She feels so bad for her son who was crying so hard to see the dead kitten, thinking it was his fault. If it weren't for Caesar, it never would have happened. She can hear that Caesar is awake. She can hear his morning radio show playing from his open kitchen window as loudly as if the radio were in her own home. She begins to write. She writes, "Your sex show kept me up all night, and if you really want to watch that stuff you should go to the store and buy curtains." She writes it fifty times.

"I'm done!" her son announces and holds up his page.

"Good. I'm done too. Let's put them into envelopes." She quickly folds her letter and seals it into an envelope so her son can't read it.

After breakfast, on their way out the door to drive to school, she tells her son, "You go on ahead and get in the car. I forgot something in the house." She runs back into her bedroom. Through her open window she can see Caesar's open window. She can see his unmade bed. She takes her envelope and tosses it through her window and out over her small strip of grass and right in through Caesar's open window, where it lands on his wrinkled bottom sheet.

She goes back out to the car. Her son has already strapped himself into his car seat and is holding his race cars.

"How about I take you late to school? How about we go to the store first? You can pick up two race cars if you want to. You can pick up the same exact ones even," she says and turns the car on.

"Yippeee! Let's go!" her son says.

She can see Caesar with her envelope in his hand coming out of his house. He comes up to her side of the car and leans in her window before she can drive away. "We're off to the store to buy race cars!" her son says, leaning over from his car seat to tell Caesar.

"Race cars! That's great. I'm off to the store myself," he says.

Sarah drives onto her street. The Santa Anas are picking up again. She can feel the bone-dry desert air coming in through her open window. Warm as another person's breath, it feels as if someone she couldn't see were very close to her and sighing heavily.

NOW IS THE TIME

COLLEGE APPLICATION — CIRCA 1979

Dear Great College that I really want to get into: Do you see me in my typing class? *Now is the time for all good men to come to the aid of their country*, but instead I type, *Now is the time. Now is the time. Now is the time.* Can you see my mother on the toilet with the lid down crying when I was a girl? Our father has left her for another woman. Dear Great College, is this really what you want to know? Because it says here, this is what you want to know. Hear the thunder noise my body makes as I bend over in our rusted metal shower stall? See our loft? See how the skylight glass ripples in a storm? Notice how when our father comes back it is not to take us to a movie or a ride in the park or give us money for food or to pay the rent. It is for the antique ceramic Navajo bowl that used to be his parents and that the Indians used for cooking. Smoke-colored stains go up its sides. Can you hear the rhythmic sounds of our mother's fists on our father's back as he's going out the door, the Navajo bowl still in his hands? Can you keep from touching our pretty German shepherd? She is in pain. Our mother cracked a broom over her back because the dog went on the floor again. See my older sisters? They are taking one side of their split ends and splitting them up the shaft of the hair strand so now they have two hairs, one still on their head, the other curled and held between their fingers. I am changing the channel from *Lost in Space* to *Days of Our Lives*. The backs of my knees are sweating. The heat coming in through the skylights makes our house greenhouse hot and the garbage in garbage bags in a pile in the corner of our house stink, and maggots appear to grow out of nowhere. The tower of garbage, let me explain, Dear Great College, is there because we have no garbage pickup where we live. We live in a loft building where only artists are supposed to work during the day, but somehow, we do live here even though families are not supposed to live here at night, cooking dinners, watching TV, sleeping under the glass of the skylight that is reinforced with chicken wire. My sisters are sitting on a train up to school with their French horn and their oboe at their feet, leaning on each other, fast asleep. Dear Great College, can you get that bottle of pills out of my brother's hand? He has dug his hand in deep into our mother's purse. I cannot get the pills out of my brother's hand, even though he is laughing so hard. I am not strong enough. With the pills, he runs away to his room, locking the door. A packet of cigarettes from our mother's purse is broken. Flakes of tobacco are now on my fingertips.

I'm back in typing class. *Now is the time. Now is the time. Now is the time*, but the teacher says I'm going too fast. I'm missing letters. I'm typing, *No is the time, no is the time, no is the time*, instead.

"Be careful," he says. "Typing is very important. You might need it for a job someday," my typing teacher says. I shrug. I type, *There is no way in hell I am ever going to be a secretary*, but

I type it wrong by mistake. I type, *There is now way in ell I am ever ging to be ass ecretary.*

Dear Great College, see me in grade school, where the boy next to me is so good at drawing with pencil the gazelles he says roam the plains of Africa? The teacher singing *Dixie* to the class after recess, asking us to put our heads on our desks in the dark? See me hide? I am small enough to fit on top of the refrigerator when we play hide-and-go-seek at home with our friends. They never see me up there. They never think to look up that high. When they take me down my palms are dirty from grease that is stuck there from fried food my mother has cooked over the years. Smell the fried flounder? This is my favorite. I help dip it in egg mixture, flour, and breadcrumbs. I wave my fingers at my mother, the tips thickly covered in batter. My mother smiles at me, the cigarette in her mouth moving down, pointing to the floor, to our vinyl tiles meant to look like bricks, while her lips curl up.

Can you see my brother locking himself in his room with a gun? No one saw that coming, but maybe I should have known he wanted to kill himself since that time with the pills. He comes out a day later deciding to live. See him holding two beer bottles, which were empty until he peed in them, and now he's headed to the bathroom to empty them out?

One night we stay up all night on the rooftop watching the building next door burn down, my leg shaking. I am so scared our building is going to catch on fire next.

Want to see my cat? Her name is Jesse, named after Jesse James because my mother's friend who gave her to me says Jesse James is her great, great relative. If I had enough time, I would tell you all about Jesse, but that would be like a children's story all about an amazing super cat, and I think what you want here is just a glimpse of me, right? (Maybe, at the end of this essay, I will draw you a picture of Jesse, the amazing super cat, or, better yet, maybe I will get that kid in my class who draws so well with a pencil to draw Jesse the Amazing Super Cat roaming the plains of Africa.)

Dear Great College, I have abilities. I know how to cook. My sister has taught me how to make onion-and-mayonnaise sandwiches, and when all we have is just flour and water, I know how to make pancakes.

Dear Great College, here are more of my achievements: I can snap my fingers. I can do a backbend, a cartwheel, and touch my thumb to my wrist. I can fly, well only in my dreams, and even then I just kind of rise off the ground just by believing that I can do it. I see my mother down below, the men on the sidewalk turning their hands into fists, holding the curled ends to their lips, making smooching sounds in her face. She is pretty.

I also see my sisters on our rooftop popping tar blisters in the summer, our brother walking with his guitar at his side, off to play in an Irish band with a lead singer with a voice like the sweet voices of the girls she sings about in her songs who run in green fields off to meet lovers standing on hillsides in Ireland. I know about the Irish. My father is one. My teacher Frank McCourt in high school is one. Mr. McCourt puffy-eyed and quiet during first period. Some of the other kids preferring to sit on the heaters by the windows while he teaches. Me having to change gears in order to listen to him. Me having to get my Irish ears on to understand his accent. Me wishing he taught every class I had to take, just so I could listen to him. Me writing because he makes me want to.

Dear Great College, I haven't volunteered all these years. I suppose you will think I am not the applicant for your school in that case. Or maybe you will consider this volunteer work— me in grade school saying to Rebecca, "I'll pull that five dollars sticking halfway out of Eric's back pocket after school so we can go to Bertha's and buy bagfuls of penny candy." Me saying to Rebecca, "Do you want mini wax Coke bottles, candy necklaces, or marshmallow circus peanuts? It's on me."

Me being the one to say okay, I'll be the one we try and levitate and my sisters and their friends all standing around me as I'm lying down, lifting me up, high up, in my house with just the tips of their fingers. I think I can reach out and touch the chicken wire in the skylight glass. They are lifting me so high.

Dear Great College, and here is where things start to intersect. My volunteer experience and my sports abilities— swimming at the top of my list. Me being the one to say okay, send me over the fence first when we all go to the Leroy Street pool at night to swim with the other kids who cannot sleep because of the heat, who leave the house to get cool, the street lamp lighting up our hands seen wavy under water. The cop's flashlight bouncing against the brick wall by the pool deck like the ball over words when the cartoon song plays. Me being the first to get out and run. The chain-link fence going clang, clang, clang as I climb. Me being the one to say okay, I'll be the first to swim in the fountain in the park in the dark. Me feeling plastic bags sliding under my feet when I step in, and then when I crawl around like an alligator, I feel the sharpness of bottle caps cutting into my palms. Me saying okay at the boat lake in Central Park to swimming in the dark green water, a wooden oar of someone's rental boat I grab onto making them scared a monster lives in the deep, but it's just me, a girl in her clothes reaching up with a skinny white arm, her hair covering her face, seeing through long dark strands she moves away from her eyes with both hands. Just a girl in the deep of the lake on a hot summer's day.

Academic abilities, you ask? Dear Great College, let me tell you I am not the girl next to me who wears plaid jumpers and patent leather shoes and brags about her grades the whole time that she cheats from the textbook she holds under her desk while taking an exam.

I'm the girl who can go to her room and study even though the TV is loud, my mother watching variety shows, the eleven o'clock news. Even though my brother is playing guitar in his room with the door open, the refrains being refrained over and over again because he's not satisfied that he knows all the notes. My sisters practicing French horn and oboe. One sister blowing out the spit from her valves, the other sister moistening the reed in her mouth, walking around with it in her mouth as she cleans out her glass garter snake tank. Boris and Natasha curled around each other looking at us through the glass. My sister saying, "Boris, Natasha, vould you like more water? I get you some directly," in her Russian accent. Me saying *"Dasvidaniya,"* to them before I go to the bathroom to get ready for bed. Me turning on the light in the bathroom, watching the sink come alive. The cockroaches crawling all over the sides of the sink. How they love our toothpaste and the bristles of our toothbrushes. How I have to knock them off my toothbrush before I use it. How I run the water and send them down the drain saying, *"Dasvidaniya,"* again because I'm still in Russian mode. Oh, and I guess here, Dear Great College, is where I should mention my foreign language abilities.

I can understand my mother saying *"merde"* after she cuts herself closing the window when the weather turns cold and the dirty glass in the rotted frame breaks and her hand bleeds. *"Merde"* after the power gets cut because we didn't have the money to pay the bill, and the candles we use walking through the loft waver in the breeze, and the wax falls on our sweaters, turning us spotted white.

"Merde, merde, merde" after she talks to her French mother who is always drunk at night and lives uptown in a hotel room with a dog named Thumper whom she feeds treats of Pepperidge Farm pirouette cookies. When I visit her I steal her dog's cookies when she's drunk too much and lays her head back on the couch and closes her eyes.

You ask, Dear Great College, what I wish I were better at doing. There are so many things. Not having given up my bicycle so easily when the boys in the gang in the park chased me down with their knives calling me *puta*. Not having let the hot dog man lift me up to the lamppost, touching my breasts as he did, taking my picture as I looked at the rest of the park, the people, the arches, the water in the fountain catching light casting gold flecks on the leaves of nearby green bushes speckled by soot, offering me Hershey bars with almonds he kept in the drawer of his cart after he then helped me down. Saying no to my brother when he took me to his room and made me sit on top of him while he lay down, his belt buckle hurting me as he held me by the waist, moving me back and forth over himself.

I wish I was better at countries and states. Everything west of the Hudson is just a guess. Idaho could be Ohio could be

Iowa could be Illinois could be Ireland could be Iran, Iraq. I'm not sure. I'm better at the local geography: the deli next door owned by the Greeks who serve Yankee bean soup; the liquor store on the way to the park selling Popov, my mother's label; the tobacco shop at the corner on the way to the Lexington line with the man who has to hold a box to his throat so that his words come out as vibrations so that when my mother asks for a carton of Chesterfield and he repeats it just to be sure of her order. It sounds like Ch-essssssss-ter-field, and I think maybe the man should be laughing because it's all got to tickle like crazy. One day my mother comes home saying the man in the shop asked her out on a date. We want to know what he said so she holds her hand to her throat like she's holding the box he holds to his throat and she says in a buzzing voice, "You are very pretty. Would you like to go with me to dinner?" and so now we talk to our mother that way all of the time. "You are very pretty," we buzz, holding our throats, repeating the tobacco shop owner's words and then telling her other things, telling her what we covered in school today, "The Opium Warzzzz," my sister buzzes. What we ate in the lunchroom, "Grilled cheezzzze," I buzz and then I think, what if the man in the tobacco shop becomes my new father? How would he treat me? Would he find out about the money I stole from Eric's pocket? Would he buzz to me, "You are a dizzzzzgrace"?

Dear Great College, you state that the suite style of living at your college may be an integral part of my experience. You want to know what I would contribute to the dynamic of my suite. "P-I-G," I say. I like playing it at night before we fall asleep. Our loft, being a loft, is wide open for the most part, and we can hear each other in our beds down the length of it.

We do it with fruits, say orange. The last letter is *e* and if you can't think of a fruit beginning with *e* then you're out, and you are given a *p*. If you spell "pig," you've lost the game. (Just in case you are wondering, "elderberry" is all I can think of for a fruit beginning with *e*.) If you can't think of anything you can try and fake it and say something like "Errol Flynn Fruit," and if anyone challenges you they have to get up in the dark out of their warm beds and try not to step in the dog pee while going to get the dictionary in the dark or light a candle to see by and prove you wrong. In my suite we would leave our doors open and have long games of PIG so that everyone could feel safe at night before falling asleep because what could be safer, I think, than seeing the tip of your mother's cigarette glowing red as she inhales while lying in bed at night, then exhales saying, "Fig or pear or *pomme*," at the same time the smoke comes out, and us saying "Oh, Mom, *pomme* is not English," and her saying, "*Merde*, but you know what I mean. I can't think of the word in English right now." Oh, and cooking of course. I could make my suitemates all mayonnaise-and-onion sandwiches and pancakes out of just flour and water.

Dear Great College, you ask what excites me intellectually. Where to begin? Maybe with the skylight glass. How does it ripple in a wind and not break? Maybe with Frank McCourt. How is it he can quote so many writers' words from memory? How is it he doesn't care where you sit in class—the desktop, the heater by the windows, the floor in the back beneath the bulletin board—but other teachers want you seated in rows? His voice is so soft. We are all quiet. We don't want to miss hearing one brogue-pronounced word. When he first walks into the room in the morning, sometimes he just stands looking at us for a long time. We can't help but smile. We know soon he will tell us a story. Maybe I should begin with geometry. Maybe with my tutor, whom my teacher made me sign up for, who in fact never tutors but puts his hand on the inside of my leg and whispers in my ear, "Will you marry me?" and why does that teacher wonder why I still can't prove a theorem? Why my formulas are wrong? You see, Dear Great College, all of this excites me intellectually.

You ask to elaborate on one of my work experiences. Do you see my friend Martha? Do you see us on the Avenue of the Americas, her wearing a sandwich board, me handing out flyers for discounts on fried chicken? Do you see the black and Puerto Rican boys talking to us, mostly to Martha who is half black and beautiful, and they walk to her side to see in through the spaces of the sandwich board? They want to see her ass, her legs. Do you hear her telling them to get the fuck out of here? Do you see the owner of the chicken place coming out, telling us he'll fire us if we don't stop talking to boys and to get them away, they're blocking the sign? Do you see us quitting, telling the owner we can't keep the boys away, and it's too hot to stand outside on the sidewalk all day, and when the owner asks for the flyers back that I didn't hand out, I tell him I handed all of them out even though I didn't, even though I threw them in the metal wastebasket on the corner. Do you see the owner throwing the money at us that we earned for our morning's worth of work, the bills floating in the air, smoky from the chicken frying on the grill?

Do you see us with the cash we earned for our few hours of work, going into Woolworth's, taking our time because it's so nice and cool with the store being air-conditioned and buying material to sew our own bikinis? Martha has convinced me that it's easy, but afterward, when we test the suits in Martha's house in her bathtub we've filled with water, the cotton of my suit runs red when it gets wet. When I'm standing up, Martha says it looks like I'm bleeding all over, the red color running down from my chest, down from my hips, and down my legs. The bathwater now pink.

Dear Great College, you ask me to describe one of my extracurricular activities. I really only have two friends in high school, and that would be Martha, whom you've already met, and then there is Dana, and sometimes the three of us do things after school. Do you see Dana, almost fat but not quite, with her big blue eyes and a wide smile with perfectly straight teeth and who lives way uptown on the upper West Side with just her mother in a pre-war building with huge floor-to-ceiling windows? Do you see how those windows are open one evening when Martha and I are on our way to meet Dana at her house and go to a play, to go see *A Midsummer Night's Dream*? Do you see how Dana, after a fight with her mother about cleaning the bathroom, opens the huge floor-to-ceiling window? Do you see her jumping out the window? That's what she is doing—falling, hitting the pavement eight stories below, not far from the stoop of her building. Do you see Martha and me on the subway train making our way up to Dana's house and getting there right after Dana's body has been taken away? Do you see how the police tape is cordoning off a few squares of the sidewalk? Do you see Martha and me going in the building and knocking on Dana's door and no one coming to the door and Martha saying to me, "Something is wrong." So, we knock on the neighbor's door, and the neighbor, who is crying, lets us in, and Dana's mother is there on the couch crying, and it is then that we learn that Dana jumped out the window and is dead. When we finally leave the building, and we go past the cordoned off police tape, Martha grabs onto my arm and says, "Oh my god, the blood," because it is then that we notice the red stain of blood soaked into the sidewalk that is made up of cement and broken seashells. I can see the ridged bits of clamshell the blood hasn't touched. They look like small white ribs locked into the ground.

Dear Great College, do you see Martha and me now? She is over my shoulder. We are reading your application together. She wants to go to your college as well. We are thinking of what we will say. We are on a Peter Pan bus up to visit your campus. We are putting behind the tall buildings of our city, the fires burning, the garbage at home, swimming in the fountains, the mother on the toilet crying, the father holding the Navajo bowl, the brother with the pills, the sisters with their snakes and their instruments, the friend falling to the sidewalk.

We are saying, "Yes," if you say, "Yes." We are ready to answer that question, that very last question on your form, the one that asks: Describe a place where you are perfectly content. The Peter Pan bus doors are opening, and we are stepping out onto your campus. We are here now in that place where we feel perfectly content. See how we admire your trees, the great lawns, the gentle curve of the mountains in the distance, the academic buildings with teachers, so many teachers inside of them, waiting for us, wanting us. Will they all be as good as Frank McCourt? Wouldn't it be wonderful if they were all as good as Frank McCourt? Warm, welcoming wood-sided buildings filled with teachers talking softly, telling us stories, letting us sit anywhere, letting us write anything. We wish the Peter Pan bus would drive quickly away. We don't want to think about having to board it again and go back. Please, please, please, Great College, accept us. We think we've answered all of your questions as best as we could. Now is the time.

FORTY WORDS

WHEN I WAS A GIRL, I had a doll that was my size. She had a wardrobe that matched my own. When I wore the rabbit fur muff and the rabbit fur hat and went ice-skating, she wore them too. My limousine driver would watch me skate with my doll sitting beside him. Sometimes I told Michel that she had to sit on his lap, and when I skated in circles, I waved to her, and Michel, thinking I was waving to him, would wave back. When it grew dark, I didn't want to go home. I did not want to go back to my apartment where the heat was always on high and coming out of the vent continually, making the drapes in my room shudder. Michel would come to the railing holding my doll, and he would call for me, telling me it was time to leave. Central Park was not a place for a ten-year-old girl at night, he said.

"We must go home and get you some dinner," he said.

"We want a pretzel," I would say, and so he promised my doll and me a pretzel hot from the vendor if I just came off the ice.

In the limousine I fed my doll some of the pretzel, which she did not like, and so I forced some of the pretzel into her mouth, the big grains of salt falling onto her muff, getting lost in all the whiteness, but my doll did not mind. She kept smiling as we drove down the streets, the lights from the signs above the store windows and the lights from the streetlights the only things making her change, making her face take on the yellow, green, and red colors of the lights. Sometimes I tried to smile just like she did. I wanted to learn how to continue smiling even though someone might be forcing something into my mouth I did not want or making me do something I did not want to do.

My *nounou* would try to come and tuck us in at night, but I did not want her. I wanted Michel. I would sit on my bed with my arms crossed, trying to put my doll's smile on my face, and refusing to listen to *Nounou* tell me to lie back and get into bed. My smile must have looked sad, though, because *Nounou* would look at my face and say, "Don't do that. Don't cry. I'll go get him." So *Nounou* would go down the hall to Michel's quarters and bring him back to me. Michel smelled of scotch then, and his eyes would be red. He would not have his black suit on, but he would be wearing a flannel bathrobe over an undershirt, and his cheeks would be mottled and flushed as if it had been him who had been circling the rink out on the ice in the cold.

"Mademoiselle Rebecca, do not let the bedbugs bite," he would say to me, and then to my doll he would say, "Mademoiselle Cinderella, sweet dreams."

Nounou's job was easy because I did not let her care for me. It was Michel I made play with me and build towers with my blocks and play charades where, in order to do so, he had to take off his suit jacket and roll up his cuffs so that he could easily put his fingers against his inner arm. He repeatedly tapped them there, one or two or three at a time on his pale skin, so different than the hairy top of his arm, letting me know how many syllables spelled out the title of his charade.

I named her Cinderella because I liked the fairy tale of how she changed from being poor to being rich. I liked believing that people could change like that, so quickly. If I saw a homeless person on the street, with a broken-down cardboard box for a bed beside a building's vent, I liked to believe that the next day if I walked by the building, he would be gone, that like Cinderella, someone had changed his fortune. When I saw the homeless person, I would beg Michel to give the person some dollar bills. I did not let Michel try and walk by quickly, as he sometimes tried to do. Instead I dug my hand into his pockets, pulling out what I could. Sometimes it was just a half-eaten roll of white Life Savers, which I knew Michel sucked on after he had had a drink after lunch, and I would set the half roll of Life Savers on the uneven cardboard beside the homeless man.

I learned about submarines because of my parents. They were away making a film about them. My father directed films, and my mother wrote the scripts, or sometimes she just doctored them. Before I knew what that meant, I had asked her what was the matter with the script. Why was it sick? And she had thrown back her head and laughed, and I saw how perfectly white and straight her teeth were and how perfect the roof of her mouth also was, like the ribs of the great whale skeleton in the museum Michel would sometimes take me to. My mother and father were often away on location, and for the longest time I thought "on location" was the name of a place, a part of the world I hadn't seen yet, but a place where all movies were made. My father was small, smaller than Michel, and bald. I wished that Michel were my father instead, because he was tall and always looked handsome in his black suit, with his head of thick, black hair. When he wore his chauffeur's hat, he was even taller. Once my father woke me in the middle of the night and stood in my room. He wanted to say hello to me after having returned from being on location, but he was not tall enough to block the light coming from the bulb in the crystal fixture in the center of the ceiling of my room, and I had to shield my eyes to keep the bright light from hurting me.

My mother told me that submariners could not send telegrams to their loved ones above the waves. Sending a telegram might make them detected by the enemy. But the families, every ten days or so while a submarine was on patrol, could send a telegram to their sailors. The telegram could not be longer than forty words. My mother said the families were instructed not to send upsetting news in those "familygrams," as they were called. The familygrams were mostly about day-to-day things that happened at home that would make the sailor comforted that life still went on, the same as usual, on terra firma. "Johnny doing well in school so far. All A's. Trees turning colors here already. Have had the woodshed filled."

Cinderella and I often played submarine. Sometimes I made her hot bunk. My mother had also told me that because there were more sailors than bunks onboard for the men to sleep, the men took turns. There was no night or day in the depths, and so in a twenty-four-hour period, three men in a row would share the same bunk. When it was a man's turn to sleep, he would wake the sailor in his bunk up and make him get out and then he would climb in after him. The mattress beneath the sailor was always warm from when the other sailor had been sleeping in it, and some said they even continued dreaming what the other sailor had been dreaming. When I got up out of bed for school, I told Cinderella it was time to hot bunk, and I put her to sleep on my mattress where I had slept. When I came home from school, I woke her and told her we had received a familygram. I had written the familygram in school instead of doing my math problems. I had tried to think of everyday things to write in the familygram that happened in people's lives. But the only thing I knew how to write about was my life. I did not know the daily lives of my parents since they were often on location, so the familygrams to my submariner self were written by myself as a girl. "Went ice-skating again today. Michel bought us pretzels. A squirrel ate from my hand. Gave a homeless man three dollars. Went to the museum. Was scared in the dark looking at the Eskimos where behind the glass they stood on fake snow and their dogs pulled sleds with their lips peeled back and their glossy tongues hanging out and their teeth sharp." And because it was over forty words, I cut it down and crossed out the part about the Eskimos and just said, "Went to the museum and was scared in the dark," which I was. I was afraid that, somehow, I would be captured and made to be a part of the frozen scene behind the glass. I would be made to put on my Cinderella smile and stand behind a sled, my arm holding a whip raised in the air and the whip never coming down but forever striking out.

I made Michel hot bunk too, after school, when I played. He pretended to snore and not get out of bed when it was my turn to sleep, and so I screamed like a Klaxon in his ear, saying *ahwooogah!* and shaking him and telling him that we had reached crush depth and he had better get up and bring us back up or we would die; we would be crushed like a tin can. If he was really playing the part, he would keep a straight face, and then I would shake him or pinch his nose to stop his snoring, or I would run and get a glass of water and throw it in his face yelling, "We're taking on water! Quick, fix the leak!" Sometimes, though, he would start to laugh, and then I would start to laugh too, and, sputtering, still pretending like I was on board the sub, I would keep saying things like, "Reverse the engines! Seal the valves!" at the same time I was laughing.

A few times I came home from school and there was a familygram on my pillow beside Cinderella's head. I knew it was Michel who wrote the familygram because I knew his loopy penmanship, but the familygrams pretended to be from someone's parents. They said things like, "Miss you so much. We are so proud of you. Can't wait to see you when you come into port." I would put the familygrams in a cigar box and then stow the cigar box under my mattress because I knew that on a real sub that's where a sailor stored his possessions, in a compartment beneath his mattress.

One weekend, after lunch, I made Michel play submarine with me and I made him the first to hot bunk. Then I went to the pillar in my room, which I pretended was my periscope. "Enemy ships!" I yelled, and then I ran to Michel, tugging on his arm, screaming like a Klaxon and screaming that we had to "Dive, dive, dive!" I couldn't wake Michel, though. He must have had a lot to drink at lunch. His mouth dropped open and he snored. It wasn't until *Nounou* came into my room later and saw him sleeping soundly on my bed that she yelled at him and told him that if he didn't get out of my bed she'd call my parents on location and tell them that he had finished off a bottle of scotch all by himself. Michel sat up and wiped his mouth and then headed out the door. I stopped him though. "What were you dreaming?" I asked him.

"It was a great dream, Rebecca. I dreamt that I was rich and I was back home in France, visiting my wife and my daughter. I had presents for them. A new car and beautiful clothes and a doll like yours for Nina," he said, smiling.

Right after Michel left, I climbed into bed, feeling the warmth he left behind. I closed my eyes and tried to dream what he was dreaming, but I couldn't. *Nounou* was being loud in my room, picking up my clothes that I had left lying about the room, groaning and holding onto her lower back when she had to pick up my rabbit muff off the floor. "*Nounou*," I said, startling her because she thought I was asleep. "Why don't Michel's wife and Nina come here and live with us?" I knew that sometimes *Nounou* and Michel would stay up late and share a bottle of wine together, and they would talk in French. They both came from France, from small towns by the sea. It was my parents' idea to hire French people to be my nanny and my driver. They thought I would learn French from them, but I didn't want to learn French. I never answered them or listened to them if they talked to me in French, and so the only people Michel and *Nounou* spoke French with were each other.

"He cannot go back," *Nounou* said.

"Why not?" I asked.

Nounou sighed and sat on my bed beside me, holding my muff, and putting her own hands inside of it, but of course her hands did not fit all the way, and her thin wrists stuck out, the knobby bones on the sides of them looking as big as the caps of knees. It was the first time I let her sit on my bed. It was the first time I let her tell me a story. Before she started, I told her to wait and to bring me my doll. I wanted Cinderella to hear the story too. If there was something in the story that later

I didn't remember, then there was the chance that Cinderella would remember it for me, and I had a feeling it would be a story I would not want to forget.

It was *La Saint-Sylvestre*, New Year's Eve in France. All the bakery shops had festive cakes called *galette de rois*, or king's cake, made with puff pastry and filled with almond cream, displayed in the windows. Inside each cake was baked a trinket, the kind you might find dangling from a charm bracelet. If a person was served a slice of cake containing the trinket, that person was king for a day and got to wear a paper crown. Families had invited over friends or made plans to go out to dinner. Champagne was ordered by the caseload, and mistletoe was bought and strung up in doorways so that lips and cheeks could be kissed.

The rain in Biarritz had started to fall early that morning, and the skies stayed dark throughout the day while the waves reared up high and threw themselves against the cliff, covering the rocks in white foam that hardly had time to slide back into the sea before another wave came and beat the cliffs again.

Michel was not a chauffeur then. He was a clerk who worked in a firm that made sure that agreements between businesses were fair. That afternoon, a new client had arrived in town. He had been invited by the owner of the firm to celebrate *Saint-Sylvestre* and to drink champagne and eat foie gras and king's cake with him at an expensive restaurant that looked like it was built into a cliff. The restaurant had a view of the sea from windows that went from the floor to the ceiling, and the windows had to be washed every day so that the salt from the spray from the ocean did not collect on the glass and cloud the view. The owner of the firm, unfortunately, would not be able to make the dinner date on time. He was on a winding road outside the town calling Michel from a pay phone, telling Michel he had to meet the client there at the restaurant because he had driven over a smashed champagne bottle along the way, and his tire was now flat and had to be repaired.

Michel kissed his wife and his daughter, Nina, and said not to worry, that he would be back in time to have king's cake with them and their guests and to kiss Nina under the mistletoe when the clock struck twelve. Before he left, he took his large black umbrella with him. It was a heavy umbrella whose point was fitted with a metal ferrule that when the rain was light and Michel walked with it like a cane, the ferrule clacked loudly on the sidewalk.

It was difficult to be heard over the crashing waves. The water from the force of the waves splashed against the windows as loudly as if people with buckets were standing outside the windows whose sole purpose it was to send the water buckets flying at the glass where the customers sat trying to have a conversation over their duck foie gras. Michel did not talk much, and neither did the client because it was so hard to be heard. In place of talking and shouting, they drank and nodded their heads in the direction of the wine bottle when the waiter made ready to pour them some more. They ordered *galette de rois* for dessert, and it was the client whose slice of cake contained the trinket. Since he was king, the waiter brought him a paper crown, and the client, drunk now, wore his crown the rest of the evening.

When the *maître d* came over to tell Michel he had a phone call at the front desk, the *maître d*, in order to be heard, had to bend so close to Michel's ear that Michel felt the waiter's breath slightly lift up the stray hairs by his temples. It was the owner calling again. He was still waiting for the tire to be repaired. He asked that Michel entertain the client, and after the restaurant he should take him to a lively bar in town that would celebrate the new year with streamers and dance music and endless glasses of champagne.

They walked to the bar from the restaurant, the rain lashing against the large umbrella, which they shared, and which Michel had to hold almost sideways like a shield against an armed enemy headed straight for them.

In the bar, after a few drinks, Michel asked the client if he was tired and would like Michel to walk him to his hotel, but the client insisted that he was not tired at all. The client repositioned the crown on his head and said to the bartender, "More champagne for me, the king, and my loyal subject," and Michel found himself in the bar after the first stroke of midnight and then many hours past the stroke of midnight. The client could barely stand, and Michel, almost as drunk himself, found the bar spinning around him, and so when a fight broke out, and he did not know how, but he and the client ended up in the middle of it, where bottles were smashed on people's heads and women screamed and tripped in their high heels trying to run, he knew he should get the client out of the bar. As the umbrella had worked to fight against the furious rain, Michel, in his drunken state, reasoned that it too would work in the bar to fend off the attackers. He sprang it open. Holding it out in front of himself, he grabbed onto his client and said, "Let's get out of here."

They were almost at the door when they were suddenly pushed back, as if the whole crowd in the bar was pushing on the canopy and ribs of the umbrella, trying to stuff them back inside. Michel almost fell backward, and then from behind, he felt himself being supported. The crowd behind them sent him forward again, but with unexpected speed. He grabbed onto the handle hard, with both hands, causing the canopy to collapse and shut. In that same moment, he saw a man right in front of him, a man bending over and struggling to stand, who was also being pushed toward Michel by the drunken crowd. Michel saw how the end of the umbrella went clear through the man's eye. He heard how the man screamed and saw how the man reached up with both hands wrapped around the umbrella. Michel let go, and the umbrella fell to the floor along with the man's eye while his blood spurted forth. "You took out his eye!" the client said, now turning to Michel, hardly seeming drunk now, seeming so sober now that Michel was almost tempted to ask him if he had been pretending all this time to be drunk up to his gills.

The man turned toward the door, screaming, and the crowd, which only a moment ago was a mob that could not be separated, now parted and made an aisle for the man who had his hand over his eye socket and whose blood was spurting through the spaces between his fingers. Michel could see that someone was holding the door open, and the cool air from the outside was blowing in. Michel ran toward the door before the man could. He ran outside. He heard shouts coming from the bar. People wanted to stop him. They yelled for the police. They yelled for a doctor. They yelled that the man had collapsed and that he might be dead. Michel ran home.

He ran into the house and opened his desk drawer in his office. He took his passport and extra cash he kept there in case of an emergency, held together with a rubber band. He had his car keys in his coat pocket. His car was parked on the street in front of his house. He ran outside. As he drove off, he turned and looked in the windows of his living room. His wife had left a table lamp on for him, and above a doorway he could see a bunch of mistletoe, held by twine, hanging in the air.

That New Year's Eve was the last time he saw his wife and Nina. He bought a plane ticket to New York. He took a room at the YMCA and counted his money. He would have to find a job soon, one that would not require him to have work papers. One that paid him in cash and preferably gave him room and board. When he saw the ad in the paper for someone who spoke French to be a full-time driver for a young girl who lived in a good neighborhood, he called right away.

"He has not seen his wife or Nina in over a year?" I asked *Nounou*, and she shook her head.

"He will probably never be able to go back to France without being arrested, and he knows this. If he tries to even call them or write them a letter, he will be found."

"What if I write to them and tell them to come here?" I asked *Nounou*.

"It would be complicated. They would have to do it in secret. Besides, they don't have the money for the trip," she said.

In order to make Michel feel better, I wrote him a familygram, as if I were his wife and Nina in France. I didn't know much about France, so I had to take a book out from the school library. I wrote, "Went to visit the Lascaux Cave paintings. Saw the red cow, the Chinese horse, the black bull whose legs are crossed. Wish you were here with us. The garbage men are on strike, and with the rain, the sewers overflowed, and now the rats are living on the beach and coming out to sunbathe with the tourists. We are so proud of you. We miss you so much." And because my familygram was over forty words, I shortened it, taking out the part about the striking garbage men and the sunbathing rats. I slid the familygram under his door. Later, when he came to tuck me in for the night, he told me and Cinderella to sleep well, and then he said, "Life on this submarine is sometimes difficult. Don't you think?" I nodded. "But since we are living down here under the sea, all of us so close together every day with no one else to talk to but each other, we are close. We are like family. Maybe, in fact, we are closer than family, and that makes being a sailor all the more special," he said to me.

The next time my parents came home for a visit I stole from them. They went out to a dinner party, and I went into their room and I found money in the pockets of their suits, and I found money in one of my mother's handbags that had a strap made of pearls. I found close to fifty dollars. I saved it. When I had one thousand dollars, I would give it to Michel. I would make him rich, and somehow with the money he would be able to send for his wife and Nina.

Days later, my mother left the apartment to go use the pool on our rooftop that was covered in glass. She left her wallet behind that was made with leather so soft I at first thought it was brown velvet. Inside her wallet there was a few hundred dollars, and I took almost all of it, except for a twenty-dollar bill and the change. From my father's dress coat pocket, I found another hundred dollars. I put the money under my mattress. I figured that maybe by the end of the month I would have the thousand dollars for Michel.

A few days later I was able to hunt again through their pockets and wallets, and I now had a total of five hundred dollars. I was halfway there. I wrote Michel another familygram, a short one. "We can't wait to see you soon when you come into port. We have been waiting so long for this day."

When my mother sat me down on my bed and asked me if I had taken money from her, I tried to put on my Cinderella smile. Then I shook my head. I shook my head to all of her questions, except one. She asked me if I knew who had taken the money. Was it *Nounou?* she asked. I did not shake my head. If I had shaken my head then she would have gone on to ask if it was Michel, and what if she didn't believe me that it wasn't Michel? What if she thought it was Michel? Then she would get him in trouble. She would send him away. He would never see his wife and Nina again. "So, it is *Nounou?*" she asked, prodding me. I picked up my doll and put my finger against my doll's lips, so she would not tell.

"Don't be afraid, darling, to tell me," my mother said. "You will not get into trouble. Was it *Nounou?*"

Then I looked my mother in the eye. I said, "I will never betray my fellow submariners, even if you torture me."

"God, what an imagination. You're going to grow up to be a screenwriter, aren't you? Just like your mother," she said.

"No!" I said. "Not just like you." I would never be like her. I would never leave my daughter alone so many months in a row so that I could be on location. I would live my life with my daughter the way submariners did. I would never be farther than three hundred feet away from her, the length of the longest submarine. I would talk to my daughter every day. I would eat every meal with her. I would climb into her bed after she

96

got out of it and continue to dream the dreams she was dreaming. I would shoot Tomahawk missiles at her enemies if they dared to come close.

A week later I had a new *nounou*. She was also French, and I was also to call her *Nounou*, but because she was new, I called her New *Nounou*. Michel said that the old *nounou* had gone back to her seaside town in France. "She is lucky and happy to be back with her family," he said. "Do not worry about her."

"She was a NUB anyway, a non-useful body on board this boat," I said.

My parents were gone too. They were already back on location. New *Nounou* tried to speak French with me, and, again, just like with Michel and the old *nounou*, I refused to listen. We were not living in France. My classmates were not French. If my parents were so interested in me learning French, then I should be living in Paris, not New York. They wanted me to learn French because, they said, everything they loved was French: the food, the wine, the art, the language itself. "If you do not learn French, we will feel as if there is something we neglected to give you while you were growing up. Not teaching you French would be like not having you vaccinated for smallpox. There would always be the risk that you would suffer from it, be less healthy for it."

"Then why do we live in New York?" I asked, and my mother said that in her line of business, and my father's line of business, the only choices were New York and Los Angeles. "And Los Angeles, ugh, we would never do that to you," my mother said and shuddered, her thin shoulders visibly shaking beneath her cashmere sweater, and explained to me how it was just a sea of stucco buildings barely visible through a heavy layer of yellow smog and sickly looking palms infested with rats' nests. "And the restaurants," she said, "the restaurants are in strip malls!"

Like the old *nounou*, New *Nounou* liked to drink wine and stay up late with Michel and talk about France. I had to take French class at school, so there were some words of their conversations I understood, but they were small words, *"Oui"* and *"Mon Dieu"* at the most. I considered New *Nounou* to be a NUB as well: she served no useful purpose on board, and I did not ask her to hot bunk with me and Cinderella or to play with me at all.

There was no way to get money for Michel to see his family again while my parents were away. I did not have access to my mother's purse or my father's wallet. I began to sell some of the things from my mother's closet to a girl at school named Lily. I sold Lily a ring of my mother's with blue gems in it. My mother would never miss the ring. I'd never even seen her wear it. The ring was big on Lily's ring finger, and even on her forefinger, but she bought it anyway. She paid me ten dollars that she had taken from her mother's purse after I told her how easy it was to do. Later that day, though, the ring slipped off Lily's finger on the playground when she took off her gloves before coming inside. The ring was now lost. Maybe that was the best outcome, because I had worried that if Lily's mother had seen the ring, she might ask how she got it, and the mother would call New *Nounou* and tell her that I was stealing from my mother's jewelry box.

Michel drove me to the skating rink after school, and again he sat with Cinderella while I went in circles on the ice. It was a very cold day, and at one point, I was the only one on the ice.

I could see Michel blowing into his hands while sitting on the bench waiting for me. On the ride home he started sneezing. Thinking back, I should have never let him wait for me in the cold that long, because that night he was too sick to come and tuck me in, and New *Nounou* had to go to his quarters, bringing him broth and aspirin. I knocked on his door because I couldn't sleep.

"Permission to enter sick bay, Chief," I said, and then I entered his room. New *Nounou* had his shirt open, and she was rubbing menthol balm onto his chest, and she was doing it slowly, in broad circles. New *Nounou* was blonde, and mostly she wore her hair up in a chignon, but this evening her hair was down and shining gold in the lamplight. Through his watery eyes, I could see Michel looking at her, smiling even though he was sick with congestion and a fever.

"We might have to pull into port and get you to a doctor on shore," I said.

"No, the corpsman is doing a wonderful job," he said, meaning New *Nounou*.

"Ah, the corpsman, is that what I am? Is that good? Do I get extra rations? A longer shower?" she asked.

"You can have whatever you'd like," Michel said.

"No, Corpsman doesn't get special treatment," I said, even though I wasn't sure.

"Rebecca, I cannot tuck you in tonight, but I want you to go to bed right away. Tomorrow we will have an inspection. There might even be a fire we'll have to put out at the same time," he said.

"Yes, Chief," I said and went back to my room. I stayed up though, listening for New *Nounou*'s footsteps on the way down the hall from Michel's quarters and back to her room. When I finally did hear her going back to her room, it was late. The clock by my bed said it was past two in the morning.

New *Nounou* said she would walk me to school in the morning so that Michel could rest. After I was dropped off, Lily asked me if that was my mother. "My mother? No!" I said.

"She's beautiful. I wish she were my mother," Lily said.

That afternoon, after school, Michel said he could not play inspections. New *Nounou* was in the kitchen making him soup, and she told him to stay in bed until it was ready. In fact, she had told him to stay in bed all day, because now he had a cough. I told him he had better man up. He had better pull his weight. We were all a crew, a family, and we needed his help. He said I could manage without him. I went to the bathroom and plugged the tub and turned on the water. Then I did the same for the sink faucet. I stopped up the toilet with toilet paper and flushed it five times in a row so that the water started pouring out of the bowl and onto the tile floor. Very quickly, the whole room flooded. Water poured out from under the bathroom door and into the hallway. I went up to Michel's door. "Flooding in the re-actor compartment!" I yelled. "We're taking on water at three hundred feet." I could hear Michel and New *Nounou* talking behind the door.

"She shouldn't be bothering you now. She needs to know when it is not time to play," New *Nounou* said.

"Not now, Rebecca. I need to rest. Tomorrow we'll play," Michel said weakly.

"That's right," New *Nounou* added. "Go do your homework now," she said to me.

Not long afterward, there was a loud knocking at the front door. It was the superintendent of the building telling New *Nounou* that the water was cascading down into the apartment below ours. It was shorting out the lights down there as well, and sparks were flying.

Michel called me into his room. He was furious. He coughed and sputtered while he yelled at me. He said New *Nounou* would have to call my parents and tell them what I had done. "New *Nounou* could lose her job," he said. "Now go to your room and stay there," Michel said.

I pulled the money out from under my mattress that I had been saving for Michel to bring his wife and Nina to see him. I opened the window. Below me, on the street, I let the money go. It sailed around a little bit. Then it fell to the sidewalk. There was no one on the street to pick it up. I closed the window and then wrote a familygram. "Sorry. Can't make it to your arrival in port," I wrote. I called for New *Nounou*, and when she came, I handed her the familygram and told her to give it to Michel.

While New *Nounou* was in Michel's room, I put Cinderella in my bed.

"You have to hot bunk now," I told her. I put my coat on and grabbed my ice skates. Michel would usually drive me to the skating rink, but it didn't matter. I knew how to get there myself.

It was a Friday night, and the rink was crowded. Teenagers were there who skated in large groups and pushed through the crowd. The music that blared from the outdoor speakers wasn't music the rink played during the day. The music was loud, and all the teenagers knew the words and sang along to it. Every once in a while, they would grab hands and do the whip, and like the arms of a galaxy they spun out and sucked whomever was in front of them into their core. I was sucked in. I tried not to fall, but the teenagers were big. They wore their long coats open, and their coat lapels spread out like they were raven's wings that they wanted to wrap around me. I tripped over someone's huge skates. A cold blade cut across my face. The blood poured out quickly, covering the ice, and then the blood went through the ice, getting into the top layer. Some girl shrieked, and I looked up at her. She covered her face with her mittened hands. The mittens were made out of mohair, and at first, I thought how maybe she was holding a soft furry kitten up to her face.

In the hospital they wanted to know my name. "Nina," I said in a French accent. They wanted to know where my parents were. I told them they were away at sea. "Both of them deployed?" the nurse asked.

"*Oui.*"

"But who's taking care of you? Where's your home?" the nurse said.

"Biarritz. It's in France," I said.

The nurse was confused. "Honey," she said. "We need to find who's responsible for you."

"You can't contact them below the sea. You're not supposed to tell them anything upsetting, *mon Dieu.* They just want news of everyday life. They want to know what the weather is. They want to hear how the leaves are changing. How the dog chased a rabbit and didn't come back for hours, and when he did come back, he had the rabbit in his mouth and mud in his fur. Things like that," I said.

The nurse brought in another woman. She gave me hot chocolate. She put her arm around me. She smelled of the outdoors. More distinctly, she smelled of cold air and pine, as if she had just cut down a Christmas tree, and the sap and the cold had clung to her. The woman said she was here to help me.

"But the doctor has already treated me," I said.

"Let me be clear. I'm here to help you remember where you live. Who your parents are," she said.

"Even though we are poor, I live in a house by the sea," I said. "There's a restaurant by the cliffs and such high waves splash up against it that the windows have to be washed all of the time to keep the salt from clouding the view. On New Year's Eve we eat *galette de rois* cakes. I always want the slice with the trinket. I want to be king for a day. My father is Michel C. One day he took a man's eye out with his umbrella. It was not his fault, but still, it made him run from the police. My mother did not want to be without him, so she ran with him. He let her go with him. My mother is beautiful. She is blonde and she usually wears her hair in a chignon, but when she wears her hair down, even the sunflowers bow over, their seeded centers nearly touching the grass because they recognize she is more beautiful than they are. They joined the navy. No enemies can find them under the sea. They take turns sharing the same bunk. If my father gets in after my mother, he feels the warmth of her body, and when he dreams, it's a continuation of the same dream my mother was dreaming."

The woman sighed, and when she did it was as if she released more of her smell into the air, as if the tree I imagined she cut down had now been dragged in through the door and was in the middle of the room with us.

"What will become of me?" I asked. "Will I have to sleep in the museum? Will you put me behind glass next to the Eskimos?"

The woman, whose name was Dolores, laughed. "No. We'll take care of you. You'll stay with me for a couple of days until we can find your parents or until they contact us. Would you like that?" she asked.

"It depends. Do you have a limousine?" I asked.

"Hah, no," Dolores said.

"Good," I said.

"Do you have a penthouse?" I said.

"No, a railroad flat," she said.

"I'd like to see it. I'd like to stay with you very much," I said, thinking how Dolores's apartment probably smelled of pine and cold air, unlike mine that was hot with the heat coming up strong from the vents, and I tried to smile the way Cinderella would smile, but I could feel that I wasn't doing it correctly. My lips were pressed too tightly together, and it must not have been a happy smile because when Dolores looked at me, she put her hand under my chin and said, "It's going to be okay."

When we got to Dolores's house I asked, "Do you have pencil and paper? I'd like to write my parents a familygram."

"Of course," Dolores said.

"Dear Mama and Papa. Went skating today. The trees are bare, but it was nice because it made the music sound even louder. Drank hot chocolate. Visited the museum. You would not believe there is a girl Eskimo behind the glass who looks just like I do. The same hair. The same smile. Can't wait to see you when you come into port." Then, because it was over forty words, I cut out the part about the trees and the hot chocolate, and when that was still over forty words, I cut out everything but "There is a girl behind the glass."

After a few days, Dolores said she had a surprise for me. I was going to fly on an airplane. We flew to California. On the plane, water droplets became trapped between the double-paned windows and made it hard to see the clouds or the land below. "Does it make you nervous not to see what's outside the window?" Dolores asked. I shook my head. I thought of sailors on submarines, of how long they would be on a tour of duty without being able to see out any window at all.

Once on the ground, we went to the luggage carousel, and I saw my mother there. She was waving so much, the gold chain bracelets on her wrist made a jingling sound.

"Look, guess who that is!" Dolores said, and she pushed me forward so that I would walk in the direction of my mother. We said good-bye to Dolores, and then my mother put me in the back of a limousine. Cinderella was already in the car, sitting on the seat. "I got you a new Cinderella. Isn't she lovely? She's just like the old one."

Instead of a fur muff and a fur hat, this Cinderella wore a yellow jumper of light cotton, and on her lap was a beach ball of many bright colors that stayed in place beneath her hands that were the same size as mine. My mother told me how happy she was to see me. "You'll come live with us on location now," she said. I touched Cinderella's face. It was the same face as my Cinderella at home who was hot-bunking in my bed. I traced my finger along this Cinderella's lips, my finger slightly going upward with the path of her smile. Then I put my own finger to my lips and made sure the curve of my smile was the same as this Cinderella's. "Good, you're happy too," my mother said, and then she slid the window open between us and the driver. When the driver turned around, I saw it was not Michel.

In French, which made my mother's voice sound higher, like she was a girl my age, my mother told the driver where to go.

We drove past tall palm trees whose thin trunks swayed and bent over so much that I thought they would break, or that their long leafy tops would brush the roof of the limousine, but they didn't. We drove past the ocean. I could see the white tops of green waves that when they rose up were deeply curled, as if the waves were forming over an enormous invisible pipe. I thought of submarines beneath the sea, where everything was calm inside that steel frame, and the sailors were moving steadily onward even though the waves above them were roiling and smashing up against the shore.

BEAUTY SHOT

Maya had been attacked once. A man had followed her up the stairs of her building and held a long knife to her throat. He made her open the front door of her apartment. What he didn't know was that her dog was behind the door. It was a dog trained to attack. Maya's mother, wanting her daughter to be safe when she moved to New York City, had given her the dog already trained. When Maya said the German word that told her dog to attack, the dog went for the man's throat. He dropped his knife trying to get the dog off him. Maya saw the dog hanging off the man's neck as he ran down the stairs and out onto Second Avenue. She chased after them. She was able to follow because there was a trail of blood on the sidewalks. The blood crossed the avenue and was on the sidewalk in front of Gem Spa, the soda fountain shop, where a few hippies or yippies, she never knew the difference, were standing and talking and smoking. She followed the blood all the way down the length of Eighth Street, all the way up Broadway and to Grace Church, where it seemed to stop by the iron gates that enclosed a yard with a few lovely cherry trees growing. They were in bloom, and when she breathed in deeply in order to make a long, loud whistle for her dog, her nose filled with their scent. Her dog came from behind her, barking happily to see her and rubbing against her so that she could be petted. Maya knelt down and put her face up to her dog's and rubbed her neck. When they started walking home, her hand felt wet, and when she looked down, she saw there was blood on her palm and all over her dog's back.

She thought the dog might have killed the man because so much blood had been on the sidewalks and on her dog's fur. That night the hippies or the yippies protested the war. They gathered all of the metal wastebaskets from the street corners and put them in front of Gem Spa. Then they lit them on fire. Even from her place, which was across the street, Maya thought she could feel the heat from the fires as she looked out her picture window. Her dog came up under her hand as she watched, wanting to be pet. Her dog's fur was still wet after the washing she had given the dog in the bathtub where the attacker's blood had run down the drain of her claw-footed tub. The hippies or the yippies sang songs. They sang "Last Night I Had the Strangest Dream," and she found herself singing the words as she stood with her dog watching the fires burn. Then they chanted. They said, "One, two, three, four! We don't want your fuckin' war" over and over again.

Maya did not think much about the war. She didn't know anyone who was in the war, and she didn't follow politics. "Don't get involved with those anti-war hippies," her mother had told her. "They're only protesting because they're young, and they've got nothing better to do but take drugs and link arms and sing for peace." Maya assured her she would not get involved. She was in New York to learn how to make films. She took a job with a filmmaker so she could someday learn how to make films herself.

Sometimes the chants of the hippies or the yippies stayed in her head because they were catchy. She repeated them as she shampooed her hair in the shower. She had no desire to join the protestors, but that night she was thankful for their burning fires. When she lay down on her bed that was near the picture window, the flames kept her room bright, and tonight she was afraid of sleeping in the dark. She took the knife the attacker had dropped, which she had cleaned in the bathtub at the same time she had cleaned her dog, and put it on the floor near the head of her bed. It looked like a machete, she thought. The handle was made of ebony. The blade curved up at the tip, reminding her of the way silk slippers a genie might wear curled up at the toe.

She didn't want to go to the police. She didn't think she could remember the face of the man. She never really saw him. She only felt the machete blade at her neck and she only sensed that he was much taller than she was. All that he said to her was, "Open your door now, or I'll cut you on the stairs." She wondered if she did go to the police if they would take the dog from her, because it had attacked the man. That night the dog lay beside her bed with her head facing the door. She could see the licking flames in her dog's eyes.

She wanted to take the dog with her everywhere now. When she went to the grocery store, she tied the dog's leash up to a street sign and told the dog that she would be back. The dog sat and waited and jumped up to greet her when she came out of the store holding a bag full of groceries. She wanted to take the dog to work with her and asked her boss if she could bring him into the office. Her boss was making a film about the parks in New York. He told her what parts of the film he wanted her to find, and she would go through canisters of film he had taken. He wanted the parts where children were rolling down the grassy hills and hollering through tunnels, listening to their own echoes. He wanted the parts where people in the heat of summer dove off the bow of their rented rowboats and swam in the dark water of the pond. He wanted the parts where a girl held a red balloon tightly while she went up and down on a wooden carousel horse. "Maya, find me a beauty shot," he'd sometimes say, and she knew what he meant: she should find some shot he took of mist over the lake in the morning, of a carriage horse's caramel-colored mane as the carriage horse trotted on a cherry blossom–covered lane. The dog was not a problem. She lay beside the large canvas bins that held the strips of film in the midtown office. She turned her head when she heard the groan of the elevator stop at their floor, but she did not bark. Maya would always give her dog the crusts from her deli sandwich, and the dog always took them gently between her teeth and ate them quickly, without making a mess.

One night her boss asked her to go to a concert that was being held in the bandshell of the park. Maya brought her dog, and her boss filmed the concert while she held his Nagra reel-to-reel tape recorder bag slung over her shoulder and held out the mic above her head to capture the sound. She let the dog loose, so that she did not have to hold onto her leash and at the same time take the sound. The dog trotted behind her, and when Maya stopped, the dog stopped and sat beside her on the ground. Hippies were at the concert. The men had hair like the women, long and flowing. The hippies came up to the dog, their peace sign pendants hanging long from leather cords and almost hitting the dog as they knelt down to pet her. The dog was nervous from all the attention of the people dressed in kaftans with flowing sleeves that grazed the dog's head and with the scent of cloves on them from cigarettes they had smoked. The dog kept looking up at Maya and panting. Her panting almost like speech, Maya thought. As if the dog were telling her she wanted to go home.

When the concert was over, Maya's boss was pleased with the footage he had taken. He had close-ups of women wearing beaded headbands watching the concert and mouthing the word "peace" into the camera. He had shots of children on their father's shoulders as the fathers swayed to the music and the children clapped. "Let's get a drink," he suggested to Maya, but Maya wanted to take her dog home. She did not like how her panting had become faster and shallow, as if her dog could not breathe the hot summer air that seemed to be even hotter in the park because the people were grouped so close together watching the concert. "Come on. Just one drink," her boss said. "You have to do as I tell you. I'm your boss, after all," he said, smiling, but Maya was afraid a part of her boss wasn't kidding. She was behind on her rent, and she felt she could not take the risk of being fired right now.

Sitting across from her boss at a table in a bar, she could see how one eye was rimmed with a red circle from where the rubber eyepiece on his camera had been held up to his face. It made him look older than he was, and it made him look like he had been crying. She thought the bar would be better for the dog, but it wasn't. There were sports fans there watching a game, and their cheering every once in a while, would make the dog move from a sitting position to a standing position, and she would let out a slight whine, so slight that Maya was sure she was the only one who could hear it.

Maya drank a gin and tonic quickly, hoping it would mean she could leave the bar that much more quickly and go home, but her boss saw how her glass was empty and ordered her another and one for himself. "I know I'm not supposed to ask you this, considering I'm your boss. But would you like to spend the night with me?" her boss said after he had swallowed down his second drink. "I mean, both you and the dog, of course," he said, laughing a little. Maya laughed a little too, because she was embarrassed for him. Why hadn't he at least tried to seduce her instead of just asking her? Was he that insecure? Had he not done it in so long? She looked at the sports fans. One kept pounding the bar every time a player missed or a player made a shot. There seemed to be no difference: one pounding was as loud and as strong as the next, whether it was for the point or for the loss.

"I have to get home," she said. He nodded. He took another drink of his drink. "Well, then. I'll see you tomorrow," he said. He stood up and he left the bar. She stayed where she was. The game must have ended. The men were not cheering. They were sitting and drinking at the bar. Someone must have turned on the stereo because soft music started playing, some kind of jazz. Her dog lay down by her feet. She noticed the bar had paintings on the wall. They were for sale. She liked them. They were of scenes of wildflowers in fields and skies with clouds that seemed more like wisps of smoke than clouds. She ordered another drink. This one tasted better than the last two. She wondered if the bartender had switched to a different kind of gin, one whose flavor she could taste just by breathing in over the rim of her glass. She reached down and petted the dog even though the dog's eyes were closed now. It was a Saturday night, and she knew that back at her place her dog probably would not be sleeping as soundly. The hippies in front of Gem Spa were probably lighting their fires in the trash cans. They were probably singing, and maybe there would be a fight or cop cars cruising by, their flashing lights creating kaleidoscopes of color on her walls.

The bar did not seem like it would close anytime soon. More people entered and ordered drinks. The jazz tempo changed. It was livelier and louder now. The dog was noticed. Women wearing spaghetti strap gowns came over to pet her. They had just been to a show, they said. Their polished nails were creamy pastel colors, and when their fingers moved across her dog's head and coat, it looked like so many sweet candy-coated pieces of bridge mix raining over her, sliding around her fur. Maya was invited to join them. There was Adam and Seth and Keith and Cindy and Doris and Bonnie. She said their names as they were introduced, but the minute she said them, she forgot them. They said the tunnel home was jam-packed with traffic, and so they decided to stop here for a nightcap until everything had cleared. "The gin and tonics are very good," Maya told them, thinking she sounded like she had been coming to this bar for years.

Adam or Seth or Keith ordered her one, even though she had told them she had had enough. She wasn't even standing and she thought she could feel the upper half of her body swaying as she sat at the table. The wood of the table beneath her hands was warm, and she thought how it might even be nice to lay her head on the warmth of the table. The women were inviting her dog to put her front paws on their laps. "Come on up!" they said in high voices, but the dog looked at Maya and did not jump up. "She'll rip your dresses," Maya said, but it came out, "Sill ip your dresses." Maya laughed at herself, and everyone laughed with her, and then they clinked their glasses together and drank more. After that, though, there was a long silence. Maya looked at the pretty shimmery spaghetti strap dresses the women wore. The material looked like iridescent scales of fish were sewn onto it, and when the women moved it seemed to Maya like they were moving underwater, and their bodies were flashing as if caught by rays of sun. "What do you think about the war?" Maya asked them, because she had been thinking about going back to her neighborhood and how the yippies or hippies would be out.

"Oh, I am so sick of all this talk of war," one of the women said, and the rest agreed.

"Don't you think we should be trying to stop it?" Maya said. But one woman said, "We should be trying to order more drinks. That's what we should be doing," and she raised her hand high, trying to call over the bartender, even though Maya, the entire time she'd been there, had never seen the bartender come out from behind the bar to serve anyone.

It was a shame she had to use the ladies' room, Maya thought to herself, because if she didn't have to use it then she wouldn't have had to stand and make her way across the bar to the back, past a lot of people. The dog wanted to come with her, but she told her no because she did not think the ladies' room would be big enough for the both of them. "Stay with Boris and Candy and the other woman," she said. "Hah, Boris and Candy. I like that. I'm going to call you girls that from now on," she heard one of the men say as she stood and the room reeled and the floor seemed to tilt as if she were walking in the aisle of an airplane turning in midflight.

She was wearing a miniskirt and she was thankful she was not wearing pants or anything with buckles or snaps. She almost didn't make it to the toilet seat in time. She shivered as she relieved herself. It took such a long time to go. She stared at the black-and-white tiled floor beneath her feet, and it seemed to move. Then suddenly she felt sick, and whether or not she was finished using the toilet, it didn't matter: she had to get up from the seat and turn and lift the lid or else she would have vomited on the floor. She felt sweat break out on her back and her neck and chest, and when she was done, she took some tissue and ran it under the faucet and used it to swab the places on her skin that had broken out in sweat.

When she walked out of the bathroom, bright lights were on in the bar, and the bartender was putting chairs up on the tables. She winced. The lights seemed as bright as the sun. Everyone was gone from the bar. She ran into the street. She yelled her dog's name. She ran back into the bar. "Have you seen my dog?" she said to the bartender. He shook his head and took off his apron and tossed it onto the floor, where a pile of bar towels was already sitting. "Nope," he said.

She ran toward the tunnel. When she got there, she could see that the traffic was clear now. Cars were speeding into it. She was tempted to go into the tunnel, walk all the way to the other side, but she could not be sure that those people had taken her dog. Maybe her dog was on the streets near the bar, running around, looking for her. She started to feel sick again but held it down.

The bar was close to her boss's office. She thought maybe the dog had gone looking for her there. She went to the outside of the building. She looked in through the revolving glass doors. Everything was dark. She looked up and down the street. She tried to whistle, but she couldn't get her lips to do it right. She yelled her dog's name again, this time shrieking it. She went back to the bar. It was closed now. She slid down the wall. She sat with her legs apart. If anyone walked by, they could have seen up her skirt, but no one was on the streets now. It did not matter. She slept with her head up against the building for a while. The sound of hooves woke her. A horse-drawn carriage was passing. The horse had a purple plume of feathers in its headpiece, and the feathers danced and floated as he moved. At the same time, the sun was rising, and it rose first as purple and hazy. "A beauty shot," she said to herself, knowing that if her boss were with her, he would have said it himself.

When she walked home down Fifth Avenue, she called for her dog. People turned their heads to look at her as she cupped her hands around her mouth. She held an empty leash. Walking past Gem Spa, she stopped to ask the man working behind the counter if he had seen her dog. Her voice broke when she asked. The man, a hippie with a mustache and long beard and wearing a dashiki, told her that he hadn't seen her dog. He gave her a free egg cream though, and then he told her he had something else for her. He asked for her hand, and he shook it, and in her palm, he left a small pill. It was the blue of a robin's egg.

"You'll feel better. I take one when all this shit about the war brings me down," he said. She walked home holding the pill, thinking how she did not necessarily need to feel better. What she really needed was her dog back.

Before she climbed up the stairs to her place she turned around, making sure no one was following her. Then at the top of the stairs, she turned around again. There was no one there, just the black-and-white tiled wall, reminding her of the bar and its tiled bathroom floor where she was sick. Inside, she put the pill on her dresser and forgot about it. She looked through her photographs. She looked for one of her dog. She only found one of herself and the dog, and the dog's head was half out of the picture and sideways. Looking at it, no one would be able to tell what the dog looked like. She wanted a photograph that she could tape to the lampposts in her neighborhood and the midtown neighborhood where she had lost her dog. She wanted to post a reward for her dog. She would pay $200 to get her back. It was at least one of her paychecks. She thought of lying, writing that she would pay $500 to have the dog back and that if the dog were found, maybe she could borrow the rest of the money to claim her. Maybe her mother, who always asked about the dog, or her boss would loan her the money. But in the end, the photograph was not good enough. She took white paper and wrote "$200 for lost dog" and drew a picture of her dog with pencil, and it looked like a child's drawing, but she copied it and taped it to lampposts everywhere anyway. She called the ASPCA and asked if they recently had a dog brought in that looked like her dog. "All the dogs look like your dog," the woman on the phone said. She went to the ASPCA. She hated looking in all of the kennels at the dogs who were not her dogs. She hated the dogs. She knew she should feel sorry for the dogs with their runny eyes and their dull coats that she could not bring home that needed homes, but instead she cursed them because none of them were her dog.

The only thing that lay by her bed at night was the machete, with its curved tip like a genie's slipper. She moved it from the head of the bed to the side of the bed where her dog used to lie. She wanted to be ready to lift it up if she needed it to defend herself.

Her boss did not invite her out filming in the park any longer. After he filmed the Bread and Puppet troupe putting on a performance on the green, with their huge papier-mâché heads making them look grotesque, and after he filmed the children hiding behind their mothers' backs as the puppets, gigantic on stilts, spoke to them through microphones that distorted their voices, he packed his camera and took her sound equipment off her shoulder and told her good night. Feeling very light after not having the Nagra reel-to-reel sound equipment bag on her shoulder any longer, she decided one evening to stay in the park a bit longer. She climbed a rock, a huge piece of granite that had names written on it and that was smooth from so many people having sat on it. From that high up, she thought she could see so much of the park. She could see the zoo and the carousel and the boat pond. She could hear the animal clock strike at the zoo, and she could hear the carousel music and the oars of boaters splashing in the water. When it was too late for her to be in the park alone, after the sun had set, she stood on the rock. Because no one else was nearby, she called for her dog. It was a long call. She made it as long as she could and did not stop until she needed to breathe.

That night, there was singing on the street again and fires in the trash cans. She could not sleep because it was so loud. People were running in large groups down the center of the street, blocking a sea of taxis and cars. The drivers leaned on their horns and did not let up. She heard police sirens and people screaming, "It's the pigs." She heard a woman's voice yell, "Take off your shoes! You'll run faster." She heard someone banging on the downstairs door, and then she heard the door opening and the door slamming against the black-and-white tiled wall. Someone was running up the first flight of the building's stairs. Their footsteps scuffed and pounded on the slate steps. Someone was either thrown or threw themselves at her front door. She heard a thumping sound, and her door jiggled in its frame. If her dog were here, she thought, she would be barking. She would be right up next to the door, and she would have her shoulders set wide and her ears straight up and her tail out straight, and she would be barking so loud and so sharply that it would hurt your ears, and you would hear her bark inside of your chest, vibrating what was inside of you, your lungs and your ribs and your heart.

She lifted up the machete. She walked right up to the door. She heard something slide down the length of the door. Whoever was there must have slid their back down her door. They were sitting down now. She could hear them breathing loudly. After a while, their breathing slowed, but it was still loud. She could hear her kitchen sink, which had a leaky faucet, drip a drop of water to the sink bottom in between his breaths. She sat down cross-legged facing her door. She left the machete in her lap, with her hand still on the ebony handle. The crowd outside was chanting, "Bring our boys home!" Then they chanted, "Hey, Hey, LBJ, how many kids have you killed today?" The sirens grew louder. The police must have been right outside. Her place danced with the sirens' lights. She heard someone whisper her name. They said it again louder. "It's me, Brian, your boss," the voice said. She did not believe him at first. She thought someone had found out her name and had found out her boss's name and was tricking her. "Can I come in?" he said in a louder voice.

"Brian?" she said.

"The cops are thick out there. I think one's after me. I helped the others light the trash can fires. I threw a soda can at the back of a cop's head. The cop turned just in time to see I was the one who did it. All I could think to do was run. Luckily, I remembered you said you lived across from the Gem Spa and I remembered what address I sent your checks to," he said.

When she let him in, he looked at the machete and said, "Whoah, where'd you get that from, the cane fields?" He took the machete and hefted it. "You might do better with something lighter. Something that would not make you tired just to hold it," he said. Then he noticed the blue pill on her dresser. "What's this?" he said. She shrugged. He rolled it between his fingers. "Where'd you get it?"

"Across the street, at Gem Spa," she said.

"You mean you ordered an egg cream, and this is what you got?" he said.

"Something like that," she said. He laughed, and when he did the sirens' lights lit him up, and triangles and squares of blue and red light flashed on his face.

She let him hold her that night while they lay side by side on her bed, still in their clothes. She told him she did not think it was a good idea that they do any more than that. She asked him why he was down here at the protests, and he said he had a brother who had been drafted and was over there and he just wanted him to come home. "It's so simple," he said. "I just want to see him walk through my door one day soon. I keep thinking if I imagine it every night, then it will come true. He'll come home in one piece." He asked about her dog, and she told him how her mother had given her the dog and how the dog knew the word for attack and how the dog had once saved her life. Her boss did not interrupt her or ask more questions, but she talked more about her dog anyway. She told him how the dog had hung from the man's neck all the way down her stairs, all the way down the street, past the Gem Spa, all the way until the churchyard. She told him how the man's blood was in her dog's coat. She told him how she thought the man was probably dead. Her boss spoke then. "Yes, I imagine he is, or maybe he is still alive but in bad shape," her boss said.

"Oh, no, I am sure he is dead."

"You mean you hope he is dead," her boss said.

"Yes, but maybe sometimes it's the same. Maybe this time it's the same because I will never see that man again, because he will not come back, knowing this is where the dog lives," she said.

"Yes, maybe it is the same then," he said, and she could feel her boss nod his head against her own as they lay spooned. She could hear what must have been his chin rub against her hair.

Sometime in the night, the streets became quiet. The fires in the trash cans burnt down, and the police left. She and her boss were able to fall asleep. In the morning he kissed her forehead before he left her place. She noticed later on that the blue pill was gone. She wondered if her boss had taken it with him or if he had thrown it away so she would not take it. When she met up with him later at the park to take some shots of the sun coming through the leaves and some shots of kites being flown by a man from India with children running behind him as he ran to catch the wind with his kite, she asked him where the pill was. "I threw it away. You have no idea what's inside that pill," he said. He was right, she knew, but she felt he had no right to throw it away either. She was never planning on taking the pill, but maybe it wasn't such a bad pill. Maybe it would just make me feel better or sleep better or be awake better, she thought. She was tired often. She would wake up every morning and visit the ASPCA and look at the dogs in the kennels, and then she would take long walks near the bar where she lost the dog. She would just walk and look for the dog. At night she dreamt she saw the dog running down the empty streets, but the dog was a ghost and did not stop even though she kept calling out to her.

One night she got a phone call. A kid was on the line. He sounded like he was a teenager. He said he saw her flyer and he had her dog. She thought it was her own fault. What did she expect when she had drawn such an amateurish drawing of her dog except for kids to respond to her flyer? The kid wanted to meet her at the playground all the way across town. "Meet me by the boat," he said. She knew the boat in the park. It looked like it was made of sand, but it was just sandy-colored concrete. The children could climb up in it and walk the deck and look through portholes at passing cars on the avenue. When she met the kid, he looked older than he sounded on the phone. He was sitting on the side of the boat, with one leg crossed over the other. She had the two hundred dollars, but she was almost sure that the kid would not have her dog. She was right, and when she went up to him and said, "Are you the kid who called me?"

"I need the money first," he said.

"It doesn't work that way," she said.

"Give me half the money then," he said.

"And then what?" she said.

"Then I take you to your dog and you give me the rest of it," he said.

"How do I even know you have the right dog?" she said. He handed her the flyer she had drawn.

"Is this your dog?" he asked.

"That's a bad drawing," she said.

"Well this is the dog I have," he said. She looked at the kid's face. In a few years he could go to war. She thought he looked like her boss, Brian. She thought they had the same chin. It was a chin that was square, and you could see the outline of his strong bones beneath the chin. She imagined the kid could even be Brian's brother.

She didn't care about the money all of a sudden. She imagined that after she gave it to him, he would just run. She could see him running in the sand to get away from her, the sand flying up behind his tennis shoes as he dug into the sand as fast as he could. "Take the money, go to Canada, get far away from the war," she thought to herself. He did not run though. He walked ahead of her, counting the money as he walked, and then stuffing it into the back pocket of his blue jean cutoffs. It was a dumb place to keep it, she thought. She could see some of the bills peeking out from the pocket. They would have been easy to slide out without the boy even noticing. She wondered how this kid could be so smart about trying to get the money but so dumb about where he kept it. She realized then how you could never be sure about people. Just because you had some information about them didn't mean you could guess what they would do next or in another situation. There were no pieces to the puzzle when it came to people, because in the end there was no fixed picture to see. Instead, people were like some kind of a blur, something in motion all of the time that was always changing.

He took her down a street lined with brownstones. He stopped at one brownstone and went down the basement steps, and as he went, though, he reached out and held her arm, helping her down. She flinched at first, remembering the man who had attacked her, but then she let the kid help her. She was surprised at how gentlemanly his grip felt on her arm. She did not think a kid would be so polite or so strong. It was one of the less well-kept brownstones on the block. Out in front, wrappers and cans littered the area inside the metal fence that surrounded the square patch of earth a tree was planted in. The door down to the basement had unfinished scraps of boards nailed to it, which probably served to patch up holes in the wood. She followed him down and into the basement and hoped that her dog was really down there because if the kid tried to hurt her, then she knew her dog would protect her. It was dark in the basement, and coming from bright sunlight, she could not see a thing for several moments.

"There he is," the kid said, and her heart sank, of course, because her dog was not a "he," and so this dog she could not see was not her dog. Then, at the same time, the kid pulled a string and turned on a bare bulb, and she saw her dog, but only for a flash, because then she ran to the dog and buried her face in her neck. Her dog was thinner, and her coat was the same dull color as the dogs in the pound. She got down on the dirt floor of the basement and sat there while the dog licked her face and wagged its tail. "I'd like the rest," the kid said, and she gave it to him. He said, "Thank you," and then he ran up the steps. She turned and called up the stairs, "Thank you! Thank you so much!" she said, and she really was thankful to this boy, this kid, this almost man.

The walk home took them a long time because sometimes she would just stop on the sidewalk and bend down and hug the dog and pet her and tell her she was such a good dog.

When they finally neared her neighborhood and they walked past Gem Spa, the man who worked there who had given her the robin's-egg blue pill shouted out, "Hey, is that a new dog you got?" and she said, "No, this is the same dog. I found her." The man waved her over and held out an egg cream he had poured into a plastic dish. She gave it to the dog, and her dog lapped it up on the sidewalk, licking the dish even when it was already clean, so that the dish moved down the sidewalk, crossing over the black burn marks from the trash can fires with every lick of her tongue.

She called her boss that night and told him about the luck she had finding her dog, and he was happy for her and said he could come by with some champagne and they could celebrate, but she did not want to see her boss, and she told him thank you anyway, but she and her dog needed some time to be together again. She called her mother to tell her about the good news, and her mother said, "That's some story. Are you sure it's the right dog?" and she told her mother yes while she had one hand on the phone and one hand petting the dog.

When she brought the dog to work the next day, her boss said the same thing. "Are you sure that's the same dog? I swear your dog was darker. Your dog wasn't this blonde," he said.

"Of course, I am sure. Of course, it's my dog. Why does everyone keep saying that?" she said.

"Isn't there a way to be sure? What was that attack word in German your dog knew that you never told anyone? Can't you use it with this dog and see?" he said.

"I can't just have the dog attack when there is nothing to attack, and if there is something to attack, like a person, then that person will be hurt for no reason," she said. "Besides, it is my dog," she said.

The dog now liked to sleep with her on the bed instead of next to her on the floor by the bed the way it did before. She thought the dog changed to sleeping with her because she was so upset by having been separated from her that she never wanted to be far from her again.

One evening, she was working in the office and her boss stepped out to get a coffee. The phone rang and when she answered, it was her boss's mother. Maya had never spoken to her before, and the mother did not ask who she was. "Tell him to call me back," the mother said, and Maya could tell the mother was trying to say it at the same time she was trying to keep herself from crying.

"Is it about Brian's brother?" Maya said. Brian's mother burst out crying then. "I'll tell him to call you when he gets back," Maya said. She thought how she would tell him when he got back. When he got back to the office, with not one coffee for himself but two, one for her as well, she would tell him the news of his dead brother, and he would drop both of them. Both coffees would hit the hard tiled office floor and bounce, and their tops would pop off. Coffee would splash as high as the bins that held the loose cuts of film, and it would stain the bins' white canvas sides. The entire office would smell of the coffee. She would stay with him until very late. He would want her to stay. When he called his mother back, she would go down the hall to the restroom to get some paper towels, and she would hear him crying from that far away. But she never did tell him his mother called. She figured she might tell him later or tomorrow, just so he could keep thinking his brother was alive for a little longer.

That night they went to film a firework display in the park, and her boss was excited. He was telling her ways he would intercut frames of the exploding fireworks with shots of musicians banging on drums and children playing chase through the tunnels. They didn't finish until very late. Then she and her dog walked home, without her ever having told Brian to call his mother. Her ears were ringing from the rockets and all the packs of firecrackers the kids along the street were lighting and throwing at the feet of passersby. She was thinking of how it would be nice to be at home, inside her place with her dog lying by her side and away from the fireworks, but when she got close, she saw that it would be impossible to get to her building. Cops and hippies and yippies were blocking the street and the sidewalks. Suddenly the cops started chasing the people, and they started running toward her. She turned and started running, but she fell in the clogs she was wearing and twisted her ankle. The dog stopped when she stopped, and the dog whined. A cop came up close to her and had his club out and struck her on the back. She could not breathe because of the blow. She could not get up. The cop raised his club again. That is when she said it. She said the German word to her dog that would make her attack. The dog continued to bark. The dog did not jump in the air and hold onto the cop's sunburned neck beneath his severe crew cut. The dog just barked. Maya said the word over and over again while the cop hit her on the back and on the legs, trying to make her get up. When the cop turned to hit the dog, the dog yelped before it could be struck, and then it ran, putting its tail between its legs and winding through people's legs, escaping. Maya turned and looked up at the cop. "Bring our boys home," she said, her voice sounding like a whisper. The cop laughed and then he hit her one more time on the back and left her there. When he moved on up the street, he started clubbing other people who would not get up. After a while, Maya could stand, and she limped back to her place and up the stairs. The cops had done a good job clearing the streets, though. Everything quieted down quickly.

Sitting or lying down hurt. For a long time, she just stood and looked out her window at an empty street with just the thin trails of smoke coming from the extinguished trash fires. The smoke rose up past the tops of the buildings and coiled against a pink-clouded sky. She made her way to her bed and lay down and then felt for the machete on the floor next to her. Maybe her boss had been right: maybe she needed a lighter one after all, one that would not be so heavy for her to wield if she really needed to use it. She picked up the phone and dialed her boss's number. It was time now to tell him about his brother. The morning light made her hand look dreamily pink as she wrapped her fingers around the black ebony handle. "A beauty shot" she knew her boss would have called it.

TOO MUCH FOR ADELE

ADELE MEETS CHARLIE AT A PARTY. He's an American who speaks to her in his poor French and tells her he would very much like to date her. Adele laughs when she hears him talk, and then she puts her hand around his mouth to help him form the sounds he needs to make his French understood.

He brings her to a pension where he is renting a room. He photographs her in bed after lovemaking, with her feet together up against the wall. He tells her she has beautiful legs. "Really?" she says, and she looks at her legs, wondering what Charlie sees when what she sees are the bony caps of her knees and a bug bite on the wrinkles of her Achille's tendon.

Adele learned English in school. She is in *terminale lycée*, which is the equivalent year of a senior in high school. She makes fun of the way Americans dress, telling Charlie that his shoes are so big and thick, they remind her of loaves of bread.

During the day Charlie kisses her under the Eiffel Tower, and at night he tells her he hasn't enough francs to take her out to dinner. She says she doesn't care about going out to dinner, she's always going out to dinner with her father anyway, and sometimes she's tired of a waiter always refilling her water glass when sometimes she just doesn't want any more. And so

Charlie and Adele buy wine and drink in the pension without using glasses at all, just trading the bottle back and forth.

Adele is the daughter of a diplomat. Her father is a liaison for the consulate. Adele's mother died when she was young, and she and her father and her younger sister all live in a flat in Paris.

Adele's sister looks like a waif with a haircut that looks like she's wearing a bowl on her head. Her legs are as thin as her arms. Adele has nicknamed her Little Gnat, *Le Moucheron*, and *Le Moucheron* pleads with Adele to take her with her when Adele and Charlie go for a walk. *Le Moucheron* walks behind them, whining for sweets or chestnuts every time they pass a vendor's cart. Charlie tells Adele he has to go back home in less than a week because he's run out of money, and when he takes Adele and *Le Moucheron* back to their flat after the date, Adele tells him to wait just a moment. She runs upstairs, her heart beating hard and in time, she thinks, with each fall of her foot on each marble step. She comes back down with a cigar box and hands it to him. Inside the box is more spending money than Charlie's parents gave him to vacation in Paris in the first place. "Now you can stay!" she says, her voice out of breath and so weak she thinks he may not have heard her.

He sits down on the low curb, his knees rising high. "This curb's so much lower than what I'm used to back in the States. It's as if all the people walking on the streets of Paris over all the centuries have worn the stone down," he says.

Now, in a louder voice, she says, "Did you hear what I said? You can stay with this money," and she taps the top of the cigar box.

"From here I can see up your dress. I can see your beautiful legs and your midnight blue panties," he says, smiling, and then he stands, clutching the cigar box by his side and kissing her on the mouth, using his one free hand to hold the back of her neck.

That evening they leave *Le Moucheron* at home and they go to a restaurant on Rue Baudin. They sit side by side, the cigar box on the other side of Charlie while they eat their meal, kissing in between bites of rabbit cooked in brandy and bacon. Charlie tells Adele about Harvard, how his parents practically insisted he go there, but he feels his years were wasted studying so hard. "And for what?" he says, throwing his hands up in the air the way he has seen so many French do since he has been in Paris, throwing their hands up as if to say, "poof" all is gone. "Ask me about Dickens and Kipling and I can tell you, but what would you do with the information? What good is it? Can it stop a leaking boat? Can it put out a raging fire? Can it move the masses to overthrow a regime? It can't even get me a job."

Charlie tells Adele about his father, a chemist, manufacturing copy ink and on the side trying to invent a recipe for instant tapioca. Adele doesn't know what tapioca is, and the only way he can describe it to her is to tell her it is like small pearls you can eat. "But human beings can't eat pearls," she says. "Are you sure you're not another life form?" she asks. And then goes to kiss him, wanting a long kiss, but Charlie pulls back. He wants to keep talking. He explains to her, his words coming quickly, how even his father, selling ink, can make more money than his son who has the framed diploma from Harvard in his room at home. Adele doesn't have dreams yet of becoming anything. What she likes best is when her father takes her horseback riding in the country around a lake where on its surface she can see the silver shadows of the trees, or when she can dress up in a floor-length gown and go to a dance with all of the other diplomats. When she graduates, she may go to *université*, or she may just live at home until she decides to marry. There have already been offers, but she doesn't pay attention to them. She's never dated an American before. She likes how Charlie tells her everything he's thinking and then asks her what she thinks about his ideas. He thinks going to France should be a mandatory course in college for all Americans. "From you," he says, "they could learn not to always be in such a rush, to sit back and enjoy a meal, to really love a woman. What do you think?" he says. She laughs. She doesn't have answers for him. She likes how he sometimes takes out his camera when they're in the pension and snaps photos of her while he's talking to her, as if the snap of the photo were some kind of punctuation mark at the end of his sentences. "You are gorgeous!" he says and then *snap*, he takes a picture. "Pass me a cig, would you?" then *snap*, he takes another picture of her while she's leaning over, reaching for a pack on the nightstand beside her, her breast resting on the wooden edge.

Charlie reads Adele a letter his mother wrote to him at the pension. She wonders how he's getting along. She imagines that with the amount of money they leant him that he could stay in France at least another month. When Charlie reads this he laughs, as the money is already long gone, and all the money he has is Adele's and sits on his bedside table still in the cigar box. On the letter paper is a sketch his mother drew of a groundhog that's been plaguing their garden. She drew it on all fours and then upright on its hind legs. When he shows Adele, she shakes her head. "This kind of animal we do not have in France. I've never seen one. Are you really from Earth?" she says.

The next day on a walk with Adele and *Le Moucheron*, he tells Adele, "If I can't stay in Paris, then I'm going to take a little bit of Paris home with me." Adele wonders what that will be. Will he take a loose cobblestone from a street?

"Come back with me to the States," he says.

Le Moucheron jumps up and down. "Hurray, we are going to America!" she says.

Adele has never been to America. She imagines everyone there looking like they come from Texas, wearing big hats and chaps because she has seen a number of John Wayne movies. She imagines the landscape alien, the earth reddish, dry and crusty, covered with the small rodent, the one pencil sketched by Charlie's mother in her letter. Charlie hands Adele back the cigar box of money she gave him. "This is enough for you to buy yourself a one-way plane ticket," he says. The cigar box feels heavier to Adele than it did when she first handed it to Charlie. She wonders if he's mistakenly put something in with it alongside the money. Is there a glass ashtray in it from his pension? One of the ugly American shoes he wears that make his feet look like they're wearing loaves of bread?

"One ticket! What about me?" *Le Moucheron* says, stamping her patent leather shoes on the slick cobblestones, wet from a mist rising from the Seine and falling on them as if sprayed from a bottle of perfume.

"My father will say no," Adele says, picturing her father saying more than just no—also cursing and throwing papers off his desk and throwing books at the wall the way he usually does when he is very angry.

"You'll be eighteen in a week. You can do anything you want then."

Adele laughs. "There is nothing I can do without him consenting. He will find out where I am. He will bring me back. He knows everyone. You have to see it to believe it. We can go to any restaurant in all of Paris, and they know him. They give him free champagne and make other couples move from seats with a view just so he can have the view."

"I'll tell on you if you leave without Papa's consent," *Le Moucheron* says. "You'll have to take me with you so I don't tell." Adele hugs her sister. *"Le Moucheron, sweet le Moucheron,"* Adele says, and she breathes in her sister, wondering how long she'll be able to remember her smell, and if the memory of a smell will last as long as the memory of how a person looks.

At home, Adele packs what she'll need. Charlie is right, she thinks. In a week's time she won't have to ask her father's permission to travel. She packs all of her cashmere sweaters. Charlie described to her how on the hill beside his college dormitory he would sit on metal food trays from the dining hall and slide down the snow. He described how the cold air made it easier to hear, and so if a person dropped a key, for instance, on the path, its sound could be heard all around campus, as loud as a church bell. She would like to live in a place like that for a while, where everything could be heard so clearly there was no question about what it could be. In Paris, sounds always seem muffled. The Seine seems to trap sounds in the early morning mist that rises up from it. The heavily draped windows in her house trap the sounds of the voices of people on the street going to work. She is never sure if it is the baker or the policeman who is calling out hello to a passerby. Even the pigeons sound like their voices are trapped. Sitting on her ledge, they coo as if something is caught in their throats that they are trying to clear by swallowing over and over again.

Le Moucheron braids the tassels bordering Adele's bedspread while Adele packs. "I will tell Papa what you're planning. I'll ruin it for you," *Le Moucheron* says.

"But I will send for you to come join me, and if you tell Papa, then you won't be able to come. Be good, *Le Moucheron*. Don't tell Papa on me. Think of all of the attention Papa will lavish on you while I'm gone. He'll take you everywhere with him, too. He'll take you to the dances. He'll let you stay up late with him in the club playing mah-jongg. Just think, you'll be the one he waltzes with, and you'll be the one he rides home with in the taxi; you'll be the one leaning against the warm fur of his collar, smelling of his cologne and the late night air." After Adele says all of this, she knows she will miss her father more than she thought when she first told Charlie that, yes, she would go with him to America.

On the plane, Charlie cannot stop talking about what she will see. Their first stop will be Hinsdale, of course. Not that there is much to see there, but he would like to show her his home where he grew up. He tells her how he feels that he is someone special and will do something amazing in life. He has known it from the time he was such a small boy. It was not something he could discuss with his parents. They would have thought him egotistical, he tells Adele.

After Hinsdale, Charlie says he will show Adele the Eastern Seaboard. He will take her to the Atlantic Ocean on his country's shores, and they will eat lobster pulled live from the traps. Of course, he will take her to New York City, too. There he thinks he will do the amazing thing he was meant to do.

"I will be the amazing person I was meant to be," he tells her. He says he will show her Park Avenue, with its endless sea of taxis and cars, and the skyscrapers that lord over the skyline and pierce the sun with their flashing spires and tops. He reaches over and kisses Adele. He takes the bag of unfinished peanuts she is holding, and he stuffs it into the seat pocket in front of her. Then, he leads her back to the restroom. When the stewardess isn't looking, the both of them enter through the narrow folding door. The plane increases their excitement; it's roaring engines right beside the restroom wall make them both shudder, even before he is inside of her. All the power of the engines, Adele feels, is inside of her now, and the power is flowing from him inside of her, too. When they are done, he is breathing heavily, and he tilts his head back under the bathroom light, and she can see the light through one of his flaring nostrils, making the cavity glow red. When she pulls her skirt back down, she laughs: while she has been supporting herself against the sink, a small bar of soap clings to her rear momentarily before it falls off, down to where a smell of urine rises from the floor and feels sticky on the bottoms of her shoes.

* * *

Charlie's mother serves Adele Jell-O salad with mayonnaise, and when Adele tastes it, she excuses herself and goes to the bathroom and spits it into the toilet and flushes. This is not any kind of mayonnaise she has ever tasted before. The mayonnaise she knows is creamy yellow and tastes pleasantly of garlic and a dash of mustard and pure virgin olive oil. The Jell-O made with the mayonnaise is green. Did Charlie's mother want to feed her the food of Martians? One flush does not destroy its evidence. She flushes again, but the Jell-O floats and separates on the water's surface. Again she flushes, but the bits of green do not submit. She is in the process of using a bit of tissue to pinch up the bits of green from inside the bowl when Charlie's mother knocks on the bathroom door.

"Are you all right?" she says in a clipped voice. Adele does not answer at first. Charlie's mother is a large woman who reminds Adele of the huge white refrigerator that is in the mother's kitchen. There are no soft corners to her. She did not even hug Charlie when she and her father picked them up at the airport. Instead she let him kiss one of her cheeks, and all she could manage was to lift her hands and rest them for a brief moment on his shoulders. When Adele first met her, Adele leaned close to her to kiss her on her cheeks, but she stepped back from Adele and simply shook Adele's hand. Now the woman has her mouth close to the hardwood door, asking if Adele is all right.

Adele wants to say, "No, no, I'm not all right. I'm not sure what I'm doing here, and who is your son, Charlie, anyway? I think I hardly know him. And what is this green Martian food called Jell-O salad you served me that's making my stomach somersault and that can't be sent down your sewers? I'm from Paris, where just about everything can be sent down the sewers! We've sent entire revolutionary soldiers down the sewers. I miss my sister, *Le Moucheron*, and I miss my father, and . . ." But instead, Adele says, "I'm fine, thank you. I'll be out in a spiffy, oh, I mean jiffy."

When she goes back to the table Charlie and his father are arguing. Charlie is asking for more money from his father to go to New York and show Adele our country's most famous city. There he will be able to find the job of his dreams; he just knows it. Charlie's father says, "But we just gave you money to vacation in France."

Charlie's mother stands from the table and wipes her hands on her apron. "I'll clear," she says. Adele helps her. From table to kitchen, Adele walks back and forth with the plates and dishes. Charlie's mother passes Adele so as not to rub shoulders with Adele. In fact, she walks so far away from Adele that Adele thinks at one point that Charlie's mother is going to exit the room, but she is obviously just trying to avoid having to be close to Adele.

Charlie's father seems like the type of man who never yells. It is Charlie whom Adele hears yelling. He accents it by pounding his fist, sending up the saltshaker so it jumps before it lands back down on the top of the table.

"Can't you see what an opportunity this would be for me and Adele?" Charlie says.

In a quiet voice, Charlie's father says, "Adele?" and for a moment Adele thinks the old gentleman wants to ask her a question, but then she realizes he is just trying to comprehend the significance of Adele in this equation.

"Yes, I plan on marrying her," Charlie says.

Adele is almost glad it is the leftover Jell-O salad she drops to the floor at that moment. It means she won't have to be served it again at the next meal. Charlie and his father just look at her and look at the green mess on the floor. They do not come running to help her. When Charlie's mother comes out of the kitchen to see what accident has occurred and she sees her Jell-O salad on her Persian dining room rug, she too just stands there looking at the green mess of Jell-O and mayonnaise.

Charlie's mother's lips become straight and tight. When she speaks, it seems incredible to Adele, because it does not seem as if any air could pass between those lips or that if it did pass through, it would sound like air released from a balloon. But in a voice that does not sound human, that is so low and monotone one could mistake it for the quiet humming motor of the refrigerator kicking in, Charlie's mother says, "I'll fetch a wet rag."

Then, all at once, Charlie and his father and Adele are bending over to help clean up the mess. They scoop up the Jell-O salad in their hands and toss it back into the bowl to get it off the rug. Picking up the cool, wobbly salad in their hands feels good. It makes Adele feel playful. She has the urge to throw some at Charlie's face. For a second, she thinks, no, I better not, but then as soon as she thinks she had better not do it, she does. A handful goes flying at his face. For a moment, he can't see through the Jell-O salad, but then he blinks. The mayonnaise is white on his eyelashes, and pieces of Jell-O make his skin lumpy, as if he has broken out in green boils. Charlie isn't laughing, but Adele is. Her laughter is loud. She knows she cannot stop it. She points at Charlie. "You have to look at yourself in the mirror!" she manages to say through her laughter. Charlie's father isn't looking at Charlie. He is looking at Charlie's mother, who, standing there with the wet rag, is furious. Instead of using the wet rag on the Persian carpet, Charlie's mother uses it on her son's face. Her downward strokes are hard. Adele can see how the force of her hand motion pulls on the skin of Charlie's face, dragging his jowls down and pulling the skin from underneath his eyelid down so that the inside is exposed and she can see his tiny veins branching like so many red streams across the curved yellow-white surface, the same color as the inside of an oyster.

Later that night, while she sleeps in the guest bedroom, Adele wakes up. She thinks she can hear a bucket of water sloshing and the sound of scrubbing. She imagines Charlie's mother is digging hard, working her elbow into the Persian rug, and the colors of the dyed wool fibers bleeding.

No one told her she could not use the phone. In the morning, when Charlie's mother and father are out at work and Charlie is still asleep in bed, Adele picks up the receiver and dials the overseas operator. She starts to cry when she hears *Le Moucheron*'s voice.

"What are you crying for? You're the one who wanted to leave," *Le Moucheron* says.

Adele nods, but she is still crying and can't speak for a moment. Finally, she is able to say, "How are you? How is Papa?"

"He's begun combing his hair over to hide his bald spot. It looks ridiculous," *Le Moucheron* says. Adele laughs. "Me, I'm fine. I tried to swing so high off the swing that Sister Matilde made me get off. She says the day will come when I should be so close to God, but now she wants me closer to the ground. How is your Yankee?" *Le Moucheron* says.

"He's fine. What about Papa, really? What did he say when he found out I was gone?"

"He cursed and called you a whore and then he went out at night alone, and when I heard him come back home I heard him fall as he opened the door, as if someone on the other side had opened the door too quickly for him, and he landed on the floor. Then he came into my room and stood over me and said, 'I know you're awake and I want you to promise me you'll never do what your sister did.' So I sat up and told him that you promised to send for me, and he said, 'over my dead body.' So now I don't get to go to America and I'm stuck here with Sister Matilde who wants me to do all of my calculations in my head when I've told her I can only do them on my paper, and she told me there are reams and reams of paper in my head, if only I bothered to look for them. That's what you've left me with, so I hope you are happy with your Yankee and your groundhogs and your John Wayne."

Adele is going to tell her that Charlie was thinking of marrying her. She wants to hear herself say it out loud and hear how it sounds, but Charlie comes down the stairs. When he hears her talking in French, he grabs the phone from her and hangs it up. "Tell me you didn't just call Paris?" he says. His hair is flat in the back from having slept so long, and his breath reminds Adele of soft cheese far too ripe, the inside almost as runny as pus, the rind yellow and gray, the smell overpowering.

"I didn't call Paris. I called my sister. She is hardly *all* of Paris," Adele says, thinking of her sister's thin arms and small face.

"You what? Do you know how much a phone call to Paris is going to cost? You might as well buy a plane ticket there for the price," he says.

"It can't be as expensive as a plane ticket. That's ridiculous."

"All right, then half a plane ticket, but still it's expensive. When my parents see the bill, they'll be furious."

Adele wonders where half a plane ticket would get her. Would she end up halfway home? Would she end up over the ocean, over the deepest part where the largest fish live and ships become lost?

They leave for New York before the phone bill arrives. Charlie's father gave in and loaned Charlie the money. Charlie's mother drives them to the train. Before they board, she hands them a brown paper bag with two sandwiches of liverwurst and mayonnaise and then she pats her son on the arm saying good-bye and then pats Adele's arm.

Along the way, looking through the train windows, Charlie points out the cornfields, how the sweetest kernels are the bicolored ones called honey and pearl, and Adele doesn't understand. She thinks she may as well be on another planet. In France corn is for animals: no one eats it by the ear, the way Charlie describes, rolling the ears in sticks of butter sitting on the table and sprinkling hickory-smoked salt on top.

When they're close to New York, Adele becomes sad. Something about a girl by the tracks bending down in her wool coat to arrange a baby doll in a toy baby stroller makes her think of *Le Moucheron*. Even walking the streets of New York by the Hudson River pier, the smell of the salty wet wood, reminds her of the Seine. Charlie takes her picture as she descends the subway stairs spotted with black circles, the cruddy remnants of gum chewed and then spat out. Her high heels she bought months ago on the Boulevard Saint-Germaine become scuffed and dull at the toes from all the walking they've been doing.

Charlie finds them a flat in Queens, and before she sees the place, she thinks it must be glamorous with such a name. At night, though, the subway shakes her mattress and jostles her bedside water glass.

She feels as if a butterfly is trapped inside of her. She can feel its wings beating against her inside walls. "You idiot," Charlie says. "You're pregnant. Didn't you know to mark the calendar?" he says. She didn't know about marking the calendar. She didn't know there were good times and bad times to make love, as Charlie now tells her.

Charlie gets the only job he can—working at a golf course, collecting lost balls and caddying for men who talk as if he isn't there beside them. They marry at city hall. Charlie forgets a ring, and instead Adele has to feel his fingers pretending they are holding a ring, gliding up her finger in front of the justice of the peace.

Sometimes Charlie comes home from the golf course with a ball in his pocket, one he picked up and forgot to return to the clubhouse. Invariably, it's nicked or has a grass blade clinging to its pocked surface. When she gathers Charlie's clothes to do the laundry, she sets the ball on the mantle, over a fireplace that doesn't work, and the ball wakes her up in the night when it rolls off from the vibration of the elevated subway driving by.

She writes to her father, but the letters come back unopened with his handwriting on them that reads, "addressee unknown," and all she can do is hold the letters in her hands and tell herself that at least she knows her father held the letters in his hands, and now she's holding them too.

All of the letters she sends to *Le Moucheron* aren't sent back, but neither are they answered.

Adele dreams of her dresses. Back home in her closet she is touching them, bringing the silk cloth of skirts to her cheek.

The pictures Charlie takes of her stop; the film costs money, of course. She wears his shirts and pants now, the baby growing, sometimes making her twinge, making her feel as if someone was inside of her with a needle and thread, making stitches, piercing the deep folds of her flesh.

In the corner drugstore she sees women working at the cash register. They look tall behind the counter, standing on a platform so they can see potential thieves pilfering high-ticketed items out and down the aisles or just the bums on Sunday mornings trying to steal mouthwash made with alcohol when the liquor stores are closed. Adele thinks she could do that, stand on the platform, counting out change to customers and telling them to have a nice day.

Charlie laughs. "Who will hire you with your belly like that? You won't fit behind the counter."

The days are becoming shorter, and snow flurries sweep through one evening, the flakes resting on her hair, collecting on her shirt. On the shelf her protruding belly forms, they sit like crumbs that fall after biting into a slice of baguette.

Charlie doesn't get up to go to work one morning. She shakes his shoulder. It takes a while for him to wake up. She wonders if he just thinks her shaking him is the elevated train coming by. "Do you think people golf when it's below freezing?" he asks her when she tells him the time. "I'm out of a job," he says.

He buys the racing form and sits with a slide rule at the kitchen table for hours, making marks besides the names of horses that sound more to Adele like ways you should behave when you need to be strong rather than the names of animals. Names like "Ride the Storm," "Grit Your Teeth," and "Raise the Flag." In the early afternoon he leaves for the track, taking a shoebox with him that holds all of the money they own. While he's gone, she walks into the drugstore, asking to speak to the manager. The manager, an Asian man with hair that looks as soft as her brush for putting rouge on her cheeks, doesn't seem to look below her neck. She's wearing one of Charlie's coats, so maybe it just looks like she's fat instead of with child. She can start the next morning. He'll teach her how to align the products on the shelves. He'll teach her the register.

Charlie doesn't come home that night. In the morning she leaves him a note saying she's working at the corner drugstore. She's learning how when someone gives a bill larger than a dollar, you're supposed to lay it crosswise over the bill compartments while you pull out the change. That way, if someone tries to roll you and tell you they gave you a twenty when all they gave you was a ten, the bill is out, and you can show them as proof.

When Charlie comes into the drugstore, she thinks he's coming up so close to her to give her a kiss, but what he does is open the half swing door up to the platform where she stands at the register, and he grabs her by the arm and pulls her out. He pushes her out the half door, even though she's telling Charlie her shift isn't over, that she's got three more hours. The manager comes over and asks if there's a problem, and Charlie says, "No problem, Confucius. My wife's quit, by the way," and the manager looks at Adele, and Adele shakes her head and starts telling the manager she hasn't quit, she'll be back in a minute, but the manager doesn't hear her, because by now Charlie has pushed Adele halfway up the block, and the train is driving by overhead, and the whole street is shaking, and metal is shrieking against metal.

The money is all gone. Adele wants to know why he bothered to bring the empty shoebox home. He tells her it's not his fault. All of his calculations were right. His system is foolproof. It was the jockey's fault. The jockey, who never held tight on the reins in his entire career, must have held tight on them today, because the horse he was on stayed back in the field at the start of the race and never made a move up to the front.

Charlie gets out pen and paper and starts writing a letter to his parents asking for more money. Adele can feel her baby move, as if it's trying to turn completely around inside of her. A foot sweeps up under her rib cage. When he's done writing his letter, he gives Adele pen and paper, too. "Write to your father and ask him for money," he says.

"He won't open the letter. You know that," she says.

"Tell him about his grandchild on the outside of the envelope, and he'll give you the money," Charlie says.

She writes the letter while Charlie is sleeping, his mouth open, his snoring sounding exactly like wood being sawed. In the letter she asks for a ticket to go back home. She gives the address of the drugstore she worked at as the return address. When she tells the manager of the drugstore, he says he understands. He tells her to come by every day after three when the mail comes to check and see if the letter has come. He will keep it for her.

It comes close to Christmas, when the shop windows have wrapped boxes in the windows under decorated fir trees and when a Santa on the corner rings a bell all day long next to a round pot people drop coins into. She doesn't have the money for the subway even to get to the airport, so what she does is she walks by with a penny in her hand, pretending to drop it into the pot, but instead she pulls up a handful of change, cold to the touch, and she smiles at Santa and he tells her, "Merry Christmas."

She doesn't bring anything with her, just the clothes of Charlie's that she's wearing and her passport. She climbs the subway stairs and waits for the train, listening to Santa's bell ringing.

At the check-in counter she explains to the attendant that her passport picture looks different than her own face because, of course, the weight she has gained due to her condition makes her look like another person. The attendant says she can order Adele a wheelchair, and Adele says she's fine. She'd like to walk anyway. Really, she'd like to be able to run, just in case Charlie comes to find her. She'd like to be able to duck into the ladies' room so as not to be seen.

On the plane, the doors cannot close fast enough. Even on line for the runway behind other planes, she thinks she's not safe, and Charlie will bound up on the wing and bang on her small, round window, smashing it, and reaching in to drag her back to Queens.

"What are you wearing?" *Le Moucheron* says when she first sees Adele step off the plane in Charlie's jeans and his old button-down shirt. She doesn't answer her sister. She hugs her instead. "What did you bring me?" *Le Moucheron* says.

"A niece or maybe a nephew," Adele says and opens wide her coat, showing *Le Moucheron*.

"I was thinking more of a cowboy hat," *Le Moucheron* says. Her father stands back, waiting for her to finish saying hello to *Le Moucheron*. She goes up to him.

"Papa, I am so sorry," she says.

Her father nods, and then he says, "You will give up this

child. I know people who will take good care of it, who will find it a home."

They don't drive to Paris. They drive up into the mountains. They reach a house surrounded by pine trees. A woman with small beady eyes, and who wears a kerchief over her head like a gypsy, leads her in through the front door. The woman's name is *Madame Boucle*, and after *Le Moucheron* and her father leave, she puts her hand on Adele's belly and says, "Two months."

During the day Adele gathers firewood for the house, and *Madame Boucle* makes sure that Adele eats proper meals. "A healthy child is always easier to give away," she says. Adele can see what must be the heel of the foot of her baby through the skin on her belly, stretching it, but it is stretched in such strange shapes and at such odd angles that it is as if what were inside was not healthy but something freakish that, once born, would summon its spaceship from up above and disappear back to its planet without a word of hello or good-bye to the woman who carried it for so long.

One night, in the middle of the night, the baby's hiccups wake up Adele, and Adele has trouble falling back to sleep. She can't help thinking about to whom her child will be given. She can't help thinking how she doesn't want anyone to have it. She hopes that when the child is born it is so lovely that *Madame Boucle* will let her stay in her house and raise the child here. She imagines how they will search for wood together, the child holding a small bundle in its arms and Adele holding the larger bundle that she lets fall from her arms and onto the hearth.

She is not sure of Charlie's face now. She can see his nose, but the image of the exact shape of his eyes is fading from her memory. She sees a fox one evening run in front of her when she's taking a walk, and she thinks the fox's eyes and Charlie's eyes are the same, and it isn't until later that she realizes that couldn't be true, that people's eyes aren't gold like the fox's eyes. If a person's eyes were yellow, they wouldn't be of this Earth.

That night *Madame Boucle* tells her when the time comes, not to worry, she has delivered over one hundred babies and they all came out perfectly healthy. "Really? All of them?" Adele asks, and *Madame Boucle* says, "Well, almost all of them."

Her father sends a letter with money for *Madame Boucle*. He has enrolled Adele in a junior college near their flat in Paris. When she returns, she can start right away. *Le Moucheron* sends her a box of chocolates, with a few of them missing and half-eaten, and a note that says, "I thought you shouldn't eat all of them."

Her water breaks in front of the woodstove while she's bending down stoking the coals. The hearth beneath her is already hot, and the rock hisses when her water hits the surface. She doesn't know what to do with the pain: it is so huge, she thinks it would be helpful if someone could just take the pain from her and move it somewhere else. She wonders how long she can feel the pain without dying. *Madame Boucle* tells her to push, and what comes out from Adele is feces. "I'm so sorry," she says, and *Madame Boucle* says, "I told you, I've delivered over a hundred babies. Nothing is new to me. Push again," she says. "You will be so happy when this baby is out of you. Think of that. Think of how you will bounce around the room. You will be light. You will fly like a bird."

She shivers when the baby comes out, all of her vibrating. *Madame Boucle* doesn't let her see it. She washes it and wraps it and puts it in a bassinet across the room and then she sits at Adele's feet again. "Here, we're almost done," she says. She delivers the placenta and then she begins to sew Adele. The sewing takes a long time. "You tore yourself ten ways," *Madame Boucle* says. Adele tries to sit up, to see the baby in the basinet. "Lay back. I can't do this with you moving around," she says. Adele looks over at the basinet, just turning her head. The basinet is wicker, and it slightly shakes, as if they were back in the flat in Queens when the subway drove by. When she's done, *Madame Boucle* puts on her coat and takes the baby in her arms and heads for the door.

"Where are you going?" Adele asks.

"The monastery, where else?" *Madame Boucle* says. Adele has seen the monastery on the hillside. Most of the time, though, she has only seen the bottom half of it, as the top half is so often covered in low-lying mist. Adele stands and begins to walk and find her own coat. "You're not going anywhere," *Madame Boucle* says. "You're not to set eyes on this child. If you so much as set eyes on it, it will never find a good home. It will never love its new mother. You don't want to curse your own child, do you?" she says.

Adele sits back down on the end of the bed, where it's wet with her fluids and her blood. In a bedpan she can see her placenta filling the pan up to the enamel sides where it was poured in. *Madame Boucle* closes the door, and Adele can hear her footsteps crunching on the trail that goes up behind the house. Suddenly Adele stands and swings open wide the window facing the hillside.

"Is it a boy or a girl?" she yells at the figure of *Madame Boucle* walking up the trail. The cold air hits Adele, making her colder where she's still wet between her legs and where she still has sweat on her chest and at her temples from all of her pushing. *Madame Boucle* doesn't answer her. The wind has blown Adele's own words back to her.

She doesn't remember the pain of her labor when the pain of her breasts begins. Her breasts feel like they've turned into rocks, and she imagines she's been living in some fairy tale out here in the woods where a spell's been cast on her and she's slowly turning into stone. For three days afterward she soaks cloth diapers in a pot of boiling water on the stove and presses them against her breasts to relieve the pain. *Madame Boucle* has taken the placenta out to the woods and thrown it down a hillside, and at night Adele hears what she thinks is the howl from a fairy-tale wolf coming from where the placenta was thrown. "Look at you, so springy," *Madame Boucle* says when Adele walks across the room to the stove to get more hot compresses.

When Adele goes outside, she stands and stares at the monastery. She looks at the bottom half, the only part she can see below the clouds. She cannot make out any people walking around the monastery. All that she can see are stone walls, and she feels she truly knows the hardness and pain of that stone, because of the days she had rocks for breasts.

Her father comes in a new long sleek black car to pick her up. *Le Moucheron* sits with her in the back on the ride home, showing her how there is a place where you can rest your cigarette and crush the stub and a headrest on the seat back where Adele can lean back, which she does. The pine trees shoot by as her father drives quickly, and *Le Moucheron* hums a tune Adele's never heard before.

In the flat in Paris she leaves the window open at night and ties back the drapes, listening to the sound of all of the people speaking her language. One evening her father comes to get her. "Wear your yellow silk dress that goes to the floor," he tells her. He takes her to a ball. Men invite her to dance on the dance floor, which is a raised circular platform. It reminds her of the platform in the drugstore in Queens. From up above she can look down at all of the people. She sees how they tip glasses to their mouths, how they stand with their hands in their pockets, how they light each other's cigarettes, how they put their arms on the small of each other's backs.

Driving home, her father is in a good mood. He keeps telling her how many men admired her beauty. "You will meet the right man in no time," he says.

One man she danced with, who was in the navy and stationed on a submarine, invites her to dinner. "Go," her father says. The naval officer tells her about the high seas, about the relentless waves, about the hot bunk he shares with two other men. He kisses her, and his lips are wet and salty, as if he were keeping seawater inside of his mouth when he kissed her.

He asks her if she'd like to have lunch with him a few days later. She says, "Yes. Can you drive?" He borrows her father's car, and she tells him there's a town, high up in the woods, with a beautiful monastery, where she'd like to go for lunch. She packs food for them, as there will be no need to stop and waste time at a restaurant along the way.

On the steep road she presses him onward, telling him to keep driving even though he's afraid the car won't make it up the incline. "This is the best new car there is. My father only buys the best. It will make it," she says. She can see the monastery at the top of the hill, but the naval officer stops the car and pulls on the emergency brake, afraid to go further. "Let's walk then," she says. She takes his arm. The walk up the road is difficult. The wind is strong, and it's against them. Adele's swing coat flies back at the hem, flipping the coat back so that the silk lining is exposed.

The monks don't answer the door. "They're probably at prayer. We don't need to go inside, do we? We can see how it looks from here," the naval officer says.

Adele presses her face up against the door.

"Where is my child?" Adele yells so that she'll be heard over the wind and through the heavy wooden door.

"What are you saying?" the naval officer says. The door swings open. A small monk wearing thick glasses has opened it.

"We've come for the child that was born a fortnight ago. It was delivered by *Madame Boucle*," Adele says.

"What are you talking about?" the naval officer says to Adele, and then he turns to the monk and says, "I'm sorry, I don't know what she's talking about."

The monk shakes his head. "There are no children here," he says. He begins to close the door.

"My child, he's here. *Madame Boucle* brought him here," she says. The monk steps outside of the doors, closing them partway behind him, where they move slightly back and forth in the wind. Then he turns to Adele. He speaks in a whisper. "Your child is no longer here. He was given away," he says.

"He?" Adele says.

"Yes, he," the monk says. "I'm so sorry," he says.

"What's that then? Is that him crying? Don't you hear it?" Adele says, lifting her head and then turning to the naval officer, grabbing his arm. He shakes his head.

"Come, we should go back to the car," the naval officer says, turning now so that he's facing down the road.

"You still have him, don't you?" Adele says to the monk.

"No. He was only with us a night. The family came for him right away."

"But that's a baby crying. I can hear it," Adele says. The monk turns and opens the huge wooden doors on their metal hinges. He opens and closes them partway a few times so that they creak. "This is what you're hearing. It's the wind. It sounds just like crying, doesn't it? But I assure you, it is only the wind," he says, and then he stands so that he is behind the doors, closing them shut against Adele.

On the way back down the road, Adele sobs into the naval officer's stiff jacket.

The naval officer drives while she lays down in the back seat of the car. When they arrive home, her father is in the courtyard, waiting for them. He asks them how their lunch was. The naval officer says it was a delightful afternoon but that maybe the warm spring sun was too much for Adele. Her father takes her upstairs and lets her go to her bed. *Le Moucheron* bounds into the room, showing Adele her new skirt she is wearing that, when she twirls, flies up around her. "Do you like it?" *Le Moucheron* asks.

"Very much," Adele says.

"You're sick, aren't you?" *Le Moucheron* says. Adele nods.

"I'll come back later," *Le Moucheron* says.

"No, stay with me," Adele says and reaches out to grab her sister, but *Le Moucheron* quickly moves away.

"You didn't stay for me. You left for America. You left me alone," she says and she skips out of the room.

In the night, Adele leans out the window looking at Paris, wondering where her child is, if she will ever meet him in her lifetime. She thinks how maybe one day she will pass him by on the street, but they will not know each other. How is it then, we call ourselves human? she thinks, that we will not know our own child when we pass him in a crowd?

A letter comes from Charlie. The envelope contains signed divorce papers that her father arranged for Charlie to authorize. In return, her father will send Charlie a large sum of money.

"Well, that's over and done with," her father says when he's standing in her room showing her the papers. After he leaves, she goes into her closet. She shuts the door and sits in the dark. She brings up the silk skirts of her dresses and holds them against her cheeks. So soft, they are like water, she thinks, and she's not home and she's not in America. She's only made it halfway in between. She's in the deepest part of the ocean—the part where the largest fish live and ships become lost.

THINGS THAT ARE FUNNY
ON A SUBMARINE BUT NOT REALLY

(FSBNR)

THINGS THAT ARE FUNNY ON A SUBMARINE BUT NOT REALLY: the torpedo man named Grenadier who lives in South Carolina and thinks North Carolina is the North. The XO who hates my bucket hat printed with cherries but would rather me wear it than the other one I have that says, "Bigfoot is real." The swim call we have where no one swims, but instead we sit topside and smoke, and Baitz tells us the story of how he was beat to shit as a boy, and we all tell him if he were our son we'd beat the crap out of him too, and he tells us that's why he loves us. The gay guy, Manning, who tells me I'm fat, and he'd never do me, and I'm actually relieved for once for being fat. The one exercise bike we have that is in such a tight space that you have to lean your head to one side in order to use it so you always look like a dead man in a noose. The *Would You Rather* game we play, and Grenadier says he'd rather be with all of us on the boat than at home with his wife who used to be a stripper and wears more clothes to sleep in than she ever wore stripping, including wearing her underwear and socks to bed. The stupid Brooklyn accents we decide we're going to talk with the entire underway. The fucker who stole my headphones, even though I bought them in bright pink so no one would want them.

Things that are Funny on a Submarine But Not Really: the shit-ass becoming an expression we use for both a person and a thing that we can't shit-ass remember the name of, so, shit-ass, pass me that shit-ass thing over there. I need it to fix this broke-dick shit-ass thing in front of me. The email my father sends me telling me that when I'm done being a radioman on this submarine I should really go to college, and I wonder if there's a shit-ass college for me out there. One that will let me tell guys like Baitz to shut the fuck up, because we don't care. How my mother and father keep asking me where we're going on the sub, like I could really tell them, and I tell my mother she's probably some Russian spy because she always asks me where we're headed.

Things that are Funny on a Submarine But Not Really: the exercise we do where we're constantly being pinged by sonar for over a week round the clock, and I still can't get the song "Pretty in Pink" by the Psychedelic Furs out of my head because we just watched five eighties movies in a row, and *Pretty in Pink* was one of them. The way the gentle snoring of Grenadier across my rack reminds me of waves rolling onto shore. The way, when we're close to the surface to receive transmissions, Grenadier's always checking to see if he got an email from his wife, and when there isn't one and he looks upset and I tell him what the fuck, Grenadier, you don't even want to be with her, and he just looks at me and says, "Fuck you, Davis."

The way we're all cleaning and playing loud rap music and dancing around and then I play *Rodeo* (Four Dance Episodes) by Aaron Copland, which is what my dad likes to play, and everyone just shuts up and listens to the rest of the music. The next swim call in the evening when I'm swimming, floating on my back and looking up and realizing I've forgotten what the moon looks like, and think maybe the next time we surface there might be two moons and I'm in another world. How everyone here from Texas loves Texas more than they love any woman. The survey that says seventy percent of men rate the movie *Predator* as more important than getting married. Talking about tatts and Kentucky Fried Chicken and how when we're back in port we're going to get as much of both of them as we can. The email I get from home saying my room's been ransacked, and my sister took my desk, the shelves, the dresser, and even my favorite plaid flannel shirt. How an LT is talking to a group of five of us and says he knows Brisbane well, and what's the first thing we'd like to do when we pull in, and how all five of us say, "Whores" at the exact same time. The coners who work at the front of the boat who decide to become a frat called Alpha Phi Nu and walk around calling each other Brad, Chad, and Brett.

Things that are Funny on a Submarine But Not Really: the way Tintin, my buddy in radio whose real name is Smolensky, has a cowlick just like the cartoon Tintin that always sticks up, even when he hasn't showered for weeks and his hair is heavy with grease. How the COB lets me stand on the sail off Hawaii, and in the wind the old U.S. of A. flag keeps clanking on the shaft of the periscope, sounding like someone trapped beneath the hatch and banging a hammer on the steel to get out. How everything is an acronym in the navy and little words get cut, so COB is short for chief of the boat.

Things that are Funny on a Submarine But Not Really (FSBNR): the way, off watch, I make everyone watch *Cool Hand Luke* instead of a bad submarine movie, and later we learn Paul Newman didn't even eat one of those eggs in that famous egg-eating scene. The way everyone now thinks *Cool Hand Luke* is a really good movie. How the bad submarine movie sunk even lower in standings after watching old blue-eyed Paul Newman become a hero in prison. The way Tintin tells me he wants to marry one of the strippers at the club we always go to on shore. I ask, "What's her real name?" since none of the strippers uses the names their parents gave them, and he says for real, it's Kitten.

Things that are FSBNR: a large naval exercise with an Asian superpower—half a dozen subs in an arena and we all simulate shooting at each other. Typhoon making landfall nearby makes it hard to keep at periscope depth, that and ten-to-twelve-foot swells making depth control a nightmare. A fire drill where I'm first responder manning a hose; then I'm relieved by a guy with an O2 mask, so I run aft to escape from the heavy simulated smoke when I see another fire in the crew's mess so I route another shit-ass hose to that fire and start fighting it, but then when I'm relieved I'm told I died. *But* the COB compliments me for saving the ship. So then everyone starts calling me Dead Man, and for so long I haven't had a nickname, and then I get stuck with Dead Man, which, if you try to tell people is not your nickname, they just call you it more, so I don't say jack and hope that Dead Man fades away.

FSBNR: Tintin telling me how he and Kitten are planning a wedding in his hometown in Iowa, and I tell Tintin, "You know, marrying a stripper rarely works out," and I remind him about Grenadier, who would rather be with us than at home with his stripper wife who sleeps in socks and a T-shirt. Tintin says I'm wrong, and I'm jealous, and I tell him yes, you're right, I'm both of those things, because now he's redder in the face than usual, which is pretty red considering he's a redhead, and I think how I bet I could fry an egg on his face, and the yolk would turn hard. Which gets us all talking about how if the sub ever sank and we had to switch to cannibalism how would we rate the crew on how good they tasted and how would we prepare them. We figure the officers rate the highest as far as marbling and tenderness go. The XO overhears us in the crew's mess and tells us he can understand our stupid talk. He makes me take off my bucket hat with the cherries on it while he talks and he says that these things happen when we're under so much pressure considering we are the most combat-ready submarine in case war breaks out. It's nice to be second to none, but jeez, being the literal tip of the spear in this theater can be exhausting. We're in another exercise for a week where we get pinged all day by sonar, and I'm sick of the sound, and Tintin asks how could that bother me in the least because I'm a dead man already.

FSBNR: the way we talk about food underway, and I tell the others how my mother's the best cook, and so they start thinking about all this food that if they threw it at my mother, what could she make with it. "What if I throw her a reindeer? What can she make with that, Dead Man?" Grenadier says. I tell them how my mother would marinate it first in soy sauce, ginger, garlic, sesame oil, honey, and red pepper flakes, then broil it to perfection. They throw more food at my mother—a swan, a guinea pig, a marmot. Then we have a discussion about what kind of shit-ass animal is a marmot, really. We talk about how when we're all done with this submarine, we'll meet at my house in the woods and we'll camp out in a tent, and we'll sleep fourteen hours every day and have my mother cook for us for a week straight and we'll get out my shotguns and shoot skeet and my rifles and shoot targets like our old TV I once shot up because it turned into the poltergeist in the TV one day and only broadcasted snow and fast-moving horizontal lines. But really, I know we'll never do all that, and the future is far away, even for a dead man, and maybe I'll never want to do all that with these assholes anyway. "Fuck you all, I take back my invitation," I say to no one in particular but to all of them, really. Baitz who is picking some scab on his arm. Tintin who is looking at a picture for the millionth time of Kitten, and when he shows us the picture, none of us recognize her because she's not just wearing a bra and thong but actual clothes—a wool coat and knit hat and boots that look like she could wear them on the moon and hop from crater to crater. Me, I don't even want to go to my own party in the woods in the tent. They can all come; then I'll leave. I'll get in the car and just drive who knows where. Maybe I can just climb the Appalachian Trail by myself. I know where to catch it off I-91. I'll bring my father's Glock, just in case, but really, I'll be fine and never need to fire it. I'll walk for miles like Forrest Gump and find Jenny at the end of the journey.

FSBNR: standing watch off Hawaii, knowing the seamount range with mountains named after classical composers is not far away and thinking why isn't there an Aaron Copland mount? Thinking there really should be an Aaron Copland mount and wondering why Liszt got the highest mount, at 5,190 feet.

The whale's tail I see from the bridge when we're leaving Hawaii, and how it's not perfect like all the pictures I've ever seen in books, but it's cut here and there, barnacled and scarred. The liberty brief we get from the COB for our port call where

Thompson asks what the drinking age is and Rieger yells, "Fifteen," and I yell, "No, that's the age of consent." And then the COB, after an hour of these nonstop jokes, looks like he's ready to go back to bed.

The way I see an email for Grenadier on his account from his stripper wife that says she wants a divorce and I know I have to keep it from Grenadier until we're back at home port because you don't ever relay bad news underway. Grenadier talking more and more about his stripper wife like he misses her, like for once he'd rather be with her than with us. He says, "At least I have my two girls" and Thompson asking him if it's cheap for Grenadier to clothe his family of strippers because probably all he needs to buy is some G-strings. Grenadier trying to land a punch to Thompson's face, but we all saw Grenadier getting spun up and held Grenadier back and told Thompson to go hang out with Brad, Chad, and Brett in the cone. Even with a fight almost starting, we still use our Brooklyn accents, like nothing will break us out of character.

FSBNR: later, telling Tintin about Grenadier's email from his wife asking for a divorce, swearing Tintin to secrecy, but telling him because I think Tintin should know how a marriage to a stripper is doomed. Tintin telling me he's sorry I haven't experienced true love yet. Me saying, "Yeah, you're right. I haven't experienced true love yet because it doesn't exist," and then Grenadier saying, "Yeah, that's because you're a dead man, Dead Man, and you're not living in our world." On the bridge I see dolphins swimming in front of us and think how I'd rather be them than me. Tintin's right. I'm not like the others sometimes. I'll come in early from a night at the strip club and just read random shit on the computer and drink by myself. I'll call home and ask how they are, happy to hear not much goes on. My dad talks about walks with the dogs and a bear he's seen on the trail, the kid from my high school who killed himself on the snowmobile. When they ask what's new with the boat, I tell them same old, same old and say good-bye, saying I love them before my mother can tell me to stop smoking and before they can ask me about what college I'm going to go to after my time is up.

FSBNR: me driving the boat and getting tossed out of the chair when the chief tells me he owns my time, and I tell him how you cannot own something which cannot be held or touched. I have to clean for an extra hour and then I'm like the Cool Hand Luke of submarines doing time in the hotbox, only unlike Paul Newman, I would have eaten the hard-boiled eggs for real. Hard-boiled eggs rock. My mother makes them in the top part of the Japanese rice cooker. They come out perfect. How you have to hand it to the Japanese. Even their cities are clean. How in Yokosuka I ate sushi three times a day and when I paid them the money I held it out with two hands and bowed and they took it with two hands and bowed too, and how that makes the whole thing, the buying and selling and the meal, all the more good and special.

Colleges that will never take me: the usual, Harvard, Yale, etc., because of my bad high school grades. Colleges I'll never apply to: liberal arts colleges that have safe rooms for students who feel targeted, because after five years of being on the boat, I'm probably the one who's going to say something that's going to make someone run to that safe room. How I'm reading Nietzsche and he says, "He who fights with monsters might take care lest he thereby become a monster. And if you gaze for long into an abyss, the abyss gazes also into you." And maybe how after five years on this boat, I'll be the monster. How I have to tell Grenadier, who thinks North Carolina is in the North, what an abyss is. How then I make them all watch the movie *The Abyss*, because it's a cool movie. How Nietzsche also said, "To live is to suffer; to survive is to find some meaning in the suffering." How Doc is the only other one on board, it turns out, who's read Nietzsche, and when he asks me, while bandaging a cut on my head I got from being 6'3" and forgetting to duck enough when going through a door, what meaning I've found in the suffering on this boat, I answer, "That movies from the ninties were just better than what they are now." And Doc tells me, actually, *The Abyss* is from 1989.

FSBNR: talking to Tintin about being bounty hunters when we get out, but then we arrive at the conclusion that we would end up shooting too many bounties. With our high-security clearances from working in radio we could work CIA maybe, but then we realize we'd have to get a college degree for that. We then realize that, fuck, there are a lot of bounties out there that need shooting anyway, and if not us, then who?

How scrubbing bulkheads, I listen to Van Halen's "Best of Both Worlds." Eighties hair metal is keeping this nuclear submarine clean.

Would you rather cut off your arms or cut off your legs? We think about this one for a while. Being able to still jack off becomes one of the main reasons for keeping your arms, or maybe it becomes the only reason.

FSBNR: looking through a shit-ass old book on the bookshelf in mess about Guam that reads that the island's motto is "Where America's Day Begins" because of how close we are to the international date line. When I talk to my family back home in the States and I'm about to go underway the next day, I sometimes make the mistake and tell them I'll call them tonight to say good-bye. Then I have to correct myself and say, "I'll call you when it's your tomorrow," because their tomorrow is not mine, and neither is their yesterday, and pretty much, for that matter, our todays are never the same.

FSBNR: all of us talking about Wendy's burgers, and Baitz says how when he gets back, he's going to eat like a whore. The forty-eight hours we're up straight for drills and watches, and the game we play where we talk about what we'd trade for twelve hours of sleep a night. So far, Thompson would trade his new Jeep Wrangler, and Rieger his soon-to-be son, and the XO a medal he got for Distinguished Service. Me, I'd trade my sister, the one who stole my plaid shirt.

FSBNR: a storm where I get so seasick that I'm ready to swim back to base, to our brown, snake-infested island that's always too hot, just to make the sickness stop. How we've been away so long that we start talking about what we miss the most like we were in boot camp again and being homesick for the first time.

FSBNR: the awful beards and moustaches we're growing because we don't have to shave out to sea and there's no point. The marriage Tintin is planning with Kitten the stripper that's going to be in Iowa, on his family's farm. We're all invited one minute, and then the next he tells us we all drink too much, and there's no way he's inviting us all because the bar tab would be too high. Then he gets the idea to invite us by lottery, and then he decides he's even going to sell the lottery tickets. How he makes the tickets out of a blank page he rips from the back of the Guam book. How we start buying the tickets with packs of cigarettes and Red Bulls but what buys the most tickets is my extra-large-size bag of Atomic Fireball jawbreakers that I brought on patrol. I'm not sure I want to go to Tintin's wedding someday anyway, because I don't want to think about how a few years from now they'll end up split like Grenadier and his wife. I sell my lottery tickets to Woods, the JO, for a pair of headphones that are pink and that I swear are the ones someone stole from me earlier on.

FSBNR: the way I wonder sometimes if we're sailing over wrecks of those Japanese destroyers and cruisers from the great naval battles of WWII. Even though, back then, we had radar range finding for their guns, the Japanese still tried, in the bitter end, to beat us with the skill of their sailors.

FSBNR: cleaning toilets so freedom can endure.

The news we get that Gregg Allman from the Allman Brothers just died, so I crank up "Mountain Jam" in his honor, and everyone else cleaning starts moving their sponges and brushes and mops in time with the music. The way the whole boat is honoring the man, and I wonder if Gregg Allman ever thought that would happen? Some rusty sub sailing the Pacific full of enlisted cleaning like crazy for an engineering workup about to happen, blasting his "Mountain Jam" on the day he dies?

Trying to remember how Prince died, but no one can remember, so we settle on Prince died because he had too much sex. His heart gave out while pleasuring fourteen women at once. We can't stop laughing because we've been awake on duty for twenty-four hours straight. Then I get a déjà fu, not déjà vu as in past, but "fu" as in future glimpses of myself. I'm in college, after getting out of the navy. I'm sitting in a lecture hall and wondering why I'm here. The lecture hall is packed with overprivileged kids wearing the latest fashions and trying to suck up to the teacher. The class is some bogus class like "Rock Music's Effects on Today's Culture," and the teacher asks me what I know about Prince, and I tell him how he died pleasuring fourteen women at once, and then I laugh, and I can't stop laughing, but of course, no one else is laughing, and I'm looking around, wishing I was back on the boat with my shipmates because I'm a fish out of water in the great big lecture hall.

Baitz says he has a déjà fu as well. He's in his apartment and his dad has beat him to a pulp. "That already happened before," Tintin says. "So technically, that's a déjà vu fu," which gets us laughing even more.

FSBNR: the way a submarine is really boring almost one hundred percent of the time, and that's how we like it, because if it's not boring then it's bad. Really bad. Like how the alarm that goes off when we aren't supposed to have any drills because the date is the same as our hull number and we're celebrating and the captain told us he'd be giving us a rest. Like how I head to the head and upon opening the door, find Grenadier naked, collapsed in the shower, and at the same time the message comes over the comm: "Silence on the line. Fire in crew mess," and then the alarm sounds. I wish Grenadier had at least locked the door so I couldn't have walked in on him, but he hadn't. The message says this is not a drill, and all stations immediately rig for fire. It could be the clothes dryer on fire. I don't know. I don't even know what I'm looking at. It's Grenadier with his wrist cut, and there's a steak knife lying next to him on the stall floor. The blood's pooling around him. There's a look on his face like he's sleeping. I try and hold the door open and yell for Doc. At the same time, I try and apply pressure to Grenadier's wrist. No one hears me yell. They're running to their stations. I should be at my station, helping get the hoses. I pull the alarm in the head, but everyone's going to think it's just the same alarm for the fire and not a separate alarm for Grenadier here, bleeding all over the deck. I could get on the intercom and call for help, but Doc's not going to be able to get through with everyone stampeding in the passageway anyway. I realize I am the only help and I have to stop Grenadier's blood. The only thing I have to tie off his arm is the sleeve of the poopy suit/jumper/uniform I'm wearing. I grab the steak knife and slice into the cloth at the shoulder, stupidly cutting myself at the same time, but I cut away enough so that I can rip from the sleeve down. "Grenadier. Fuck, Grenadier. Fuck, fuck, fuck," I say while tying his arm, which is hard to do because now my hands are shaking, and I think I'm going to faint and so I bang my head against the metal shower wall a few times so I don't. During drill, it takes no longer than a few minutes to put out a fire we simulate with red LED lights, but the alarm is still ringing, which means it's a pretty big fire. It could be the dryer. Some fucker probably left a gum wrapper in his pocket when he did a laundry load. It doesn't take much. I sit with Grenadier on the deck, leaning him up against me. "Grenadier, did you seriously do this over a fucking stripper?" I say. I think how Tintin must have shown Grenadier his email from his wife, even though Tintin and I agreed not to give it to Grenadier until we were back in port. I think how if I were in a college and this happened, there would be help right away. There would be some dorm adviser who could come help and take over for me. There would be the campus police who could come in a minute. I could just stand up and walk away, get back to whatever I was doing, playing video games, getting ready to go to a party, doing Adderall, going to a diversity meeting, doing whatever the fuck college students do. The alarm hasn't stopped. The fire's been going too long. Are we all going to die? I don't want to die. Grenadier might die. I have to find Doc now. I stand up, moving Grenadier off me. I stumble into the passageway. At least there's no one running up and down it any longer. They're probably all in the galley and mess now, helping put out the fire. The emergency lights are on. There's smoke coming from the passageway to my right where the galley is, but the other way it's clear. I grab two breathing masks. I run back into the head and put a mask on Grenadier. Then I get on the comm. I tell the JO who picks up that Grenadier's in the head. He's dead or he's dying, I say. The JO says I should get him a mask; the fire's still burning. "I got him the fucking mask already. He cut his wrists. He needs Doc, fast," I say.

"Bring him to the wardroom. I'll find Doc and tell him to meet you there," the JO says and hangs up. I throw off my cherry bucket hat and fit the other mask over my head. The mask smells like it's been hanging on the bulkhead of a submarine for a few decades. The distinct smell of amine seems to have concentrated inside of it so that I'm suddenly reminded of a car garage in my hometown that has oil stains all over the cement floor and two grungy mechanics who smoke cigarettes while they work. The alarms are still going. This fire is taking too long to put out. I tell myself to think of it as just a drill. It doesn't work. I know it's a real fire. What the fuck are they doing? Haven't we had enough fire drills that they know what to do?

Grenadier has moved. I'm not sure if he fell that way or he moved himself. He's now lying with his head closer to the door. This makes it easier to lift him up from under the arms and drag him. I'm glad Grenadier isn't big like me. He's only as tall as my kid sister, but still he's heavy. I think I'm moving too slowly through the passageway, so I imagine it really is my kid sister and so I better move faster. This helps. I'm running with him almost. What makes it easier to drag him is the blood that's all over his backside. I get him to the wardroom and then lay him on the deck.

When Doc finally comes, we hoist Grenadier onto the table. When Doc examines the cut on Grenadier's wrist he says, "Well, at least he didn't go up the road and instead went across the street." When I say, "What?" Doc explains, while covering Grenadier with blankets, that Grenadier cut himself across the wrists, not up toward the elbow where he'd hit the artery. "He botched the job. He's going to live," Doc says. Just as he says it, the alarm goes off, and the message comes over the comm that the fire's been put out.

Manning, walking by, steps into the wardroom. He sees Doc working on Grenadier.

"What happened?" Manning says.

"Tried to slice his wrist like a steak," Doc says.

"You found him?" Manning says to me. I nod. Then I feel very tired and faint.

When I wake up, I'm leaning back against Manning, who's holding me in his arms. "You're going to be all right. You fainted and I caught you," he says, and I'm so thankful someone's here to help me that I smile up at him.

FSBNR: the way I yell at Tintin for telling Grenadier his fucking stripper wife wants a divorce, and Tintin says that he was really trying to get them back together again. He was in the middle of helping Grenadier write an email reply about how much he loved her, which Tintin thought he could do really well since he was writing it from the perspective that Grenadier's wife was really Kitten, Tintin's wife-to-be.

FSBNR: walking around with a one-armed poopy suit and trying to get back the other sleeve to sew back on. Having Manning tell me my biceps are all right, for a straight guy, but I should still lose some weight if I want to get it up the ass, and everyone laughing. Me telling Manning I'll put his mother up my ass, and everyone laughing.

FSBNR: having to wear my "Bigfoot is real" hat now, because I lost my bucket hat with the cherries on it when I had to put on the O2 mask. Asking Doc if he still has my sleeve from when he took it off Grenadier's arm, and Doc saying I should check the galley, as maybe they're using it as a rag. Asking Doc how Grenadier is doing and if I can see him, and Doc saying, "No. He's busy finding meaning in suffering right now," and I should come back later. The way I find my sleeve still bloody, crumpled up in a corner, and wash it and hang it to dry overnight. The huge stitches I use to sew it back onto my poopy suit the next day and the way I do such a poor job that the sleeve is too short so that now I look like Frankenstein. The way Manning says of my sewing that he's glad to see me expressing my feminine side, and everyone laughing. Me telling Manning that he can fuck himself.

FSBNR: the fact that because of Grenadier trying to kill himself, we get to head back to port early to get him to the hospital, and upon hearing the news we all yell for joy and ask Baitz if next time we have to go underway he'll do the same for us that Grenadier did and cut his wrists like a steak.

FSBNR: being back in port and getting on the pier and seeing the turquoise water and feeling the sun on my head and thinking how all I want to do is go to my room and sleep for twenty-four hours while running the air conditioner full blast. Calling home to tell them we're back on shore and my mother saying, "What time is it there?" and me saying, "It's your tomorrow." The way my dad asks again if I've thought any more about college and I tell him how yes, I actually thought about college while on this latest underway, but I don't tell him exactly how I thought about college and about how I thought about being in a class where the professor asked about Prince or about how it would be different if I were in college and found my roommate with his wrist slit or about how if I were in college I'd probably be kicked out for offending someone, so it would have to be a special college, a college I'm not sure exists, but that also has classes about fighting with monsters, gazing into abysses, and finding meaning in suffering.

"Good to hear," my father says, and then tells me how the leaves back at home have been changing. The big maple in the mint field is bright neon orange. The dogs have been playing in the stream every morning. The night before a coyote stood right outside my parent's bedroom window and howled so loud that it woke them up from a dead sleep. I lay in bed listening to them talk. They sound old. They have me on speakerphone, and my mother yells at my father to stop hogging the phone and holding the phone up to his ear, because she can't hear what I'm saying. They argue while I wait for them to stop. Then the air conditioning stops, the lights go out, and we get disconnected. It happens on this island sometimes. The brown snakes, which have overtaken the place, have been known to climb the power lines, wrapping themselves inside a transformer, catching on fire, and causing a short. I lay a long time in the dark, trying to sleep in the heat. When I can't, I imagine I'm on the boat again in my rack, Grenadier snoring across from me, sounding like ocean waves.

SECRET LANGUAGE

SHE ATE ONLY CHOCOLATE. Her mother, Catherine, tried blending together a concoction of fruits and vegetables and eggs and a scoop of chocolate ice cream, but the daughter refused to even put her lips to the glass. The next week Catherine heard a noise in the kitchen in the middle of the night. She walked in to find her daughter sitting on the floor with the bottom freezer open and the chocolate ice-cream container on her lap, trying to scoop out mouthfuls of it with the tip of a ballpoint pen— she was not yet tall enough to reach the silverware drawer.

Late into the night they sat in the bath together, listening to Jesús, the father, snoring from the bedroom. Catherine took a wet soapy cloth and gently wiped the chocolate from her daughter's face, and then she rubbed hard, trying to wipe away the blue pen marks as well. They stayed in the bath a long time, and when Catherine began to feel sleepy in the warm tub water and yawned, her daughter giggled loudly and stuck her finger in Catherine's mouth. When Catherine nearly bit the girl, and the girl yelped, Jesús slept through it all. He always slept soundly after a day outside on the poles. Catherine imagined that it was probably tiring for him to be in the high hot sun and the strong wind that sometimes came off the ocean and swayed the poles side to side and made him tighten his safety harness and shout into the receiver of his test phone in order to be heard. Catherine imagined it was also tiring to be out on the poles on cold mornings that frosted the leaves of the trees planted in a line in front of the cathedral that Jesús could most likely see from his place high on the pole, and tiring, too, to be out in the rain that pocked the river water and drove the carp down deep so that you couldn't see them, not like you could on a warmer, drier day when their bony orange backs glowed brightly beneath the water's murky green.

The chocolate was Jesús's fault. He'd brought it to his daughter when she first refused to eat. "At least she's eating something," he'd say, and he would pull out a chocolate from the leather tool belt strapped to his waist and pop it into his girl's mouth. Sometimes he would bring up from his tool belt red coiled wire or blunt-nosed cutters instead, to tease his girl, and she would fly at him, her small fists pounding his chest, hitting the machine-stitched letters above the pocket of his uniform shirt that read Jesús Bernal, Técnico.

There were arguments. Catherine screamed at him when he left the tool belt on the table and their daughter found it and dug into the leather pockets, fishing out chocolate so that of course, Catherine had told Jesús, their daughter would not eat her dinner. She was stuffed to the gills on chocolate! But Jesús told Catherine it did not translate. She was doing it again, he told Catherine, trying to make her Americanisms work in his language when they did not. Catherine wondered, then, what would work? Was it stuffed like a pig? Was it stuffed like a wine gourd? Stuffed like a sausage? It was probably something like stuffed like a seagull, because to Catherine so many of Jesús's country's idioms did not make any sense. In this country, she had learned, people did not see out of the corners of their eyes; they saw out of the tails of their eyes. She thought of "stuffed like a seagull" because at the time she could see one flying by, dropping feces onto the clean sheets she knew she should have hung out to dry earlier in the day, before the dew fell. Any other housewife would have known better, she thought.

They not only fought over chocolate; they fought over eggs. Jesús wanted Catherine to learn how to cook a traditional omelet. He wanted his mother to teach her how to do it, but for a long time Catherine put it off. She wanted to learn how to do some things on her own.

Besides, Jesús's mother was irksome. She had the habit of pretending she didn't know how to do certain things when, clearly, she knew a lot. She knew, for instance, how to sew, but when Jesús asked his mother to teach Catherine how to sew, Jesús's mother said, "I'm no seamstress." Jesús shook his head then. "Mother, no one knows better than you how to whip up a beautiful dress from a bolt of cloth," he said, and he convinced his mother to sit with Catherine and show her how to cut a pattern, how to thread the machine's needle, and soon it was clear to Catherine that Jesús's mother knew a world about sewing. She was a very good seamstress after all, so good that Catherine let her finish the dress they were making because she knew her own stitches would not be anywhere near as even if she tried to complete it by herself.

When Jesús asked his mother to show Catherine how to cook an omelet, she said, "I'm no cook." Jesús told her there was no one better skilled at it that he knew of. "Please, teach Catherine," he'd said.

"I really don't know very much, but I'll try my best," his mother had said, and then she turned to Catherine and had said, "Just pick a day, and I'll come."

At times, before Jesús left the house for the poles, he gave her a list of things to do. "And don't forget to call and make me an appointment with the hairdresser," he might say, or "There's a rip in my pants, left knee, you'll see it," not even bothering to state that it needed mending. After he left and the door was shut behind him, she would imitate him. When her daughter heard her doing this, she would begin to do it too. The two of them would stand by the door, shaking their fingers at each other. "And don't forget to move that boulder! And don't forget to drain the water from the ocean! And don't forget to stop that volcano from erupting!" they would say to each other, laughing at all the things Catherine would never be able to do.

She met another mother at the park once. They were sitting on a bench together watching their daughters go down the slide. She and the other mother had marveled at the children's energy, at their ability to repeat the process of running up the structure's stairs and sliding down the slide countless times. Catherine had looked at the woman's high-heeled shoes, with their wire-thin strap that went behind the Achilles tendon. She could not imagine herself wearing them to the park; she would have tottered on them like a drunk. But still Catherine admired the woman for wearing them—she was not some housewife in wide-toed flats with rubber soles. She was beautiful. The woman, in turn, admired the scarf Catherine was wearing. She reached out and touched the soft alpaca wool.

"Did you knit it yourself?" the woman asked.

"No, I can't do anything like that," Catherine said. "I can't knit or cook. I'm a failure."

The woman laughed. "Oh, good—I can't knit or cook either. Let's be failures together!" She put her arm around Catherine's shoulder and brought her closer so that Catherine could smell her perfume, which smelled like the beach, like sand being warmed by the sun, and Catherine swore that the smell went straight to her head and made her thoughts clear.

It was after talking to that mother in the park that Catherine called Jesús's mother and asked her to come and teach her how to cook an omelet. If she failed to learn, it wouldn't be the end of the world, she reasoned. There were others like her in this country who could not cook either.

Jesús's mother spent hours teaching her about omelets. The first lesson was on picking the potatoes. They spent thirty minutes at the small, crowded market, picking up potatoes and smelling them, getting jostled as they held the potatoes close to their noses, the tips of their noses becoming dusty with traces of the potato field's dry soil. "Choose one that your fingers and thumb can cover completely in your hand, never bigger, and not so small that the fingers can reach and overlap the thumb. Size is crucial," the old woman said, but Catherine could only seem to find ones that were too small and that she could make a tight fist around when she closed her fingers. It was the old woman who had the knack for finding the right-size ones, the ones they finally brought home. In the kitchen, when Catherine reached into her silverware drawer and took out her peeler, Jesús's mother slid the peeler from her grasp.

"No, we use a knife, always. Use this," she said and handed her a small, sharp paring knife. Catherine peeled and cut the potatoes with the knife.

The next lesson was the amount of oil. "If you do not have that right, the dish is ruined," Jesús's mother said. She poured the oil into the pan, so much of it that it seemed to rise halfway up the sides.

"Okay, now I fill the pan halfway with oil," Catherine said, wanting to remember the proportions.

"No," Jesús's mother said. "What if you are not using this same frying pan the next time? You cannot think like that. You must put enough oil in so that when you add the sliced potatoes, they are slightly, just slightly covered by the oil."

"So, if I don't have enough, then I can just add some more oil, right?" Catherine said.

"No," Jesús's mother said. "You never add cold oil to a pan with the sliced potatoes and the hot oil in it already; you have to have oil that is the exact same temperature as the oil that's already in the pan. But that is impossible to achieve, so don't even bother." They hadn't even come to the eggs yet, and Catherine already wanted to get out of the kitchen and be done with the lesson. She wanted to go with her daughter to the park, where she could swing her on the swing and chase her on the jungle gym and have her reach for the monkey bars and work up her daughter's appetite so that maybe, just maybe she would eat something, maybe a slice of southern melon, a slice of northern ham. Maybe the beautiful mother in the high heels would be there. Maybe she would listen to her stories about Jesús, because there were stories about countless things—the way he walked in front of her on the street, never waiting for her to catch up; the way, when she started talking to him about something she had seen or heard, he did not stay still to listen to her but wandered through the rooms, making her follow him, making her make her voice loud to let it be heard over the sound of their footsteps.

The eggs, when they came to them, were just as trying. You had to beat them with a fork, of course, never a whisk. You had to remove the potatoes from the pan first and dab them with a cloth to soak up the extra oil, and then they had to sit for three minutes. When Catherine asked if she could just leave the potatoes in the pan and add the eggs on top of them, Jesús's mother shook her head sadly. For a moment, Catherine thought her mother-in-law wasn't well. The oil heating in the skillet had made the kitchen hot, and Jesús's mother's face was flushed.

"Are you all right?" Catherine said.

"I'm fine, dear," Jesús's mother said, but then she noticed the onion that Catherine held in her hand and her smile disappeared.

Catherine looked down at the onion. "I like onion," she said apologetically. "A little might be nice, and there's plenty of oil left. I thought I could sauté up some of the onion and then add it when I add the potatoes," she said.

Jesús's mother stared at Catherine. There was something in her eyes that reminded Catherine of a stuffed animal's eyes. They seemed scratched and dull, as if Jesús's mother had been dragged on the floor, facedown, from room to room. After a long moment, Jesús's mother finally said in a whisper, "You are the reason she refuses to eat. You are killing my grandchild."

Catherine felt her face becoming red. She gripped the paring knife in one hand and the onion in the other. She gripped the onion so hard that juice began to be squeezed from it. She could feel it running through her fingers.

For a moment she hoped that Jesús had heard and would come into the kitchen to defend her, but that didn't happen. Jesús wouldn't have gone into the kitchen. The kitchen was for women. And plus, Jesús's mother was blocking the doorway. The only way out was the open window with the clothesline and its pulley attached to the outside frame. Catherine imagined herself jumping onto the counter, grabbing hold of the clothesline and suspending herself over the alley, and then jumping down to the cobblestones below.

Instead she leaned against the cabinets, in the *V* formed by the corner, and slid down, letting her backbone hit the metal knobs on the drawers and letting the knobs hike up her sweater as she sat on the linoleum floor. I'm just a failure, she thought, and then she remembered the beautiful mother in the park and how she had thrown her head back and laughed and touched Catherine when she had said that before, how she'd said she was also a failure and that they would be failures together, and just remembering it made Catherine laugh out loud too. Her laughter brought her daughter into the room. Her daughter squeezed past her grandmother and jumped into her mother's lap, wanting to know what was so funny, asking her in English, "What's so funny?" saying, "You can tell me. No one else will know," because English was their secret language that neither Jesús nor the old woman knew.

When exactly Jesús's mother left the room, Catherine didn't remember. Catherine had spent a long time with her eyes closed, hugging her daughter and whispering English words into her ear, telling her she was laughing because she had pictured herself traveling from one building to the next on the clotheslines of all their neighbors, and wouldn't that be fun? She said this to her daughter, and her daughter agreed. "Take me with you. Let's go now," the girl said, trying to climb her mother's shoulders to stand on the counter and get closer to the clothesline and the open window and the blue sky.

Sometimes Jesús left the house in the middle of their arguments. He did not take his rigging with him when he left or his safety harness or his belt. He would take one of his rayon dress shirts and put it into a bag, along with his razor and his aftershave. Catherine would throw other things at him while he did this. "Take this, too! What if your whore's afraid of the dark?" she said as she threw a table lamp at him. "Or this," she said, "take this!" And she threw one of her own sweaters. "You don't want your whore getting cold in that ocean breeze," she said, because she knew from receipts she had found in his pockets that near the ocean is where he often went.

The ocean was not so far away, in miles maybe thirty, in kilometers, who knew—she never was sure of kilometers. When she estimated distances for Jesús in kilometers, she was always wrong. He took it as a sign of her failure to fully get rid of her Americanness. He viewed it like a coat, like something she refused to take off when she entered a room, even when the room was warm and the people friendly. She was stubborn for no reason, he said.

Catherine would show her daughter photographs of herself as a child, with her parents in America. She named the street for her daughter: Magnolia, she said. And she named the house: a colonial, she said, and she named the family car: a Ford, she said, and she named the parents Dorothy and John, and her daughter would recite these words back to her. After a few times her daughter knew all the words for the people and the things in the pictures, and she would point to them and tell Catherine the names. It was then that Jesús would ask if there wasn't something else the child should be doing.

"Shouldn't she be learning her letters? Learning to count? Learning to cook?" he said.

They would go to the ocean on Sundays. They would bring Jesús's mother. She would only go in the off-season, when it was cooler, and she and Jesús would not have to smell the sun-tan gel of the tourists and step on their ratty straw mats as they tried to cross the sand to the waves. They would go to the windy beach, too, because Jesús said the windy beach would be less crowded, so Catherine wore a scarf on her head and wrapped one around her daughter, too, but her daughter never kept it on—she would hold it out so that it flew away like a kite, way, way down the beach and sometimes over the water, blending in with the tops of the choppy waves.

They would not swim; the strong wind cooled them off too much and made the water less inviting. Instead, they would sit and watch the whitecaps, and Jesús's mother would sit in the car, saying that in there she could control the wind. She did not want too little or too much wreaking havoc with her hair, she said. Eventually Jesús would lie back and sleep, and Catherine wondered how he could, with all the wind whipping about, but then of course she knew how easily he could sleep. He was always tired—he could sleep anywhere because of all the time he spent up on the poles. While he slept, she would join her daughter and walk with her on the beach, stopping to pick up bits of shells that her daughter would put in her pockets.

Afterward they would stop for lunch at a restaurant, and the daughter would take out her shells and spread them across the tabletop. Jesús's mother would spend her time wiping the sand that had come with the shells off the table.

It was always a small, inexpensive restaurant they stopped at, the menu consisting of only two meals and no table-cloths covering the tables, so that the dark wooden tops were scratched with wear. When the food came and Jesús started to eat, he would say, "Mother, you could have made this meal yourself, and it would have tasted ten times better."

Jesús's mother would wave her hand in the air then and turn her head away, saying, "Don't be silly!"

"I bet you could have!" Jesús would insist, and his mother would say, "Maybe I would have added a pinch of sugar to the marinade. Maybe that's all."

Then Jesús would pound the well-worn table, whose unsteady legs would shake, and say, "That's the difference! You know exactly the small things to do to improve a dish. That's what makes you a great cook. Everything you make turns to gold."

Catherine once insisted on ordering a meal for her daughter, thinking that if she had her own plate in front of her instead of always having to share, she would be excited to eat it by herself. But it wasn't true. The girl didn't like having the plate in front of her. It was in her way when she laid out her shells.

The receipts in Jesús's wallet were for expensive restaurants that overlooked the sea or that were high up in buildings surrounded by glass. The receipts, always for two meals, listed razor clams and legs of lamb cooked with mustard and thyme, and wines from other countries.

Her daughter had said, "Oh, how beautiful," about the

magnolias in bloom on the trees on Magnolia Street in the photographs, but Catherine did not tell her daughter how sometimes, when they were past the bloom, the magnolias smelled like rotting meat and covered the ground in patches that turned brown and made you slip when you were walking.

It wasn't always her best sweater that she threw at him during a fight. The colors were sometimes faded with washing, the buttons loose and threatening to come off, the pockets stretched, holding the form of her clenched hands, the shape of her knuckles. She wondered, what could it matter? She should have thrown her nicest sweater at him. She should have thrown the plush cashmere at him or the one sewn with hundreds of tiny pearlescent beads. She should have shown him how much she didn't care.

He would let the sweater drop, the buttons clacking on the hardwood floor. He would catch the lamp and toss it onto the bed, where it would bounce, the fragile filaments in the bulb breaking.

Their last argument, when it came, was about many things. It was about chocolates and money and the wind, but it was really about the visit. She had taken her daughter to the doctor for her yearly exam. "Ghostly thin," the doctor had said, and then he ordered tests. The blood test revealed a low iron count.

"Anemic!" Jesús had cried when she came back with the news.

"No, he did not use that word. He said 'low iron,'" Catherine said.

"Did you tell him how she won't eat your food? Did you tell him that?" he said.

"I told him how she prefers chocolate. I told him she fills herself up on the chocolates you bring her and that afterward there's no room left inside her for a meal," Catherine said.

"So, it's all my fault? That's what you told the doctor? That I made my daughter anemic when it's because you're a failure in the kitchen that she won't eat? Is that what you told him? Is it? Is it?" Jesús yelled.

Catherine shook her head. Anemic was not the word. She wished he would stop saying it. "Low iron" was the expression the doctor had used, and what was so tragic about low iron? Who would want the reverse? Who would want high iron in their blood?

He went to the bedroom first. She could hear the telltale signs of the closet door being opened, the hushing sound of his rayon shirt being slid off the hanger.

She missed the grocery stores back home. She would think of them while she was in the crowded markets, the aisles so narrow that no two people could share them back to back. She longed for the simple green of a dollar bill. The proud receding hairline of Washington. The sharp lines of the pyramid centered with the all-knowing eye. Bills here were bright and intricate, no two denominations the same color. After Jesús left, she sat against the spackled wall in the bedroom and rested her head in her hands. The wall's plaster spackling hurt. It had been spread like cake frosting, with peaks, but the peaks were hard and pricked her skin.

Earlier in the day, before the fight and the visit to the doctor, she had planned on making an omelet. She was going to do it exactly the way she had been taught. But since Jesús was gone, she did not see the point. Her daughter wouldn't eat it anyway, and Catherine had not felt like eating at all.

"Come on, sweetheart," she'd said to her daughter. "Time to shop," she'd said, and they left the house.

They walked across the river's bridge. The sun was strong. The smell of the river rose up into the air—warm mud and carp. Catherine thought how, on such a warm day, the beach was probably crowded, the tourist season in full swing.

The chocolate shop had the air conditioner on because of the summer weather. Catherine stood in front of the cases and let her daughter point and smudge the glass. When they left, they had a shopping bag filled with boxes, and the saleswoman was coming out from behind the counter with a bottle of cleaning fluid and a paper towel to erase the fingerprints.

Catherine let her daughter eat the chocolates as they walked home. At first Catherine reached in the bag herself and handed the chocolates to the girl one at a time, but then she just gave her daughter an entire box. The sun melted the chocolates quickly, and the stuff soon ringed the girl's mouth, but Catherine didn't bother to wipe it off. She knew that the girl was not finished yet.

At home she laid the open boxes on the coffee table. The girl sat on her knees and ate. Catherine sat beside her on the floor, leaning against the couch, feeling the cold leather against the backs of her arms. After a while she got up and went to lie on her bed, leaving her daughter at the coffee table with the boxes spread out before her and half the chocolates gone. It was still early, but Catherine was tired. The heat had made her slow, and so she slept, sprawling her legs out wide because she wanted to keep them apart in this heat and because she could, because Jesús wasn't there.

Her daughter's vomiting woke her a few hours later. The girl had made it to the bathroom, but not the toilet. She had used the bathtub instead, and inside of it were large splatters of vomit that looked, at first, so much like blood that Catherine thought the girl had eaten shards of glass. But it was only chocolate.

She held the hair away from her daughter's face so the strands would not become soiled. She rubbed her daughter's back while the girl's body convulsed. Catherine reminded herself that now was the time to act.

She used a clip to keep her daughter's hair out of the way and told the girl to sit tight. "Sit tight, Mama?" her daughter said, not understanding the English expression and looking up at her mother with a very pale face.

"Yes, sit tight. It means relax. I'll be right back."

She went to the living room and saw that her daughter had eaten all of the chocolates except one. Back in the bathroom she wiped her daughter's clammy forehead with a towel and then told her that she had a gift, a surprise. She held her hand behind her back. The daughter, who had been resting her head on her arms on the edge of the tub, lifted her head, her eyes half closed from her nausea and fatigue.

"Guess what I have," Catherine said.

"Show me," the girl said weakly.

Catherine took her hand from behind her back, keeping the hand in a fist. The girl reached for her mother's hand and turned it over, making Catherine peel back her fingers. When her daughter saw the chocolate melting in her palm, she started to gag again. "Don't you want some?" the mother said and lifted her hand a little higher, a little closer to the girl's mouth. The daughter shook her head, then turned, leaning over the tub and gagging more. The sound of it echoed against the porcelain.

Afterward Catherine wiped her daughter's mouth, noticing how the chocolates had coated her teeth and gums with a film of brown. Then she scooped the girl up in her arms and walked with her into the hallway, kissing her cheek, and told her that now it was time for them to sleep, that she would feel better in the morning. Her daughter was already asleep by the time Catherine came to the bedroom door.

The sun woke them. It streamed in the open window in a broad, hot shaft that fell on their uncovered legs. They had slept late. Already Catherine could hear the neighbors hanging their laundry, pinning it to the clothesline, moving it along with the pulley, the rope squeaking with the weight of the load traversing the alley.

"It's a beach day," Catherine said. "Come on, let's put on our suits and go."

The girl sat upright.

"Our suits? Really? We can swim?" she said.

"That's right," Catherine said. "We'll go to the calm beach today, not the windy one."

In the car Catherine talked of the supermarkets back home. She told the girl about the aisles of endless food. She described the bright photographs on the cardboard boxes in the frozen-food aisle, photographs that made your mouth water. She described the chickens slowly cooking on the rotisseries, behind glass cases that couldn't keep the wonderful aroma of the cooking chickens locked in, so that when you breathed you could taste the flavor in the air. The meat of those chickens, which had been cooking slowly for so long, was like butter, Catherine said. It fell easily off the bone, hitting just the right place on your tongue before it slid down your throat.

Her daughter jumped up and down in her car seat. "I want to go!" she said. "I want to try that chicken!"

"Someday I'll take you there," Catherine said, and then, to change the subject, she said, "but first we must go to the beach!"

And she drove quickly, pushing hard on the gas, making her little car whine and whir as it had never done before, so that her daughter said, "The car is excited—it wants to go to the beach, too!" And when they crossed the bridge, the girl asked her mother what direction she thought the carp were swimming in. "Are they swimming toward the beach, too?" the girl said.

"Yes," Catherine said. "Everyone wants to go to the beach today."

The tourists were there, just as Jesús warned they would be. They were glistening in orange gel on their ratty bamboo mats, their eyes closed and their faces turned toward the sun. The sea was calm and warm. There was no wind to send up white chop or spray. They swam for a long time, and then they lay down on their towels like the tourists, their chins tilted up, trying to catch the rays. Catherine heard her daughter's stomach growl. "I'm hungry, Mama," the girl said, and Catherine turned on her side and looked at her daughter and admired how white her teeth looked now that the girl's face was golden from the sun.

"Then let's eat!" Catherine said.

She chose the restaurant she had seen the name of on the receipt she had last found in Jesús's wallet. It overlooked the ocean, and from inside they could see the fishing boats moving slowly from side to side, and they could see the seagulls flying by too, their heads turning in search of food.

Catherine ordered the razor clams and the lamb with thyme and mustard. "Chicken! I want chicken," her daughter said, and so Catherine ordered her the chicken. Her daughter ate great mouthfuls of it. Catherine could see the bumpy outline of the meat behind her daughter's bulging, suntanned cheeks. The girl smiled. She talked with her mouth full. "This is good, Mama," she said.

There were other couples in the restaurant. She imagined finding Jesús sitting at one of the tables. What would she say if she saw him? She did not know. And then suddenly she knew.

On the plane home she formed the words that she would say to him later, over the phone from halfway across the world. "I have our daughter, and we are not coming back," she said, looking out the window of the plane, her daughter eating peanuts the stewardess had given her.

THE PRESCRIPTION

IN OUR FIELD IS A BULL. It is just the head—the horns sticking out from the snow. The bull died suddenly, and the owners wanted to know why, and so my husband sent the lab a tissue sample. In the meantime, the owners butchered the bull and gave my husband the head and some meat from the flanks, but I will not serve the meat. I will not serve it even to the dog, because when the lab called, they said the bull died from cancer, and I do not want anyone getting cancer, not even the dog. My husband said that you cannot get cancer that way, but I don't think anyone knows for sure. "The head will be a beauty when it is picked clean by the coyotes, the snow, the wind, and the bugs," my husband said.

I think how it will probably end up on our bookshelf where we already have a horse's skull and a wolf's skull. The bull meat is in the freezer now, and every once in a while, my husband pulls out a frozen bag of it and throws it into the front field or the woods, saying that at least the coyotes have something to eat and will not starve this winter.

I tell my husband our daughter does not really know about the Holocaust. She does not really know about the stacked bodies frozen in the cold because when we were watching a movie that flashed back to Dachau and showed images of stacked frozen bodies, she said, "Did that really happen?" So, we agree our daughter should read a good book about the Holocaust, followed up by a good movie about it. It is our Holocaust prescription.

My husband took care of one of our dogs in the same way a while ago. The dog had become too old to get up and walk to the door to even go outside. First, my husband took the dog out to the driveway and fed him, and while the dog was eating lamb curry leftovers my husband shot the dog in the head. It was around Halloween, and there was no snow yet on the ground, and our daughter was on the front lawn carving out seeds from a pumpkin and putting the yellow pulp onto the rock wall. When she heard the first shot, she looked up from her pumpkin and saw the dog fall and then she looked down at her pumpkin and continued carving. My husband shot a second time, just to be sure, and then he loaded the dog into a wheelbarrow and rolled him out into the woods. He slid the dog out onto fallen leaves covered in frost. My husband checked on the dog a few months later and told us how there was nothing left. He said, "He has been picked clean. Even the bones have been carried off. When I die, you could do the same for me," my husband said, and I pictured rolling my husband out of the wheelbarrow and into the woods and I wondered if I would be strong enough to do it.

We drive to pick up a new used car in a neighboring state. The car is copper red with a convertible top and a key that is not really a key but a black plastic card that you are not supposed to keep with your cell phone, or the black plastic card, or the cell phone, I can't remember which, will stop working. I would rather have a metal key. A heavy key. A key that I can hear when, attached to its ring and strung with my other keys, it falls from my coat pocket to the pavement as I am reaching in, feeling around past my gloves and wallet.

The neighboring state has less snow than ours, and we remark how the lawns are still sporting green. We turn the heat down. We notice birds of prey in treetops along the guardrails, mostly hawks and owls, and even a bald eagle sitting in a nest. After we pick up the car, my husband drives it home, and I follow behind him in our old car, closer than I would another car because I know he will not mind and also because he is going slower than I want to go. I move over and then drive a long time in the passing lane, and when we return home, he tells me what I did was illegal. "You should never stay for long in the passing lane," he says. I say, "But there was no one else on the road but you," and he says, "but still." I tell him that how slow he drove such a fast car home was what really should have been illegal.

Sometimes a horse is photophobic. It'll come up lame in bright sunshine and walk with a head nod. It is rare, but my husband thought he had a case recently and told the owner to ride the horse in dawn or early evening to see if it walked better then. I think maybe I too am photophobic, because when I go to the library to borrow the good Holocaust book during the day, with all the bright sunshine spreading on the snowy fields, my eyes burn, and I stumble up the library steps.

"Did you know," my husband tells us, during a walk on a near-zero day, "that what Arctic explorers have to worry about is wearing too many layers and sweating too much? If you sweat too much, your body loses heat, and you are that much closer to death." Later we rise from our seats at dinner to look out the window and watch the snow blow off the rooftop and swirl above the woodpile, whiting out all that we can see.

At night I listen to the wind roll about inside the wood-stove and shake the timbers of the house.

With another storm, the horns of the bull are completely covered now, and the snow looks smooth and windswept like dunes in the desert.

The new used car is in the garage. It gets washed and dried and waxed and polished. "There is too much snow and sand and salt on the roads to drive it now," my husband tells us. In the garage, we sit in the car and play its stereo and honk the horn to see how loud it is. We engage the clutch and move through the gears. We walk around it, our heads hitting chamois cloths we strung out on a line to dry, as we search for evidence of wax we missed removing with soft brushes and the corners of towels. We joke about putting our daughter in the trunk when we drive, because the car is only a two-seater. "You'd fit just fine," my husband tells her, but when she makes a move to climb in, he tells her not to be ridiculous.

She has not started reading the book I borrowed for her about the Holocaust. She is reading a book instead about girls in a fashion contest.

When my daughter sits on a cushion, she is tall enough to depress the clutch. When I sit on a cushion, I can depress it also. The top of my husband's head grazes the cloth top when he's in the driver's seat. We put the top down with one hand and pretend the wind is blowing in our hair as we drive when we are really still parked in the garage, hearing the sound of the hot water heater's flame coming on and the sound of the wind blowing outside and sending snow across the icy driveway.

It is too cold today for my husband to use his Xray machine or his digital ultrasound. He cannot risk using them in a cold barn and freezing the hardware or the screens. He sits by the fire telling us how wind whips heat off the outside walls and roof of the house, and that is why our fire cannot keep us all that warm.

It is too cold to stay in bed and read because our arms, while holding up our books, become cold, so I put my arms beneath the covers and the blankets up to my chin and I look at the patterns in the wood on our ceiling and walls and watch a spider walking across her web to eat a ladybug stuck in the silk.

We could skip the book about the Holocaust and go right to the movie, but whenever we have time to watch a movie, no one wants to rent the good movie about the Holocaust, and we would rather watch a movie that makes us laugh. I wonder how we ever watched the good movie about the Holocaust in the first place. How was it, years ago, we had the energy to watch it then and we do not have it now?

My husband reads the car manual before bed and tells me we have the deluxe model with BILSTEIN shocks and a Bose sound system. The ladybug from the spider's web is gone, and now in the web is a large black fly that can only move its legs and try to crawl.

I cannot imagine who is eating the bull's head since it is buried in the snow, and no animal can probably get to it. We have not heard the coyotes howling in a while. I am afraid that the bad meat my husband left out has silenced them by giving them some kind of coyote cancer.

Our daughter has popped a band, and so I make a time for her to visit with the orthodontist. Driving there we hear on the radio that a man robbed a bank, and the police say the suspect will still have red ink on his hands and face. I think, what would my daughter and I do if we ran into the man, if we walked, for example, into the orthodontist's office and the man was standing outside, with the ink all over him. Would we run back into the car and drive off? Would we walk past him into the orthodontist's office and ask to use their phone next to the basket of smiley stickers to call the police?

On the way home we stop and buy discounted chocolate sold in bulk and chopped into irregular pieces. In the kitchen we take a pointed knife and bear down on the handle and break the chocolate into smaller pieces we mix into cookie batter. We eat the cookies before lunch and I think of the ways in which I am a bad parent and I think how I should have gotten my daughter to at least have watched the Holocaust movie by now and I think how I will borrow the movie this afternoon, but when I get to the library to borrow the movie, it is checked out. Someone else had the energy to watch the good movie about the Holocaust. Walking out of the library, back into bright sunshine, I shield my eyes in case I really am photophobic. I don't want to stumble and trip on thick ice while just walking back to my car.

There are signs that something has dug up the bull's head. My husband points out the tracks in the snow. "Oh, good!" he says when he sees the animal paw prints, and I think how he really does sound glad that something like the coyotes are getting a good meal in this cold that is so cold that I keep my head under the covers at night and sleep wearing wool socks and dream of places with waves where I ride right up to a sparkling shoreline.

For an English class our daughter has to read *All Quiet on the Western Front*, and so I am feeling off the hook for making her have to read a book on the Holocaust or watch a good Holocaust movie, because *All Quiet on the Western Front* is so full of the horrors of war that maybe some of what happened in the history of our world is sinking in. Our daughter says she is on page 119, and there is still no love interest, and she is waiting for the love interest, and so far, there is only horse meat and turnips and exploding shells and men wanting other men's boots.

Today the temperature rises above freezing, and so we open up the garage doors and back out the new used car. Its tires rumble over chunks of ice and snow, but we lower the top anyway and turn up the heat and the music and drive by trees with snow still sitting on their branches. We are blinded by the white of the snow-covered fields that we can see for acres on both sides of us, and we lift our faces up to fully catch the sun on our cheeks. I drive and bear down on the gas hard before changing gears and feel the car hugging curves that are puddled with fast-melting side-of-the-road snow. Our daughter smiles up at the blue sky, and later at home we can see how her face has some color. She eats a good meal, with red meat and green vegetables and fresh fruit afterward, and I wonder why I ever wanted her to know about what the Holocaust was in the first place.

The cold is getting colder, and wind whips around the house, and we shut the doors to the garage and keep the new used car inside. Winter is not over and I have run out of kindling to start my fires, so my daughter and I take empty crates for carrying apples and tromp through three feet of snow to a place on our property where we know dead trees whose branches range from finger thick to wrist thick have fallen. We are sweating by the time we get to the place, and I worry that, like the Arctic explorers, we could possibly die from catching a chill in this cold. I wish my daughter had worn a scarf because I can see how the collar of her coat does not close tightly around her slender neck, pale from months of being covered up by turtlenecks and scarves. The branches that we break off that are still too big, we hit against the fallen trunk of the tree, and pieces fly off that we cannot find because they have landed quietly, buried in deep snow. The sound of our sticks breaking against the trunk rings in the air, and while we hit the trunk we yell, "Hiyah!" like we know martial arts. My opponent, I think, could be anything: a bad childhood, an inattentive husband, the cold, maybe just the freezing cold.

My daughter's opponent, I'm not sure: probably just my husband and me, and isn't that enough? That's enough to keep her angry for a lifetime. My never knowing if I'm doing the right thing for her, and him always thinking he does know he's doing the right thing for her.

The next visit to the orthodontist, I don't go in with my daughter but wait in the car reading *All Quiet on the Western Front* as I pulled an old copy off our bookshelf where it was hiding behind the horse's skull and started it, and it's good, and I am not waiting for the love interest. I know enough not to wait for the love interest. On the drive home my daughter says that a woman who worked in the orthodontist's office wasn't there today. She was murdered by her own husband and put through the wood chipper. My daughter can't believe it. This is good, I think, better than reading about the Holocaust. This is closer to home. This is about the horrors of mankind in her own backyard. This will lift her head up from that book about fashion she is reading. I turn on the radio. It's all over the news. We listen as we drive, passing a beauty salon that's also a grocery store and has aisles of food behind the hydraulic salon chairs, passing a gas station that sells milk, and passing a used bookstore that's also a café. Nothing is just one thing, I think. Everything has a dual purpose, even a trip to the orthodontist, which has proven to be a learning ground.

At home, after hearing the news about the woman killed by her husband and thrown into the wood chipper, my husband says, "You see. Life is short. You only live once. It's a good thing we bought the pricey car." And then he gets on the phone and tells a client to feed her thin horse corn to fatten him up.

Evidence that my husband may be right comes pouring in. Fathers of our daughter's friends become sick. One has a brain tumor he didn't know he had except for shaking in his leg when he sat with them crossed. Another dies within ten days of being diagnosed after having gone in for symptoms of what he thought was just swollen glands and the flu. "You see," my husband says. "Our days could be numbered."

In the meantime, the bull's head in our field is still buried, but now it's under a shiny layer of snow from when the snow melted in the sun during the day and re-froze in the cold overnight. We are seventeen-below in the morning and hold our breaths when starting our old four-door car that we park outside, hoping the engine will turn over. Our daughter takes a shower and then goes to get the wood from the pile outside, and her wet hair freezes, and she breaks a piece of it off, showing us how fragile it is. At night, because of the cold, I wear the covers like a burka, shrouding as much of my face as I can. My husband does the same next to me, only his eyes and nose showing pale in the moonlight and starlight, his head covered with the patchwork of our well-worn devil's-puzzle-pattern quilt.

One day my daughter comes home with the good Holocaust movie from the school library. A friend of hers told her it was worth seeing, and so our daughter had a change of heart. We watch it with her, and all of us cry, and outside snow falls in whorls around the house as if the flakes of snow were particles of ghosts trying to take on the semblance of a human form. She says she doesn't understand how so many were killed. Why did they get on the trains so easily? My husband gives her answers, saying no one thought they would be killed. "But animals wouldn't even do this to each other. Why do we?" she asks. I don't have answers for her. I realize that all that I have are the same questions she has. A thaw begins. The horns of the bull poke through. The way they face each other, it's like they've stopped for conversation in the snow-covered field.

My husband and I fight. He thinks our daughter should study German, because if she wants to go into any science field, the best scientific articles are written in German. After watching the Holocaust movie over again, though, I'm not that inclined to have her learn German. I'm not that anxious to hear the guttural sounds that will remind me of all the people who were put to their deaths. I tell him all those science articles are usually translated into English anyway. I tell him German is not like Spanish, where so many countries speak it. I tell him the only place to practice would be in the tiny country of Germany itself. Spanish would serve her well, I say, and plus, I say, the school offers Spanish, and they do not offer German. If she wanted to learn German, we would have to hire a private tutor.

"Then that's what we'll do," my husband says.

I say, "You just told me last week that we have to watch our money and now you want to pay for a private tutor? That's crazy," I say.

"You don't understand. It will be a long-term investment for her, but I don't expect you to understand what I'm saying. Some things you should just leave up to me to decide," he says. I am so angry. I go upstairs and slam the door to our bedroom. I feel hot. I go to the bathroom and wash my face to cool down. When I'm drying it with a towel, I hear a rumble down in the garage. It's my husband starting up the two-seater. I can hear the voice of our daughter talking to him. The garage door squeaks open and then the car pulls out and then the garage door shuts. They never told me they were going for a drive. I listen to the wheels driving over the driveway, and my daughter's voice saying, "Turn the music up!" I hear my husband yell, "Wheeee!" as they drive off, the engine revving.

I sit down and read more of *All Quiet on the Western Front*. The main character has just realized that, while on his second leave, the war has crushed him and he did not even know it. A wind shakes the house as if it's trying to lift it and me inside up off the ground. They are gone for a long time. Did they decide to go to the store? The library? To rent a movie? It's close to dark. The light is beginning to fade over our pond, making it hard now to see the water rippling as the beaver that has taken up residence in it swims around. I can hear a coyote howling. The howl comes from a thicket alongside the road where there's a rock wall and in the thicket, there is also the frame of a very old rusted Ford Roadster that someone abandoned there probably over eighty years ago. I think how it would be nice to once and for all get rid of the meat in the freezer. I don't want one day for my husband to defrost it in our fridge and insist that I cook it, saying that it's good meat.

There are four big plastic bags of the meat that I take down with me to the thicket in the woods with the rusted-out Ford. I drop one of the bags at a time, spacing them out so they are each separated by a distance of at least fifty feet. The evening is the warmest we've had in a long time, and over the pond and the back field the sunset seems stronger than it has in a while, giving the evening a pink-colored glow. It would be nice to watch the rest of the sunset. There is a big rock close by that I could sit on, but if I sat on it and faced west, I'd have a huge hemlock blocking my view. The door on the rusted old Ford Roadster is missing, but the driver's seat, or at least the metal frame of it, is still there. I sit on the seat, my legs still out and hanging over the grass growing up around the car, probably looking like either I'm about to get in the car or I'm just getting out of it. I can hear the gentle ripple of the water on the pond nearby. Either the beaver is trolling around or a fish has decided to come close to the surface. The sunset becomes purple now, as well as pink. I'm glad I stayed out to watch it. There are too many days when there is a good sunset and I've been busy inside the house. There are too many clear nights I have not gone out to admire the stars and to see how they light up the fields and the pond and even us, our hands silvery and our faces silvery as we have them turned up to the sky.

When the sunset is no longer casting pink, I hear a howl that sounds impossibly close. I think how the coyotes must be too shy to get near me, but I am wrong. One lone coyote is standing by one of the plastic bags of meat I dropped fifty feet away. He is not ripping open the bag with his teeth. He is not pawing at it or trying to drag it away. He is sitting right next to the bag, on his haunches, and he has his head thrown back and he is howling.

I wish I had a camera. I wish someone else were with me so the two of us could see it together. Does the coyote somehow know the meat is bad? Is he angry over someone trying to leave it for him? He is a large coyote with a thick silver ruff of fur around his neck. I can see his chest expand after one howl ends and as he gets ready to start another. He howls the sun all the way down over the horizon, not stopping until the darkness is so pervasive that I begin to think how I wish I had brought a flashlight so when it was time to walk back through the field and up to the house I would not trip in a mole's hole or a rock embedded in the dirt whose rounded surface is scarred with lines from where the blade of our mower has scraped it for so many summers.

I wonder when he'll stop howling and begin to try and eat what's inside the plastic bag, but maybe he won't because it's still frozen. He keeps on howling. It's sad and eerie and beautiful all at once. Now that the sun has set, I think I can smell him. He smells like the fresh smell of pine because maybe he rubbed against some tree whose sap clung to his coat. Then I hear our new used car coming up the driveway. The headlights hit the wooden garage doors, and I can hear the music still on in the car and the voices of my husband and my daughter. I hear my husband loudly tell our daughter to shush and turn off the radio. "Hear that?" he says. "Coyotes," he says. The coyote next to me still howls.

"No, coyote. It's just one," my daughter says. That's when I throw my head back and join in. I'm afraid at first that my howl will sound too human, and it will scare the coyote away, but he stays. I can make my howl last a long time, breathing when I need to and still howling. I try and meet the coyote's register and sound the way he sounds. Sometimes my notes are different, but sometimes I think they sound exactly the same, as if like a nested wooden doll, he is inside my throat, or I am inside of his.

Later, after I make it back to the house by just following the lights that are now on inside the rooms, my husband asks where I was. "I just went for a drive like you did," I say.

"Wasn't it a lovely evening for a drive? Did you see that sunset? Do you feel better now? You were getting pretty worked up about the German," he says.

"Ah, yes, the German," I say and then I tell him how our daughter should learn what she wants to learn, and that in the end, words matter very little. They don't matter at all. Then, as if to back me up, we hear the coyote howl down in the thicket by the pond. It's a long, high howl. Longer than I think I ever could howl.

"God, doesn't he sound human?" my husband says.

I go up to the window and put my hands against the glass, looking out.

"You can't see him you know," he says. "It's too dark," he tells me.

I don't answer. I don't want to hear my husband talking anymore. I just want to hear the coyote in our woods.

A LITTLE GRAVE

I TOLD EVERYONE IT WAS A SHARK. But of course, it was not. There are no sharks in the waters I had swum in all my life. It was the fender of a truck that caught my bare leg as I rode on the back of my brother's Vespa. A Bimbo bread truck—the sweet smell of the loaves was strong on the driver when he bent over me and tried to stop the blood with his cupped hands as if under them there was a cricket he wasn't going to let escape. What was in those waters was oil. Not from tankers or Jet Skis or speedboats but from tourists who entered the sea with orange suntan gelée glistening on them as thick as axle grease smeared on gears and cogs of factory machinery. There were also feces in the water that summer. From somewhere, some untreated sewage line poured into the cove. Children became ill from the water. With my injured leg, I lay with the children in hospital beds that overlooked the beaches and listened while they told their mothers they couldn't wait to get better so that they could swim again in the sea.

The doctors grafted skin from my rear onto my leg. My rear now has a few patches on it of scar tissue where the doctors removed the skin. Some are rectangles. One is a square. "These shapes will be hidden by a modest bikini bottom," the doctors said. "No one will know what we've done," they said.

The skin on my rear, rather than looking cut and peeled away, looks more like patches added and sewn onto me, as if I were now mended cloth.

It looked not unlike a wound from a shark attack, my doctor, who had lived in Africa, said. He took his finger and, without actually touching my stitches that ran in zigzags around my leg, through my knee, and to the back of my leg, he pointed and showed the other doctors how the lacerations mimicked those of a great white.

When I was pronounced fit to go home, my parents came to pick me up. I had to lie flat on my belly in the car with my rear facing upward because of the pain. My nose was wedged in the space between the seat bottom and the seat back, breathing in the smell of the leather and air from the dark space there, tinged with the faint smell of mint, from some candy I or my brother, Albert, must have dropped years ago.

We lived on Santa Maxima Street. A few doors down from our house was Santa Maxima's Church, and my mother was planning on going there right after I had been helped upstairs to my bed, to lie on my belly again, so that she could pray for my quick recovery and thank God I did not lose my leg altogether and to also pray for those poor sick children in the hospital beds whose brains were filling with water from feces, she said. My brother came in to see how I was and to look at my stitches. After looking at them and then having to look away and stand out on my balcony because he thought he would faint, he said if he were me, he would tell the world it had been a shark and not the driver of the Bimbo bread truck who had done this to me.

His fainting spell gone, he reached out over the railing of my balcony and pulled the fig tree branch close to him and picked some ripe figs, which we pulled apart with our fingers and ate the red insides. We left the skins, with marks still on them from scraping the meat of the fruit out with our teeth, on my bedside table in a pile. Later Albert balled the skins together and pitched them out through my balcony doors, where they sailed over our lawn, over a brick wall, and fell somewhere into the yard of the Escribanos, our neighbors.

That night, after our parents had gone to sleep, Albert slipped back into my room and he winked at me. Then he jumped off the balcony and landed softly in our yard. He was off to meet Rafael and Roberto Escribano and go cruising on their Vespas on the street that bordered the sea, where the girls often walked arm in arm. I went to sleep and thought how it would be hours before he shimmied back up the balcony supports and into my room to sneak back into the house, but instead it was only a matter of minutes.

"What's wrong?" I asked.

"It's their sister, Little Franca. She's died in the hospital," Albert said.

Little Franca was the Escribanos' youngest. Most afternoons, Albert would go across our yard and through the garden gate of the Escribanos, where he and the blonde twins, Roberto and Rafael, would shoot off a BB gun, aiming for lizards on the whitewashed walls or the black centers of sunflowers in the garden or even the church spire that they sometimes hit. When they did hit it, and if my mother was sitting in the church at the time, she and all the others in the church could hear the pellet striking as loud as a bell. My mother would then come running over and into the yard of the Escribanos and reach up and take Albert by his ear and lead him back brusquely through our yard, past the branches of the fig tree, where the ripe fruit fell easily on top of their heads and shoulders as my mother scolded, upset at being interrupted in her prayers to God. I would often watch Roberto and Rafael from my balcony, but Little Franca was always in the house with her mother. I had seen Little Franca in the hospital, though, lying there with all the other children who were sick from the sea. She lay still, and her eyes were always closed, but I could see the movement of her eyeballs under their lids as they moved from left to right in a dream.

Albert went back to his room and I fell asleep. When I woke in the middle of the night it was to the sound of Señora Escribano sobbing and then shrieking and then sobbing again, the sounds coming to me in waves through my balcony window where my curtains, I knew, moved from the wind but seemed to be keeping time with Señora Escribano, as if the curtains were blowing back because of her cries.

Poor Dear Little Franca was buried the next day in the graveyard by the ruins. Before her death, she was always called Little Franca, but now, she is always referred to as Poor Dear Little Franca. Albert washed our Renault, and the twins, Roberto and Rafael, washed their family car for the procession that would lead us up the hill and to the graveyard, but when we came back down, our cars, we knew, would be dirty again because of all the dust up there.

It was ancient dust kicked up by archaeologists who years ago discovered the Grecian remains of buildings and columns and earthenware and chips of tiled mosaics on a site that the town turned into a museum. Tourists would trek up to the ruins on a day when the three winds came through and the sand blew through the air, whipping at them and stinging them unbearably at the beach so that they didn't want to sunbathe. The tourists would take the winding road up the hill and walk the paths along the roped-off sights, with pamphlets in hand, imagining and trying to make pictures in their heads of how the rubble they were walking next to was once so grand.

The day of Poor Dear Little Franca's funeral was a day of the three-days' wind. My father drove our Renault as we followed behind the Escribanos' car. At the gravesite, the priest's hair blew about in the wind, and he was always moving it out of his eyes with one hand, and with the other he was reading from the bible whose pages he had to hold tightly because the pages flipped frantically in the wind. Some of the tourists who could no longer bear the stinging sand on the beach had come up to see the ruins and stood around us while we stood over Poor Dear Little Franca's coffin. The tourists walked in their short shorts and bikini tops, not realizing that their tanned, sandaled feet were landing on the tops of graves.

The next day, while I was on an errand, I saw Roberto and Rafael, the blonde twins, come riding by on their Vespa. They were like two girls because their hair was long and they were both slender, and on their wrists, they wore braided brass bracelets. They stopped, and through dark sunglasses rimmed with gold wire, Rafael or Roberto, I didn't know who and had only ever been able to tell them apart when one of them was smiling because Roberto had a chipped front tooth, asked me where my brother was.

"I don't know," I answered.

I asked how their mother was, and they said she was in the lingerie shop with my mother. I imagined Señora Escribano did not want to be back in her own home where everything reminded her of Poor Dear Little Franca and where Poor Dear Little Franca, having only just died, I thought, would not appear as a transparent ghost just yet but would appear almost human, with color still in her face and shine on her hair as she walked throughout the sunny rooms of their house.

Roberto and Rafael kissed both my cheeks good-bye, and I smelled a candy smell when they came close, cherry or something, as if Poor Dear Little Franca had just ridden on their shoulders and clung, with her sticky-sweet fingers from eating candy, to their long blonde hair. Then the twins released their brake and coasted down the hilly street until they came to the bottom where I could hear the Vespa's engine being gunned as they turned the corner out of sight.

In my mother's shop, Señora Escribano was sitting on a stool. She was dressed all in black and wearing black lace over her head and face, and beneath it all, I could see the white of her crumpled tissue that would travel from one eye to the next as she dabbed at her tears. While my mother rang up a sale on the cash register, she told me to go find Albert, that there had been a shipment of negligees that she had been waiting for that had finally been delivered, and she wanted him to display them as soon as possible by standing on a ladder and pinning them to the dropped-cork ceiling. I didn't want to have to go walking the streets again on my crutches, and luckily, I didn't have to because Señora Escribano said, "Let me call Rafael. He will drive you on his Vespa."

I left my crutches in the shop, and Rafael helped me climb onto the back of his Vespa. I had never sat so close to one of the twins before and so I did not put my arms around his waist, but before we started off down the street, Rafael reached behind and took me by the wrists and made me hold onto him.

I told him to watch out for Bimbo bread trucks as he drove, but either he did not hear my little joke or he did not care to respond because he was silent. He was a fast driver who turned the corners sharply, and I was glad I was holding onto him and held him even tighter. His long blonde hair blew by my face, and strands of it entered my mouth as he drove. I thought how he and his brother and my brother had probably laughed when they learned that part of my rear had now been grafted onto my leg, and maybe they had stood up at *Punte Mongo* and drank beer and the jokes came easily, a girl who didn't know her ass from her knee, a girl who let you grab her ass anytime just by putting your hand on her leg, and so on.

Rafael didn't ask me where to look for Albert. We both knew there were typical spots to go in search of him. We first zoomed down the *Passeig del Mar* and then all the other side streets, but we did not find him. We finally gave up, and Rafael drove me back to my mother's shop, and he kissed me on both my cheeks again, but this time he still held onto my wrist as he did it, as if he were going to draw me in closer and put his lips on my mouth. I looked at him, but I couldn't see his eyes. They were hidden behind the dark sunglasses, and all I could see was the distorted shape of myself with my hair all messy about my head from driving so fast on the back of his Vespa. That night, after dinner, Albert went out. Later, my mother asked me to go into the shop and get her a packet of elastic that we sold so that she could fix the sleeves of her dress—a dress whose elastic was so worn that she had fixed it numerous times before and now she would fix again, never dreaming of balling the dress up and throwing it in the garbage, which is where it should have gone, it being faded and old and see-through, so see-through that if it weren't for the slip she always wore underneath it, one would be able to see her bra and her briefs and their tags and read the name of their bargain brand.

When I walked in the shop, I almost screamed. Albert, having finished the shop's display earlier in the day, had pinned only the straps of the negligees to the ceiling so that the filmy negligees now swung freely and spun in the breeze that came through when I opened the door of the shop. In the pale light coming from the moon in through the windows, it looked as though the negligees were the ghosts of young girls floating close to the ceiling and, like rising smoke, they were trapped and could rise no higher. I thought if anyone were ever to see the ghost of Poor Dear Little Franca, they would see her here, and I ran on my crutches as fast as I could for the packet of elastic I was sent to get, and then I ran back, shutting the shop door behind me with a bang.

I ran back to my mother and gave her the elastic. "Poor Dear Little Franca," she said after she had knotted the thread and was beginning to sew the other sleeve of her dress. "I wonder where she is now," she said.

"Where?" I asked my mother. "You don't think she was turned down at heaven and is knocking on the gates of hell?" I said.

"No, of course not. Poor Dear Little Franca will definitely go to heaven, but where en route is she? Is she already there? Were there some crucial stops God wanted her to make along the way?"

"Like what, stop at the bank, stop and buy bread?" I said.

"I don't think so," I said.

My mother laughed. "No," she said. "Not like an errand, but like some rites of passage we know nothing about."

I groaned. "Oh, Mama," I said. "Do you really think about these things?"

My mother continued to talk about Poor Dear Little Franca, and so I yawned a big yawn and stretched and excused myself and started my slow and careful walk up the stairs with my crutches.

I went to my room and stood on my balcony and looked out at the Escribanos' house. Through their windows I could see Señora Escribano sitting in her chair, still wearing black because she was still in mourning for Poor Dear Little Franca.

The Escribanos were eating dinner. Rafael and Roberto ate quickly, but I could tell Señora Escribano wasn't eating at all. Once in a while she would put her fork down and lift her head and look up at her sons and then she would look down again and pick up the fork and push the food around on her plate. The twins finished eating quickly and then left the room. Señor Escribano finished next and then stood up and left the room, too, and only Señora Escribano was now left in the kitchen. She put her head in her hands, and her fingers wove through her graying blonde hair, and it looked as if she pulled hard, she could remove her scalp, and for an instant I thought I would be watching the unfolding of some sort of science fiction scene, where after removing her scalp, a scaly frog-eyed alien's head complete with gills and shining with slime would appear in its place. But that didn't happen. She finally released her hands and stood and carried the plates of her twin sons and her husband to the sink and tied an apron around herself and did the dishes.

Every morning I would hold up my mother's hand mirror and look at myself to see if the scarring had become less noticeable. The only thing I did notice, however, was that the patches, once all red, were now varying shades, as if my rear were vast farmland seen from as high as an airplane would fly. It looked like crop fields were stretched over my rear, each growing something different, wheat or rye or corn, or laying fallow, which accounted for some of the patches being pale and others darker.

What would a lover think, I thought to myself, if I were to ever have one who would catch sight of my rear? Would he buzz and sputter over me, imitating the dual engines of a plane flying overhead, passing over the countryside of my rear? Would he always make me wear my panties? Too repulsed by the sight of my rear exposed, maybe in our lovemaking I would always have to keep my panties on and move the cotton panel to one side when he would enter me. Would he be strange and love my rear and take a brush and ink and pretend my rectangles and square were frames and paint pictures right onto my skin?

I threw my mother's mirror at the wall. It did not break. All it did was dent the wall. When she came into my room to find out what the noise was, I asked her if she knew how to knock, and would she please learn and stop barging into my room whenever she wanted.

"Go out into the sunshine, my child," she said, and then from her apron pocket she pulled out a *duro* and pressed it into my palm and left my room.

Maybe in her day a *duro* was enough to buy a meringue at the pastry shop, but I would have trouble finding anything I could buy with a *duro* in this town. Nonetheless, I took her advice and left the house to go on a walk.

When I turned the corner to go down my street, the twins came driving by on their Vespa. It was often hard to tell them apart not only because of the way they looked but because they also always shared each other's clothes. One day Roberto might be wearing a green shirt, and the next day Rafael would be wearing it, and sometimes if I had seen them in the morning and then again later in the evening, they would have also traded shirts in that short time, and I was never really sure, and it made the days bleed together so that it seemed as if there was no passage of time or there was a constant passage of it, where days and nights were sped up way beyond their normal cycles.

They stopped to say hello and kiss me on the cheeks. They were very lively, which was unusual for them, and I wondered how they could be that way after the recent death of their sister. One of them even smiled. It was Roberto. I noticed because I saw his chipped front tooth. He was riding shotgun on the Vespa, and I wondered if that's how it always was and if that was a sure way to tell them apart, where Rafael was always the driver and Roberto always the passenger.

"We're going up to visit Franca," Rafael said. "Want to come?" I looked at the back of the Vespa. There didn't seem to be room for me to fit, but then Roberto patted his lap.

"Sit up here on me," he said. And so, I left my crutches in my foyer, and sat on Roberto's lap.

The ride was bouncy. We were too many for the Vespa. I could feel the cobblestones of the street bouncing up through me, shaking my rib cage, making my jaw move, and making me bite my tongue every now and then.

When we got to her grave, Rafael stopped the Vespa, and Roberto helped me down.

We stood staring at the small mound of dirt that was on top of her grave and we stared at the small white cross at the head of it.

"It's a small grave," Roberto said.

"She was just a girl," Rafael said.

"She should have a bigger grave. She deserves it," he said. "Look at old Pares's grave next to hers. It's huge, and he was a *cabron*. It's not fair," Roberto said.

"Let's make it bigger then," Rafael said. He began to mound dirt around Franca's grave, and Roberto started to do it, too. I helped. With our hands cupped, we went to the small hills beside the graveyard, and we dug into the earth, and while we walked with it to her grave, the sandy bits fell between our fingers.

Soon, Poor Dear Little Franca's grave was the biggest one there. I was tired from limping back and forth holding dirt, so I stayed by the grave, and I started to play in the dirt. I fashioned a mermaid's tale for Poor Dear Little Franca. Its tail curled upward as if in midair, about to splash down on the emerald sea. I gave her a torso and small clamshell-sized breasts and long arms that floated beside her on the waves. Then I heard the Vespa start and drive back down the long and winding road. I turned to look, to see if Roberto and Rafael would wave good-bye, but it was only Roberto on the Vespa. Rafael had stayed with me.

He took me by the hand and walked with me to the bushes. I smelled eucalyptus. He kissed me and held my breast through my shirt, squeezing it rhythmically. When he un-zipped my pants, I tried to stop him, but he was strong, and so I let him. He wanted my front. But I turned over. When I did, he traced his fingertips around the skin on my rear that had been removed to cover the scar on my leg.

"These are perfect squares," he said. "Nothing is like that on a body, all perfect straight lines. Why didn't they make circles and curves?" he asked.

I shook my head. I could feel the sandy dirt of the ruins of Empúries embedding in my hair. I imagined later it would sift and fall from my head and onto the stone floor of my home.

Then Rafael put his face close to mine again. Before he kissed me, he breathed words into my mouth.

"Those bastards," he breathed, and I sucked in his words, letting them keep me alive.

THE UN-SON

THEY FALL IN MOONLIGHT OR ON DARK NIGHTS at off-hours, falling from trellis, eave, and cornice while the household sleeps outside the house, sweating under blankets covering from head to toe the mother, father, daughter, and son.

In *la lengua*, they are *escorpiones*.

Horse-smelling wool blankets over his face keep the son from breathing full breaths, keep him thinking that if he were sleeping, he'd be dreaming of dying while living covered that way, without air in the night on a night like a day with a moon that seemed to burn like the sun. The boy peeks. Around him his mother and father and sister are also covered in blankets, like victims of catastrophe dragged out for tolling on the lawn.

"You by earthquake, you by fire, you by flood," he says out loud, pointing to members of his blanketed family, naming the nature of their demise.

"Me by gravity," he says, imagining crushing air on his chest and ribs collapsing and forcing his bones flat into the dirt, as flat as fossils he has discovered in stone.

Blood wiped on the fence keeps the rabbits from eating carrots and lettuce in the garden, but nothing keeps the scorpions from living inside the house. At first the family batted brooms in corners of their room, knocking down the scorpions and killing them in fires burning on the hill. But they came back, nesting at night in ceilings, hanging their tails over beams, climbing walls in tubs meant for baths, sitting on hinges of swinging doors, traveling on dogs, clinging to their fur on their backs.

Spaniards put them in purses and set them loose by sleeping enemies. The boy's family sweeps them out the door, throwing them really, sending them flying out toward the arroyo and toward the chaparral. Once the boy almost swallowed one hung to the lip of a pitcher, and his sister, once stung in the heel, now drags back a foot, trailing a snake path in sand.

In *la lengua*, the boy's father, Tomás says his family is *desfortunada* because their *tierra* is a *tierra* of scorpions and can never be sold, and even during this crazy revolution, the *Federales* don't want to steal it, and everyone in town and all the towns over know that his family is up to their *orejas* in scorpions, so much so they cannot even rest their heads at night in their beds because they may be stung by a tail in their sleep.

The horses whinny and the boy, hearing them, takes his blanket off his sweating chest and goes to the garden, seeing by moonlight to pull up carrots to feed to the horses. He climbs over the fence wiped with blood and wonders if the rabbits watch him, saying to each other, "He has crossed. The boy has crossed through the blood." He imagines his mother going to the garden in the morning, finding her fence trampled and so many rabbits on all of her rows that she wonders how she is the only woman around who has planted carrot and lettuce seed and grown a garden of fur instead.

Out loud, to the horses, he says, "When will the boy come? When will he ride us through the river? That's what you're thinking, isn't it?" Diego says in the *caballeriza*.

"Well, here I am," he says, putting on their bridles.

River water splashes up the horse's legs, his legs. He rides one horse and leads three others. He cannot see the morning sun for mist and a fog that rises from the water around the horse's legs and at his ankle bones. He can hear the pebbled riverbed beneath him being tripped and hooved, a rolling, knocking sound to sleep by. He does. What wakes him is not the leads of the three horses, which his sleep has let slip from his hands and now lay in the shallow water, or his own horse that rides him under leaves of a branch that hits his face, but a dream of his uncle aloft, cloud riding, arms crossed over his chest, scorpions hanging from his skin sagged at the elbows, from his earlobes, from his beard and bowed legs, from his lips and eyelids, and even his boot tips.

When he wakes and sees the three horses standing in the water, he calls to them. *Madre Mia, Por El Amor, Maldita Sea,* he calls them and then calls them *cabrones, hijos de putas,* and the horses turn to him, and walking back to his house, he tells them of his dream of his scorpioned uncle aloft on the clouds.

"What's that I heard you calling them when I was down by the river this morning?" the mother says to her son.

"I dreamt about Uncle Miguel," he says. "Do you want to hear my dream?" he says.

"No," the mother says. "I only don't want to hear you naming horses names we have not named them."

The boy wonders if she has yet been to her garden for lettuce and carrots.

"Diego, *cariño,* get some soap for the floors," the mother says.

"I am so old," he thinks he hears his mother say as he goes to the shed for the soap, but she is not speaking.

His sister is under a tree.

"Look," she says. She points to a bird's nest on a low branch. She walks in circles under the nest, holding onto the back of her leg to help her foot along.

"Where is the mother? There is no mother," she says. She tries to climb the tree but slides down, bark breaking where her foot drags the heel that was once stung by a scorpion.

"You'll kill yourself, *La Concha*," the mother calls out from the window of the kitchen to her daughter. Diego lifts his sister to the nest. He feels her heart beating as he holds her.

"Calm down. The mother will come back," he tells his sister.

"Maybe she was killed by cats. There are cats. I have seen them," his sister says.

His father is in the field. There is a place in the field that is worn from where the father has walked in circles watching his horses. Diego has walked in this place, but his feet feel strange, as if they were walking in boots that had been walked in by somebody else, and there are small lifts and depressions that do not form to his feet, and he feels as if he is alternately being tipped over and falling backward and could step off over the edge when just walking on level ground.

Tumbled clumps of weed and straw shore up in wind against downed fence posts piled by the riding ring. Diego climbs the pile, careful not to splinter up his palms on the rotted pine posts.

"*¡Bendejo! ¡Hijo de puta!*" his father yells at a horse who rises to strike and seemingly gallop into the sky.

Diego's uncle Miguel comes through the gate and takes the lead of the horse and says, "*tranquilo*," to the horse and says, "*calmate*," to the horse and pats the horse's neck, and the horse snorts and lowers his head.

"*¡Cabron!*" the father yells and punches the horse's shoulder. The horse rears, and Miguel has to let go of the lead, and Miguel and Diego's father have to step back along the fence to wait and let the horse finish rearing and kicking and carrying on.

Miguel takes off his hat and plays with the band on the brim. Diego's father rests his foot on the lower fence rail and looks out across the field and toward the mountains. The horse moves his lathered neck up and down, and his breathing is so strong and loud that Diego imagines it fast and hot on him, making hairs move on his arms, making the tumbled clumps of weed and straw move and scuttle against the piled fence posts where he sits.

When the horse stops, Miguel holds his halter and calls out, "Tomás!" Then Diego's father comes running and sits up on the horse and then he's off. Before the horse has time to rear, Diego's father has already jumped back down to the ground and is now walking out through the fence gate, saying behind him, to his brother Miguel, "Enough for today."

Diego watches his father Tomás walk back to the house. He has long legs but an even longer torso with a rib cage that sticks far out, and everyone says it is his ribs that first enter a room and his head that follows behind. With Diego, they say they never notice him entering a room. Sneaky, like a cat, they say. Diego will enter without the sound of his steps being heard on the floor, and then you look up, and he'll be sitting in the chair as if he had been sitting there all along.

Diego helps his uncle Miguel wipe the horse down. Miguel takes off his hat and puts it on for Diego to wear, and then he points to a beam up above, and Diego knows his uncle is reminding him that is where scorpions sleep.

"You were in my dream," he almost says to his uncle, but he stops, remembering that his mother once told him to wait to tell a person your bad dreams of them because that way you will still have the dream inside you and you may dream again the same dream but with a better ending—a fortune won or a son born or a lost love found.

Miguel is a man born of a woman sworn to having had only one son. Her other child, Tomás, is not her son at all but an un-son, a boy she said when he was a babe cracked her teats with his suck till they bled, ripped her hair from her head when she bent down to clean up his bottom, and, when he learned to stand, stepped on her unhealed skin forever raw from the cut a midwife made so he could Caesar his way out—that un-son was Diego's father. And so, am I the un-son grandson? Diego thinks. And there are reasons not to care what the smelly old woman tanked on mescal or sap of the maguey tequila-laced tea even thinks, or if any of what she says is even somewhat true. "God in heaven, what a child. I'd rock him in my arms, and he would try to rock the other way. I would comb his hair, and he would command a breeze to come dishevel it. He turned my milk sour so it poured forth green-and-yellow pus and infected my blood and made fevers burn so hot in my body that my lips erupted in sores and my eyes clicked when I moved them back and forth from lack of fluid in their sockets. Un-son, yes, damn it all to hell, and unloved, unlovable, uncaring, ungrateful. Child, make me my tea, yes, my special tea. Nothing like his brother Miguel, a son who when he was born brought the air into his lungs not with a cry but with a laugh, who when he fed at my breast stroked me. I never had to bite off the nails on his fingers the way I had to do to your father because he was not like the un-son and did not rake his nails across my skin, did not maul his mother."

A lit match now, Diego thinks, on her special tea-stained dress will make her flare up—a ball of old woman cooking, burning up waxen dirt caught in the creases of her neck, her wrinkled place between her breasts, a valley of skin crosshatched, overdone by years of field sun, years of un-son.

"He is the reason the poisonous scorpion has taken up residence in your house. Throw him out, and the scorpions will leave you, and you will be able to sleep in your beds at night," she says.

"Am I the un-grandson?"

"Oh, no. To me, *cariño*, you are just a boy who lives in my town."

He is a roarer. "See the blood," his uncle says and shows Diego the horse he holds. Diego eyes the nostrils.

"I can't see," Diego says.

"Yes, you can," his uncle says.

"I don't know horses," Diego says. In *la lengua*, his father has told him he is *sin caballo*.

"I am *sin caballo*," he tells his uncle.

"*Nada de eso*," his uncle says, shaking his head.

Diego and Miguel ride to market. Strung garlic and pickled pepper and leaves for tea and straps of leather and dented bars of white soap pocked with gravel and dirt and dusty serapes and coiled wire and feed corn and blue-dyed rabbits' feet and pocket combs and handheld mirrors and salted fish and tooled belts and coffeepots and plastic cameos all lay for sale on the cloth-covered ground. Miguel shops for canvas to cover leaks in the stall and chamomile leaves for his mother. Parakeets hang in cages that look like small houses made of twisted reeds. Pointed roofs made of thatch cover the cages, and reed guillotine doors slide up and down.

"Do you want one?" his uncle asks.

"Not for me, for *La Concha*," Diego says.

"I'll take one," his uncle says, and Diego tells him not to, but his uncle has already paid the woman wearing an apron around her belly whose front pockets are her cash drawer. She pulls coins and bills up from it for change, and now all that Diego can do is pick out a bird. He chooses yellow—yellow like the lemon-yellow *allamanda*.

"That soldier's horse in front has a lame leg. Can you tell which one?" his uncle asks him.

"The left front?" Diego asks.

"The right hind," Miguel says. "See how he hardly puts his weight on it? *Le duele*. He should not be ridden. I would not want to be the man to touch that ankle to see what it is that has tied up that horse. Look how the fluid has swollen the ankle. I would not even want to be near the man who touches that ankle to see what it is that has tied up that horse. Clear me out of town for that matter," Miguel says, and he laughs. "How is that bird?" he says to Diego.

"Good," Diego says, but he is looking at the horse, trying to see how the right hind leg looks any different than the other legs, and he says when that horse is seen to he will probably be the one standing right in back of the horse, right where he could get jackass-kicked in the head by both legs, the good and the bad.

In the yard of Diego's grandmother's house there are cast-iron chairs and between them a cast-iron table that used to have a glass top but now has no top, and thick tall grass grows up through it and looks as if a cup were set on the tall grass that it would, for a second, hold it up. There is a small plaster statue of the Virgin Mary in long pale blue robes, and the robes have yellow streaks on them that still look wet from where dogs have pissed. There is lace in the window that is pulled to the side, where the old woman's face appears. Around her the house looks small, and from the outside anyone could guess everything that is on the inside: two rooms filled with more lace and teacups and woven rugs; a shot-spring bed; Jesus on the cross; a top drawer with a stopped gold-plated watch; a chipped enamel chamber pot; a flame-licked and singed metal pan dented on the bottom, blackened on the sides; a string of garlic so old, hanging from a nail, the garlic now just a moldy powder, scentless, held together by peel; an old woman in a flowered, tea-stained dress wearing bedroom slippers, a wedding ring placed on her finger so many years ago that fat has grown around it, and you wonder if it gives the woman pain.

Anna Luisa Matilda Ruiz is her name. But she was called AnnaLoo by other children when she was a child and AnnaLoo by the child who became the man she married.

Diego ties the parakeet to his saddle and follows his uncle into the house.

She won't talk to Miguel.

"Mama, please," he says.

Diego is standing on the skirt of her flowered dress fanned out on the floor. He steps off it.

AnnaLoo moans.

A fly flies to the rim of her teacup.

Miguel kneels down.

"I have chamomile," he tells her softly.

Diego looks out at what she can see from her window—rows of garden corn whose husks are shaggy and split and kernels gnarled, made grotesque by blights of smut. There are no two the same shape or size but patterned like they had been melted and might drip off the cob in wobbly dollops to the dry, silk-matted ground.

Diego takes the dented pan and gets water from the well. The well is deep, and people from the town say that someone once fell down there, and now his ghost lives in there whose scraping fingernails you can hear at night as he tries to climb the side of the well's stone walls. The water bucket now up, Diego looks for signs of the drowned man—a kerchief he once maybe wore around his neck, a bloodied fingernail—but there is nothing but a swirl of algae resting on the top.

"Mama, *por favor*, we go through this every time. I want to know how you've been. It was cold a few days ago. Did you have wood for a fire? Did you use some blankets?" Miguel asks his mother. She does not answer. "You are a strong woman, Anna Luisa Matilda Ruiz, the strongest I have ever known," Miguel says.

Maybe AnnaLoo's nose is stuffed. She breathes heavily. Her chest, blown full for air as she sits tall in her chair, is huge like Diego's father's. She leaves just her eyes for talking. Words that if they could be heard might be stories of her girlhood. But she was a girl who had a girlhood that was not sweet, that was not the kind that makes for stories to tell children before bed, but was the kind that makes for stories to remind children of how lucky they are that they did not lead the life of Anna Luisa Matilda Ruiz.

Miguel leaves. He has horses to break. He has left Diego to stay and keep her company and fix her tea. Diego watches through the window how Miguel rides so well, how he does not even seem to be sitting on a horse that is trotting but more like he is sitting on a horse that is standing still or a horse that is not a horse at all but a dead horse, stuffed and glass-eyed and nailed tight to a board on the floor.

Suddenly, AnnaLoo runs out the door, down the straight road, waving her arms, tripping and jumping, calling out, "Miguel, come back!" But Miguel doesn't hear her, and is gone.

Diego makes her chamomile tea.

When she comes back in, she holds one slipper upside down, letting rocks and dirt pour out of it.

"Get out of here," she says to Diego while she pours her mescal into her chamomile tea, barely steeped.

Diego does not leave. He stands and looks at her. AnnaLoo takes whatever boiled water is left in the pot and throws it at his feet.

"Now," she says.

La Concha cannot keep the parakeet. Diego's father has taken it from her, saying she cannot accept a gift from her brother that her brother did not even pay for himself. And then he ties Diego to the trunk of the courtyard's giant cypress and he says no son of mine will ever spend what money isn't his.

In the evening Diego is still tied to the cypress, and he can see his father walking with two horses back from the field where they have grazed, and he sees his father and the horses on either side of him, and his father's chest seems as wide as the horses' chests, and if his father were a horse, Diego thinks, the other horses would be dwarfed and cower sheepishly at his father's slightest stallion snort or bray.

At night his mother and his sister take brooms and sweep the ground of scorpions where they will lay their blankets to sleep. His father walks past him. Diego can hear the horses' hooves walking in the *caballeriza* as his father gets closer to them, going to make sure their webbings are hooked, going into their stalls and putting his ear to their bellies and his hands up along where they are tucked, listening for a telltale slosh of colic knotting up around their spines. When he comes back, he walks past Diego, and he smells of the horses, and he walks like a horse, and his head moves up and down. Diego can see the whites of his eyes rolling, looking out across the field at the mountains, at his wife and daughter in front of the house, then going to a cook fire burning in the courtyard, putting it out, grinding embers with his bootheel.

AnnaLoo sits alone in her house with her hand on her heart, feeling how it skips and murmurs, and AnnaLoo thinks how her heart has learned code and is telling great stories, and that is what death from the heart is all about, the heart turning a corner; now a master of language and appropriate pauses, it entertains, and AnnaLoo can shut her eyes and hear her heart spinning tales. The mescal bottle she drinks from is blurred with prints from her fingers, greasy with meat she has cooked for her dinner. She walks through her failed garden of corn, pulling off a smutted ear, biting into it, tasting no sweet. "Not even fit for horse or oxen. I have grown a crop fit only for mold," she says out loud. Her hand on her heart, she grabs onto stalks, imagining them as strong as sticks for walking mountain trails. The stalks bend, and slowly she falls over with them. Some stunted stalks grown only to about her knee catch between her legs. She can feel their gluey leaves drag against her skin. She thinks she sees her un-son coming toward her through the field, and she does not want to see him, but she thinks maybe when he's close enough to her, she will tell him where the mescal is and where her teacup is, and he could bring them to her while she drinks in the field on her worthless crop of corn.

It is her son. Miguel. Come with firewood he leaves by her door to keep her warm at night. He walks around the outside of the house and goes to her bedroom window, looking in to see if she is there.

She is in her corn. He finds her with her eyes closed, her hand held up for her cup of tea.

"Oh, Mama," Miguel says. She wants to tell him to come close to her chest, to put his ear to her heart so that he can listen in on her, hear the speech of her heart. But she cannot open her mouth, and she cannot open her eyes, and her talking heart tells a story to sleep by, and sleep comes to her, and it is such a strong sleep that it seems to come from up around her as well as inside her and from her field of corn and from her house and from her fields around her house and from the valley she lives in and the country she was born in.

"Where is your father?" Miguel asks toward morning, untying Diego from the cypress tree. Diego points to his father, who is sleeping in the courtyard.

"Saddle the horses," he tells Diego.

They ride under a C-shaped moon. Doves coo and the heads and handles of shovels they have tied to the backs of their saddle scrape bushes they ride by on the side of the road.

When they come to her house, they can still smell the meat in the air AnnaLoo cooked for her dinner. The mescal is on her table, and Diego's father drinks from the bottle and looks around the room. On the wall is a blue ribbon with Miguel's name written under it in pencil, the curlicue handwriting shaky from the point hitting bumps on the thickly coated white-painted wall.

"What was that for?" Tomás says, pointing with the bottle.

"I don't remember. Maybe spelling, maybe math," Miguel says.

"Math. I remember," Tomás says, and he pulls the ribbon off from the wall and licks the back of it and then makes it stick to Miguel's lapel. It hangs there for a moment and then falls.

Miguel turns and walks out the door, past the garden of corn to the open field.

"Let's go," he says to Diego and throws him a shovel.

Tomás comes later, with the bottle of mescal in one hand and his mother's hand in his other hand, dragging her through the corn, breaking stalks crashing, the horses jerking, pulling on their reins tied to a tree, Tomás stopping, looking up above the corn, yelling, "*calla*," to the horses, yelling, "*basta*," to the horses and then continuing through the corn and through the open field to the hole Diego and Miguel have dug.

Anna Luisa Matilda Ruiz is buried with foxtail stuck through threads of her dress hem and old black-tipped corn silk that clings to her hair. They pat the dug dirt down on top of her with their shovel backs after having told God to take her on in his flock. Loose dirt and small rocks roll down from the mound they have covered her under, as if she were moving from side to side, trying to find a comfortable way to be dead.

Diego's mother and his sister come walking down the road. His mother is carrying soap for the floors and a bucket of rags, and *La Concha* holds a branch of laurel sumac.

"There is dirt here from before the war and the revolution before it. Even Pancho Villa and all his bandits could not conquer this dirt," his mother says while scrubbing, using her thumbnail to scrape up what is black and hard and pooled like dried blood, saying what it is she is scraping up maybe shouldn't be scraped up at all but pushed down as far as it can go. "To hell and never back," she says.

La Concha plants the branch of laurel sumac at the head of her grandmother's grave. More leafy on one side than the other, the laurel sumac looks like it's being blown over by a breeze and is bent toward AnnaLoo in the dirt as if AnnaLoo were found by the branch like she was a body of water and the branch a willow divining rod.

In the bedroom they find a scorpion on AnnaLoo's pillow.

"*Dios*," Mercedes says, running with the pillow held out on the palms of her hands toward the garden of corn where she throws it. It lands level on top of the stalks and doesn't fall to the ground. The scorpion, still on the pillow, raises its tail.

"She never told us she had scorpions too," Miguel says to Tomás, who is busy hammering nails into a window frame. With each blow of the hammer the rotted wood splits and splinters and breaks off. Termites have turned the wood into red dust, and the dust, come up from the pounding, covers Tomás's face and covers his eyelashes, lightening them to red, lightening also his hair and sideburns to red.

"Is this my *marido*? Who is this man? An Irishman?" Mercedes says, wiping the wood dust out of Tomás' hair.

Tomás stops hammering. Standing in the small kitchen, he is tall and his rib cage huge. Each breath he takes seems to pull the air from around the room, from inside Diego's lungs, to fill up his own.

"I found a cat," *La Concha* says, coming into the house, holding up a cat who must have been born without a tail and whose whiskers were burnt off when it walked too close to somebody's flame from a fire.

"Let it go," Mercedes says, and before *La Concha* can listen to her mother, her father grabs the cat and throws it out the window.

It is quiet and everyone is standing in the kitchen and no one is talking until Diego's father says, "*Bueno, Bueno*," and then he walks toward the door of the house but turns to take one last look and sees the kitchen table and then reaches out and puts one hand there, putting weight on it, and the table rocks back and forth on one leg untrue, and then Diego's father says, "*Bueno*," again and then he leaves.

UNREAL BLUE

WE ARE GOING DOWN SOUTH. The car is named Clara. We will stay in a beach house. Our mother says she doesn't know how we will do it. We have Jody's mice and the dog and the cats all in the way back of Clara. She says she supposes we will have to be sneaks and not let motels know about our pets. Our mother wears a sweatshirt and blue jeans, and her feet are bare on Clara's pedals the whole drive down. Clara and the beach house are on loan from a friend of my mother's. The friend has taken her family to Tunis.

"That's in Tunisia," our mother tells us. When we get out of Clara to use the gas station bathroom, our mother says, "Where are my clogs? Has anyone seen my clogs?" and when we finally find them for her, they are under the sleeping dog's rib cage in the back of the car. She slips them on and clops off to the bathroom, brushing off crumbs from her sweatshirt that collected there while eating sandwiches slapped together on the highway.

We ride the whole way down with the windows wide open because Clara stinks like our garbage, which we drove to the dump and threw out right before we left our place. Our hair is bushy from wind and so is the dog's and the cat's and the mice whose fur got fluffed even with them in cages by our feet. *Ma*

Mère, our grandmother, sits with our mother in the front; really, she lays in the front, her head resting on our mother's lap while our mother drives. We stop at Stuckey's for dinner, and *Ma Mère* orders wine.

"Where do you see wine?" our mother asks her, and instead of pointing to the menu, *Ma Mère* points out the window to a bus shelter where Gallo is advertised.

"That's not in here. That's out there," our mother tells her. *Ma Mère* lowers her head. On her hair we can see crumbs that must have fallen while our mother ate and drove with *Ma Mère* resting her head on our mother's lap. Then *Ma Mère* bangs on her leg with her fist, like she usually does, trying to get rid of a pain she says she's going to have to start thinking of like a friend because it's always around.

Louisa has taken her French horn and plays it while we drive. The dog can't sleep through the music and stands in the back of Clara panting, blocking my mother's view out the rear. We're crossing lanes by having *Ma Mère* hold out her hand out the passenger window, signaling other cars, but *Ma Mère* signaling looks more like fingers tapping on the car door than a full-fledged plea to give way. Horns honk and an officer in a patrol car pulls us over.

"Ma'am," he says to our mother.

"Yes, sir, officer," our mother says.

"Are you aware you've got a faulty turn signal?" he says.

"Yes, sir, officer, I'm well aware, but she's got a blockage in her leg. It hampers her some," our mother says.

"Fix it," the officer says, and that's all and he gets back in his car and drives away. Our getting off easy we attribute to our mother's outstanding good looks and so does she.

The ocean's water is as hot as the air.

"I can't even tell if I'm in or I'm out," our mother says. And when we are in, we are always being whistled out by lifeguards with binoculars who have spotted circling sharks beyond the breakers. We collect sand dollars and stack them like blocks, creating sand dollar walls several feet high, which we have trained the dog to jump over like a trick.

"There are rats in the palms," Jody says, and she takes a jar of peanut butter and cups her hand and digs into it, bringing up blobs of it that she wipes at the base of the palms so that the rats have something to eat. So many rats come to the trees near our beach house that it sounds like a constant storm, the leaves always shaking and great fronds falling down on our roof. Compared to other houses, ours looks like it's in camouflage and we're preparing for a siege, with the sand dollar wall as additional fortification.

For days the ocean is calm, and *Ma Mère* thinks she can walk on it, and we have to pull her back, make her sit on the beach again in her chair. She has found a good stick, one with a knob at the end, that she has begun to use instead of her fist to bang at the side of her leg like some kind of grass-skirted, nipple-pierced tribal king performing rites of the ceremonial kind.

We get a postcard from my mother's friends: a tourist is standing in a square in Tunis with his arms held out and pigeons, not one but maybe five, sitting on his head, and sitting up and down his arms, all in different stages of flight or just having flown and lit down, and down the man's shirt is all stained with the gray-and-white shit of the pigeons, and Louisa points and says, "Look, there is even pigeon shit hanging off the man's nose."

"We're having the better vacation," our mother says after reading the postcard.

"We are?" we say.

"Sure. They've been robbed twice, lost their son, found him again but shorter as his shoes were stolen by highway thieves," she says.

There's a snack wagon near the lifeguard shack. The guy who runs it has arms so tan, you'd think he'd held them above flames and turned his arms slowly round and round. The give-away that he didn't is that there's still hair on his arms, blonde curly hair so thick it could be head hair instead. He doesn't give us anything for free, even if we sit by his snack wagon all day saying out loud how we wished we had a cool drink to quench our parched lips or a Creamsicle to stave off our indescribable hunger, which Louisa says she will describe for our benefit, a hunger, she says, like wild dogs attacking each other in the base of her gut, held clamped jaw to tail, rolling and rolling inside her in a frenzy of gastric juices burning like acid holes as big as craters carved out by celestial phenomena in the forms of asteroids and meteors. The tan man still doesn't seem to hear us, and when the afternoon is slow, he climbs the ladder to the roof of his silver snack wagon and sunbathes, sitting in a chair and holding an aluminum pie tin under his chin to catch maximum sun.

The snack wagon sells an assortment of postcards, most of them of the beach we are at and the color of the ocean a blue we have all agreed we have never seen the ocean before.

"That's unreal blue," Louisa says like she knows its name, and we nod our heads, it sounding like a true color, like cerulean or teal.

We find forgotten dimes in the pay phone and have enough to buy one postcard, which we all agree should be sent to our father, although I try to convince Louisa and Jody we could send it to my friend Rena first, and then Rena could send it on to our father, but it doesn't work, and my sisters shake their heads sadly at my stupidity, and we take turns writing each word, and our handwriting is each so different that it looks like we're sending our father some kind of ransom note composed of cutout typeface from magazines pasted on in uneven lines. We tell him this is where we swim. We say the waves are never as good as this picture.

"Say, 'send money,'" our mother says over our shoulders, and so we say, "send money," and our mother says, "*merde*," and we ask her how to spell that, and she says, "s-h-i-t" and so we spell "shit" and then our brother says it will never get through postal services with a curse word on it, so we try and think of words that begin with shit so we can turn it into a word that is not a curse word, but we can't think of any. My brother says Shiite might work and tells us to squeeze in an *i* into the middle of shit and an e at the end. Then we write the word "no," in front of Shiite so that our postcard now reads "no Shiite here."

"Which is true," our brother says while tightening the belt of his blue silk robe. "I haven't seen one Shiite, have you?"

Money won't come, we know. We left no return address, and all our father's got to go on is a picture postcard of some unreal-blue ocean and the knowledge of the place that it's free of Shiites.

"Money won't come because he won't send it," Louisa says, and we nod our heads and break up our postcard-writing operation and drift off to separate rooms of the house or onto the beach or to the sandy path that I choose, it being cool and shady and forested with thick-trunked trees entwined with huge ropy vines that look to strangle the lives out of the poor trees' wood.

One night we all wake up at the same time because of the sudden quiet—*Ma Mère* has stopped banging her leg. We all rush to her, thinking the worst, but she's standing at the window, pointing at a bum wandering on the beach, asking our mother in French if she remembers her father, and our mother answers of course she remembers her father, and *Ma Mère* draws our mother near and puts a hand on our mother's shoulder and says in French, "Vois-tu? There he is. My husband. Wave to him," she says. Our mother waves to him and puts her arm around *Ma Mère's* waist, and the two of them watch the bum, reeling, drunk, trying to make his way up the beach.

In the morning the bum is at our breakfast table. There is so much sand in his pant cuffs that it spills at a regular rate like a timer onto our kitchen floor while he eats cold leftover pizza our mother has served him on a plate, but he eats it over the pizza box instead.

His name is Manolo, and he is not our mother's father.

"But he is hungry," our mother says, and *Ma Mère*, from her chair in the living room, says, "*Oui*, he is hungry," so we have to let him stay, and our mother finds some of my brother's shorts that she packed that he never wears, and she gives them to Manolo to wear.

When Manolo swims he walks into the water as if he were walking into a room. He pulls open an imaginary handle and then turns to shut it behind him. In shallows he sits with the water up to his chest, smoking a cigarette he has kept dry the whole time behind his ear.

"Call him uncle," our mother says.

"Uncle?" we all cry out.

"He could be yours. He looks so much like my father," she says and she makes him special meals cooked with saffron that stains the wooden spoons yellow.

"That's what it does to your insides too," Louisa says, holding up the yellowed wooden spoons, showing us how we are yellow bellied.

When our vacation is over, Manolo is packed into Clara with us, holding the mice cage on his lap, speaking in Spanish to the mice and my sister Jody telling him they don't know Spanish, only some French now, and Manolo pokes his fingers through the holes in the wire cage trying to pet their sides, saying, when he does, "*Que suave, que suave.*"

On the long drive back North, *Ma Mère* talks to Manolo in French, and he answers in Spanish, and my sisters and I speak pig Latin, Jody throwing in some ASL she learned in school, demanding we look at her while she signs.

Back in the city, Manolo wants to sleep in Clara parked on the street, saying he feels comfortable there, and when it's time for us to return Clara to our mother's friends, our mother asks to borrow it for more time, lying, saying she's got errands in New Jersey and Connecticut. But finally, the car has to be returned, and Manolo says formal good-byes, getting on his hands and knees, kissing our mother's feet and fingertips and kissing the tops of our heads and hugging our brother and then standing back and feeling our brother's robe between his fingers and nodding his head with approval.

When he says good-bye to *Ma Mère*, she begs him not to go and she holds on so hard to his frayed shirt collar that a piece of it rips and comes off in her hands, and he leaves and she's still holding the shirt collar remnant and crying and then she touches the cloth and says, "*Que suave, que suave,*" and closes her eyes.

My sisters and I go to the park. The three of us hold out our arms, seeing if the pigeons will fly down and perch in a line up and down our arms like they did to the tourist in Tunis. But the pigeons don't. They stay close to the ground, pecking at crumbs that were once white but are now smudged gray with dirt. "My arms are tired," Jody says. "I can't keep this up," she says.

"You can do it. Just leave them up," Louisa says. "They will come," she says, and then she helps us. She lifts the tips of her fingers under the tips of our fingers and holds us aloft.

ACKNOWLEDGMENTS

SOME OF THESE STORIES ORIGINALLY APPEARED IN THE FOL-
LOWING PLACES:

"Things That Are Funny on a Submarine But Not Really (FSBNR)" *Conjunctions Online* (February 18, 2020)

"The Good Word" *One Story* (September 2008) and *The Best Nonrequired Reading 2009*

"By the Time You Read This" 2015 *Pushcart Prize XXXIX* and *Conjunctions* #60

"Forty Words" *Zoetrope* (Summer 2016)

"Caesar's Show" *Conjunctions* #65

"Unreal Blue" *Cream City Review* Volume 31, Number 2 (Fall 2007)

"Secret Language" *McSweeney's* #39

"Beauty Shot" *Kenyon Review Online* (May 2014)

"The Un-Son" *TriQuarterly* #133 (2009)

"Too Much for Adele" *Conjunctions Online* (July 2016)

"Oyster City" *n +1* (May 2012)

"A Little Grave" *The Lifted Brow* (January 2009)